GILLIAN ARCHER

Rough Ride

A True Brothers MC Novel

First published by Gillian Archer 2018

Copyright © 2018 by Gillian Archer

All rights reserved. No part of this publication may be reproduced, stored or transmitted in any form or by any means, electronic, mechanical, photocopying, recording, scanning, or otherwise without written permission from the publisher. It is illegal to copy this book, post it to a website, or distribute it by any other means without permission.

This novel is entirely a work of fiction. The names, characters and incidents portrayed in it are the work of the author's imagination. Any resemblance to actual persons, living or dead, events or localities is entirely coincidental.

Copyright © 2018 by Gillian Archer

ASIN B09TWQBXHY

Excerpt from Build by Gillian Archer copyright © 2019 by Gillian Archer

This book contains an excerpt from Build by Gillian Archer. This excerpt has been set for this edition only and may not reflect the final content of the edition.

Cover design: Y'all. That Graphic.

Cover photograph: ArturVerkhovetskiy via Deposit Photos

Proofread by Crystal Blanton, Indie Authors Book Services

gillianarcher.com

Second edition

This book was professionally typeset on Reedsy. Find out more at reedsy.com

Contents

Rough Ride Blurb	v
Prologue	1
Chapter 1	4
Chapter 2	17
Chapter 3	28
Chapter 4	41
Chapter 5	54
Chapter 6	63
Chapter 7	74
Chapter 8	86
Chapter 9	95
Chapter 10	104
Chapter 11	116
Chapter 12	125
Chapter 13	134
Chapter 14	143
Chapter 15	153
Chapter 16	163
Chapter 17	168
Chapter 18	179
Chapter 19	189
Chapter 20	195
Chapter 21	201
Chapter 22	210
Chapter 23	216

Chapter 24	223
Chapter 25	235
Chapter 26	245
Chapter 27	252
Epilogue	258
Dedication	261
Acknowledgments	262
Also By Gillian Archer	263
BIO	264
Read on for an excerpt from Build	265
Build Chapter One	266

Rough Ride Blurb

Amber:

Two years ago I would've made a play for a guy like Bam in a heartbeat. But that was before my father died in a puddle of blood in the middle of a parking lot. Before his d*mn club ripped a hole in my heart that could never be filled. Before I hated everything to do with the True Brothers and their "business." Before I hated bikers.

But I still need answers about what happened to my dad, which is why I'm poking around at a nightclub owned by the Russian mafia. And that's where I run into Bam, who carries me out of the club in his stupid strong arms like I was True Brothers property.

Bam:

The last person I expected to see at Howl that night was motorcycle club princess, Amber Bennett. And I sure as hell wasn't thrilled to see who she was with—the psychotic heir of the Volkskaya Bratva. I get that she wants to know what went on with her dad, but it's club business and she's in way over her head. When I take her home and see the hell she's living in, I can't stay quiet.

Now it's my duty to step in and protect her before she gets in over her head, and she's the definition of off-limits. If only she weren't so hot. And determined to take care of everything herself. And sweetly vulnerable. Because when we cross the line, I'm forced to choose between my True Brothers—or my true feelings.

Prologue

Last Summer

Amber Bennett

I heard the front door shut and rolled over to look at my alarm clock. Two-thirty in the morning. How pathetic was it that I was in bed streaming TV shows until the early hours at the ripe ol' age of twenty while my parents were the ones out painting the town red? Not that this was unusual. My parents were party people and totally, sickeningly in love with each other after over twenty years of marriage. Whereas, I was a dedicated homebody who had an unhealthy addiction to bingeing on Netflix. By myself. A year of college hadn't upped my game at all. It was summer break, and I was in bed before *my mom and dad*.

    I waited for the usual drunken whispers and giggles as my parents walked by my door, which was always followed by the sound of their bedroom door locking—*shudder*—but this time there was only silence. That was weird. But I also didn't want to walk in on anything that would scar me for life, so I paused my tablet and listened. When the front door closed again and silence reigned a second time, I got out of my bed to investigate. Pulling the curtains aside, I watched my mom's friend, Jessica, have a heated exchange with their other friend, Emily, before they both got into Jessica's car and left.

Something definitely wasn't right.

Leaving my bedroom, I cautiously walked down the hall. The house was eerily quiet. Was anyone even here? "Mom? Dad?"

I didn't get an answer.

My heartbeat pounding in my ears, I reached the living room and found my mom all by herself just standing by the front door staring down at her hands. That alone was strange enough, but the really weird thing was her clothes. She'd been wearing a plunging, sparkly black dress when she left the house earlier. Now she had on a too-tight white T-shirt and stretchy black yoga pants. Clearly not my mom's clothes because they lacked her usual biker bitch flair.

"Mom? What's going on? Why are you dressed like that? Where's Dad?"

Her head jerked up, and I knew. Something was wrong. Something was really, really wrong. Her expression was shattered. It looked like she'd spent the last hour crying. Her makeup was long gone, and her eyes were swollen and red. I stared into the face of absolute pain, and my whole body started shaking.

"Mom? What's . . . What's going on? Where's Daddy?"

My mom shook her head. When she finally spoke, her voice was more of a husky whisper, almost like she was talking to herself. "He wouldn't wake up. I thought he was just passed out—that he'd wake up and be fine if we just got him inside—but he wasn't. He wasn't."

Tears silently poured down her cheeks, and she looked down at her hands like they held the answer or something. But they were empty.

My whole body shook with tremors as a burning sensation swept over my scalp. Dad wasn't fine? That didn't mean . . . She couldn't mean . . . "Mom, where's Dad?"

She shook her head as she stared down at her hands. "I don't know.

PROLOGUE

I think Axle was arranging something. The girls promised they'd tell me tomorrow. They said I could probably see him tomorrow."

Now it was my voice that was a husky whisper as tears clouded my eyes. "Mama? Is he . . . Is he . . ."

Mom bit her lip. "He's gone. I'm so sorry. He's gone, honey."

"No." A roaring sound filled my ears. "No, he can't be. I just saw him a few hours ago. He was fine. You guys were going out like always. He can't be gone."

"There was a Wild Rider in the parking lot of the club tonight. He had a gun. And your dad didn't . . . There was just so much blood . . ." My mom trailed off as her breath hitched, then she held out her arms to me.

I wrapped my arms around my waist and backed away. "He can't be gone. He can't. He was just . . . And you were . . . No!"

The burning at the back of my throat made it impossible to say anything more. I dropped to my knees with a cry and buried my face in my hands. Tears burned my eyes and poured through my fingers. It couldn't be true. My amazing, supportive, awesome father couldn't be dead. He couldn't.

He couldn't.

Chapter 1

One year later

Howl Nightclub, Reno, Nevada

"Breathe, Amber. Just breathe," I murmured to myself.

I didn't know which was more pathetic—the fact that everyone was ignoring me, or that I ever thought my crazy plan would actually work. But I needed information, and this was the one place in town my dad's biker friends couldn't stonewall me. All I'd been able to find out about that night was that my dad was killed by a Wild Rider, a rival motorcycle club member, and that his killer had been turned over to the Volkskya Bratva.

The same organization that ran this club.

I'd purposely come to Howl on a Wednesday because I figured it'd be empty and I could pry information out of the bored staff, but instead it was so dead what staff was here were too busy flirting to notice a paying customer. The bartender continued to murmur in Russian to the brunette and ignore me.

I scoped out the interior while I leaned against the bar and waited. The dark, moody lighting made what was on the weekends a bright bumping club instead an intimate make-out spot. Couples sat in the

CHAPTER 1

red leather booths against the exposed brick walls, vintage portraits of flappers and twenties-era burlesque models here and there. A few ornate chandeliers made of gold and dripping with crystals hung over the dance floor and a few booths. The largest chandelier was suspended over the bar's well, the gold vines and leaves twisting down until they framed the shelves of expensive liquors at the back of the bar.

Someone's hand clasped my arm, and I jumped as he pulled me to his side.

"*Ona so mnoy.*" A deep voice rumbled somewhere above my head.

My heart pounded so hard and fast, I felt like everyone in the room could hear it. What the hell had I got myself into? Stupid Amber.

"*Prosti,* Ruslan Ivanov." The bartender snapped to attention; his voice sounded so respectful in contrast to how he'd flirted with the brunette. And ignored me.

"*Da. Ya bin khatyel shampanskaye. Moy stolik. Teper.*"

The bartender's gaze went to the floor as he moved around the counter like his shoes were on fire. He grabbed a bucket and was filling it with ice when the man who still had his arm around me pressed against me, forcing me to move toward a dark table in the back corner. I looked frantically at the other patrons we passed by, but no one would meet my eyes. Heck, as we moved across the club everyone kept their gazes glued to their tables like the devil himself had suddenly appeared.

I wanted to look up at the man next to me, but given everyone's demeanor, I was afraid of what I'd find. His hand moved from my shoulder to the small of my back, where my sparkly top didn't quite meet the waistband of my skinny jeans. Goose bumps broke out across my body as he rubbed his thumb against the exposed skin there. My heart beat out of my chest. Really, all I wanted at that moment was to be home with my mom watching sappy old movies on TV like we had a million times before.

But I couldn't because my mom was most likely passed out drunk on the living room floor and wouldn't even notice I was gone tonight. Like it'd been every night since my dad died.

He paused for a moment next to the booth before he motioned with his hand for me to slide in. It was a corner booth shaped like a V with the second-most ornate chandelier in the club suspended overhead.

And I really didn't want to sit there.

Every single one of my survival instincts were screaming at me. *Get out. Run. Now.* But I couldn't. I needed information. I'd been stonewalled for so long about my dad's death; I couldn't leave at the first sign of trouble. This guy might have the answers I desperately needed.

After one more nudge from Mr. Mysterious, I scooted over the bench seat, around the table, to the far side of the booth. Once I settled, I placed my hands on the table and looked up at the most gorgeous man I'd ever seen, despite the waves of hostility pouring off of him. His gleaming brown hair was cropped close but still a little longer on top, and he had a bit of facial hair like he hadn't shaved in a week but in a *GQ* way, given the dark gray suit he wore like a second skin. I always felt so uncomfortable in dressy clothes, but Mr. Mysterious looked right at home in his suit and tie. And his face. Aside from the frown wrinkling his brow, he could've been a model with his fierce features and piercing golden brown eyes. But it was the frown that was making my palms sweat.

And the dead, unimpressed expression in his eyes.

"What's a girl like you doing in a place like this?" He asked with hardly any accent at all.

"I, uh, came for a drink?" My answer came out more like a question.

"Really? Alone. In Howl."

His condescension had a way of clearing up my nerves. And really

CHAPTER 1

pissing me off. Much like the guys in my dad's motorcycle club, Mr. Mysterious also thought he knew better than me. "Clearly. Do you see anyone else with me?"

His frown grew deeper and his eyes remained fixed on my face. Even after a beat when the bartender appeared at our table with a chilled bottle of Krug nestled in a stand filled with ice. After placing two delicate flutes on the table, the bartender beat a hasty retreat.

And reminded me that the person I was sitting across the table from maybe wasn't someone to screw with. If he had *everyone* in the bar nervous, I should probably be wary too.

"*Nyet*. I do not." He didn't make a move toward the bottle or glasses or take his eyes off me. "How about you tell me why you're really here."

The blank expression in his eyes made me uneasy. I shook my head, avoiding eye contact as I scooted to the end of the bench. "I'm sorry. This was a mistake."

But before I could stand up, his hand came down over mine, covering it with a soft but firm grip. "*Prosti*. I am sorry. That was rude. How about we try from the beginning. I am Ruslan. Would you like a drink?"

I looked up at his now friendly face and the difference took my breath away. He was gorgeous. And smiling. Charm oozed from his every orifice. And he might just have the answers I needed. It was the latter that decided it for me. Despite my misgivings, I couldn't leave until I at least tried to get some answers about my father. I settled back in my seat and gave Ruslan a weak smile. "I'm Amber."

"Amber," he said my name reverently. "Like the color of your glorious hair. It is fitting."

"I, uh, thank you."

"*Pozhalsta*. May I pour you a glass of champagne?"

"I don't know."

Ruslan cocked his head. "Do you not like champagne?"

"Yes. No." I stopped and shook my head at my babbling. "That is, I don't know if I like champagne since I've never had it before."

"There's no way to find out other than trying it for yourself." He reached toward the bottle, but paused when I shook my head.

"That's not it. I'm sure I'll like it—even I have heard of Krug before—it's just that my dad always told me to never accept a drink from a guy in a bar."

Ruslan raised an eyebrow. "You're afraid it's drugged?"

My eyes went wide, and I opened my mouth to reply, but I didn't know what to say. That was the implication, but it sounded ridiculous when said out loud. And rude. Shrugging helplessly, I inclined my head in answer.

After a beat, Ruslan let loose the most magnetic sound of masculine laughter I'd ever heard. It made me smile and relaxed the tension in my shoulders some. But given his Jekyll and Hyde routine, I wasn't letting all my walls down. I'd been around enough sketchy wannabes who hung around my dad's motorcycle club to ever trust the façade guys like this showed to the world. And he'd already let his mask slip once.

Ruslan smiled charmingly at me. "If it puts your mind at ease, I'll drink first."

Unable to find a flaw in his logic, I smiled and nodded. "That sounds good."

Ruslan reached for the champagne bottle and chuckled while muttering something under his breath that I couldn't make out. He palmed something in his right hand. After a soft snick, an impressive blade flashed out. A switchblade. The kind my dad loved to carry around. As Ruslan slashed at the foil on the neck of the bottle, my breath caught in my throat. But I already knew without looking any closer that his knife was a different model. Dad's handle had a cherry red patina while Ruslan's was black. And I was pretty sure my brother

CHAPTER 1

Jackson was carrying Dad's blade now.

The sudden pop of the champagne bottle had me flinching from my memories.

Holding the cork in his right hand, Ruslan deftly filled the two flutes, then placed the bottle back into the bucket. After tossing the cork onto the table, he picked one flute, sniffed delicately, then took a drink. Ruslan's teeth flashed as he smiled at me. *"Na zdorovie."*

His smile faltered as he took in my expression. "It was a joke, *moya zvezda*. Drinking to your health . . . What's wrong?"

"Nothing. Sorry." I grabbed my glass and took a few bracing gulps, emptying the glass.

And immediately regretted it.

The acid taste landed harshly in my empty stomach while the bubbles or the smell or something burned my nose. I slammed the glass down on the table while I hacked a lung and tried to get my breath back.

God, this was so embarrassing. Nothing said unsophisticated hick quite like spitting out expensive champagne and then coughing all over the crazy guy who'd spent the money on it. Sheesh. Could this night get any worse?

Once I had myself under control, I peeked up at Ruslan. He stared placidly back at me like he had all the time in the world.

"Clearly champagne is not your drink, *moya zvezda*. Would you like me to order something more to your taste? A nice glass of kvass perhaps?"

"What's kvass?"

Ruslan's eyes narrowed. "You've never been to Howl before, have you?"

"I-I uh . . ."

"You ready to tell me why you're really here, *Amber?*" He bit out my name like it was a curse. Like I was something he found sticking to the bottom of his fancy leather boots.

I had had it with men who thought they knew better than me. Who thought they could keep the truth of my father's death from me. Like the president of my dad's motorcycle club, Reb, or my only-older-than-me-by-eleven-months brother and new club prospect, Jackson. Men who thought that the fact that I was a woman was reason enough to keep information from me. Like I couldn't handle it or couldn't be trusted with the truth.

Fuck. That.

Taking the bull by the horns, or the Russian by the big, furry, proverbial Russian hat, I placed my palms on the table and leaned toward him. "I'm here to make sure that the rat bastard who murdered my father last year suffered and bled and cried. And if I'm really lucky—and he's still alive—I'm hoping that you'll let me get a few jabs in on my own. *That's* why I'm here."

My chest was heaving now with the force of my ire. I was pissed. I wanted revenge. And I was really tired of not having any answers about what had happened to my father.

A muscle flexed in Ruslan's cheek. Aside from that, he had no reaction to the ugly I'd just poured out all over his table. His eyes were as blank as ever. After a beat, he lifted his chin toward a burly guy standing with his back to the wall a few feet away. All the blood drained from my head as the burly guy stalked our way and stopped at the edge of the table next to me. Russian words flew back and forth between them, faster than I could keep track of.

This was bad. This was really, really bad.

Shit. Shit. Shit.

In a flash of movement, Ruslan shoved out of the booth and stood in front of me, next to his burly guard. "*Preekhahdeet.* Come. With me. Now."

All my ire and verve had drained out of me when the Russians got scary and well . . . Russian. I shook my head. "I should probably

CHAPTER 1

get going. My mom is waiting for me. She knows where I am, and I promised her I'd be home ten minutes ago. She worries. If I'm not home, she'll probably call up my uncles, Rebel and Axle. They're like family, you know. And I really don't want to worry them. So, I'll just—"

"Get. Up. *Now.*"

The entire bar went silent. Even the soft background music stopped. I looked frantically around, but again no one would meet my eyes. Everyone kept their faces deliberately turned away.

No one was going to help me.

Oh God. Oh God. Oh God.

I put my clutch on the tabletop and scooted around the bench seat. But before I could stand up, Ruslan's goon grabbed my clutch and it disappeared somewhere behind his mammoth back. He narrowed his eyes at me and shifted ever so slightly in my direction. The threat was clear. And terrifying. This man was huge, and no one seemed to care that both of them were taking me to the "back room."

My heart pounded so hard the whole walk down the narrow corridor with the goon at my back and Ruslan leading the way. What was I doing? Why was I just blindly following these two men to my inevitable death? But really, what could I do? I wouldn't get very far before either guy caught me, especially in these shoes. They'd taken my phone, and no one out there seemed to give the first shit about my predicament.

I'd never felt so alone . . . and stupid.

Ruslan's keys jangled in the silent hallway as he unlocked a large black door. After pushing it open, he gestured for me to enter.

I really, really didn't want to.

I looked from him to the open door then back to him with wide, frightened eyes. If I went into that room, I'd never come back out.

Screw it. If they were gonna do me in, I was gonna go down with my head held high. Make my dad proud. Biting my lip, I tilted my chin defiantly, then stepped inside and found . . . a regular office with a huge mahogany desk, a few bookcases, two ladder-back chairs, and not much else since the room was so tiny. Some of the tension left my body. I'd been expecting a rack or an empty room with a concrete floor and a single light bulb swinging overhead.

Apparently I watched too much TV.

I strode into the room. Ruslan followed and closed the door behind him, leaving the goon outside. Ruslan circled the desk, then sprawled in the big tufted leather chair. He laced his fingers together and rested his hands on his taut stomach like he didn't have a care in the world.

Meanwhile, I was vibrating with tension and waiting for the hammer to fall. Because it would. If I'd learned anything from my dad being in a motorcycle club, it was that men took their business seriously and didn't appreciate women calling them on it.

Why did I blurt out all that crap about my dad? What the hell was I thinking?

Ruslan surveyed me from his throne. He was deliberately keeping me on edge. His eyes lingered at my hips, my chest, then my face. He took a long time examining every feature. I couldn't tell if he liked what he saw or if he was planning different ways to carve up my body. His face was blank the entire time. It was unnerving and creepy, and I just wanted to get the hell out of here.

But still, he didn't say anything.

After what felt like an eternity, I finally blurted out, "What the fuck is your plan? Are you going to kill me or what? Because I've still got shit to do tonight if it's all the same to you."

Crinkles appeared next to his eyes and after a beat, Ruslan laughed. "Just when I think I have you nailed down, you surprise me, *moya zvezda*."

I crossed my arms over my chest like it protected me from his

CHAPTER 1

penetrating gaze. "You keep calling me that. What does it mean?"

"'My star.' You shined so bright in the bar, I couldn't see anyone else."

Coming from a regular guy, that would've been the sweetest thing I'd ever heard, but hearing it from Ruslan filled me with foreboding. He was a really dangerous guy, given the way literally everyone acted around him, and now I was on his radar. I was so screwed.

I knew better than to piss him off, especially when I was alone with him, but I couldn't seem to get my brain and tongue to agree. My fight-or-flight instincts were all screwed up. I still had a hint of sarcasm in my voice when I replied, "That's so sweet."

"And true. You are special. I could tell the moment I saw you, Amber. Please. Sit. I promise not to pounce on you." Ruslan bared his teeth in an attempt at a smile. "I save that for the second date."

"Not with me. I'm more of a get-to-know-the-guy-first kinda girl." I smiled stiffly as I took a seat in one of the ladder-back chairs in front of his desk. The rigid wood made it difficult to relax, although that might've had something to do with the man sitting across from me. I stared at the gleaming finish of his desk and took a few deep breaths, trying to calm my racing heart.

"So, you're Stitch's daughter."

My eyes jerked to his as I felt all the blood drain from my head. How did he know? If anything, I looked like my mom, with her blond hair and facial features. All I inherited from my dad was his slender build and his love of *Star Wars*. "How did you—"

"You mentioned your father was murdered last year, and given your all-American looks and age, I filled in the blanks." Ruslan sat forward and placed his hands on the desk. He looked intently at me. "I'm sorry to state it so bluntly, but I have a few more meetings tonight and must . . . what is the phrase? Cut our chase short?"

I nodded tightly.

"As far as your father's killer goes, there is nothing for you to worry about, *moya zvezda*." He waved his hand in a dismissive fashion, and I saw red.

"I swear to God, if one more man says that to me, I'll go insane. Why is it only men are allowed to be pissed off? Only men can want revenge? That asshole killed *my father*. I want to make sure that he bled. That he felt pain and anguish and a million different kinds of hell before his miserable life ended. My father was the best man—the only man I've ever loved. He didn't deserve to bleed out in a fucking parking lot like a common criminal. And I want to make sure that the fucker who did that to him died the most horrific way possible. Or at the very least, get my own jabs in before he's dead." My chest heaved with my panting breath, and after a few beats the reality of where I was and who I just shouted at sank in.

Ruslan didn't say anything for several moments as he eyed me flatly. But the muscle flexing in his jaw belied his calm demeanor. My anger slowly leached from my body as he continued to stare at me. I suddenly felt light-headed and swayed slightly in my seat.

His voice hissed when he finally spoke. "The man who murdered your father has been taken care of. *That* is what I meant when I said there's nothing for you to worry about. You do not ever question *me* about *my business* ever again. DO YOU UNDERSTAND?"

I nodded jerkily as I avoided his gaze. Fear singed my nerves. Where my rant had been all passion and indignation, his was pure rage. It wasn't difficult to see why everyone in the bar had been afraid of him. I was terrified. I bit my lip to keep my whimpers inside. I couldn't let him see me sweat. The only thing I had going for me was that he was interested in me and my swagger. If he believed I was as scared as everyone else out there, he'd no doubt lose interest, and then I'd really be screwed.

I took another second to gather myself then lifted my head and

CHAPTER 1

looked Ruslan in the eyes. "I apologize. I spoke out of turn. It's just frustrating. No one will tell me what happened. He was my father. I just miss him so much."

Tears burned my eyes, but I determinedly blinked them back. I'd cried so many tears, and I'd be damned before I let *him* see me so vulnerable.

Ruslan's expression softened somewhat and he reached across the desk to caress the back of my hand. "I understand, *moya zvezda*. But you cannot question me about my business. That is why I brought you back to my office. The little bit I can tell you cannot be shared outside these walls."

I nodded. "Okay. Thank you."

"I can assure you that the man who murdered your father wasn't cosseted—the end was not quick—and you'll never have to worry about him again. But that is *all* I can tell you."

I leaned back in my chair, breaking my contact with Ruslan, and nodded. "I understand. Thank you. It's more than my father's club shared with me. I appreciate it."

The words and my placating tone burned my throat, but I said them anyway. I just wanted to get the hell outta here and away from him.

Ruslan nodded slowly as he continued to watch me. "Now I'm sorry to say I have another meeting."

"I believe you mentioned that." I smiled charmingly and tilted my head. "If I could get my things back from your guy, I'll get out of your hair."

Ruslan chuckled. "Ah, *moya zvezda,* you are not a trouble. Come, I'll have a car deliver you back to your home."

I opened my mouth to reply when he spoke over me.

"That wasn't a request. I have claimed responsibility for you, and I can't have anything happen to you on my watch." Ruslan pressed a button on his desk and after a beat his office door opened and the goon poked his head in. Ruslan barked something in Russian and the goon nodded before backing out and closing the door again. "You may get your things from Viktor on your way to the car."

Taking the hint, I stood up and gave Ruslan an awkward smile. His declaration that he'd "claimed responsibility" for me filled me with foreboding. I knew what that meant in the motorcycle club world. But we'd just met. It couldn't mean the same thing for him. Could it? No part of that sounded good. I'd be damned before I became anyone's property.

Shit, I never should've come here.

I took a step toward the door when Ruslan sprang from his chair. Steeling myself for whatever came next, I tried not to let my nerves show.

Ruslan walked around his desk like a lion stalking his prey. Stopping in front of me, he clasped my hand, then pulled me away from the doorway. "It is disrespectful to the *domvoi* to say goodbye near the threshold."

I didn't even have time to process that before his lips were on mine. My eyes shut reflexively, and I swayed slightly toward him. But that was only because I was off balance and had nothing to do with his kiss. Mostly. Ruslan's lips were soft and supple as they moved against mine. It'd been so long since I kissed a guy, but it was like riding a bike. And Ruslan was so damned good at it. A beat later, my lips moved of their own accord with his. Despite my utter dislike for him, I felt my nipples tingle as he took the kiss deeper. Before I knew it, my arms were wrapped around his neck, and I was rubbing my chest against his as we continued to kiss.

I vaguely registered a sound somewhere behind me, but we continued kissing. Then I heard a few Russian words followed by my father's friend, Axle, shouting, "WHAT THE FUCK?"

Chapter 2

Bam

This wasn't how I'd wanted to spend my Wednesday night. I'd planned on hanging out at our club's bar, maybe getting lucky with one of the girls, then hitting the hay. I had to be at work in six fucking hours. I sure as shit didn't want to be playing bodyguard for our hotheaded VP, Axle.

Tonight wasn't the first time the guys had used my size to their advantage since I'd gotten my patch. Hell, they used it before I became a member, too. At six-six and two hundred and eighty pounds, I cast a pretty big shadow. Half the time I didn't even have to say anything; I just gave a look and assholes ran the other way. But all that went out the window when you were dealing with the Volkskya Bratva. Those fuckers were crazy and not afraid of much. A scary combination.

There was no way this "simple meeting" our prez had sent us to was gonna end quick and easy with Axle at the helm.

"We have a meeting with Ruslan," Axle barked at the linebacker standing next to the closed office door. We'd already gone through shit with the guy at the front door of the club, another one at the bar, and now this one. Between Ruslan's goon squad and the security cameras, there was no way to sneak up on this place.

But with every checkpoint, a little more of Axle's already slim patience disappeared.

"Ruslan's not available." The linebacker barked back.

I closed my eyes with a muttered curse.

"Bullshit," Axle drawled. "We got a meeting. I'm going in there."

The linebacker at the door smirked but didn't say anything.

Axle shrugged, grabbed the doorknob, and pushed the door open.

The guard cursed something in Russian, but it was drowned out by Axle's shouted "WHAT THE FUCK?"

I stood at the back of the pack behind the guard, Axle, and our other impressively large member, Tank, but whatever was going on inside of Ruslan's office, shit had already hit the fan. Closing my eyes with a muttered curse, I mentally braced myself for the inevitable fight. Everything Reb had warned us against, Axle was doing. I could practically smell the burning bridges. Hell, from here it smelled like the whole damn village was on fire. Crossing my arms over my chest, I scowled.

"What the fuck are you doing here, princess?" Axle yelled as he tussled for a second with the guard. Finally, Tank waded in and shoved the Russian aside. Axle pushed past them both and into Ruslan's office with everyone hot on his heels. "And with your fucking lips on *his*?"

I half expected to see one of the club girls, or that one chick that Axle had fucked for a month straight before dropping her for suddenly being "too clingy." But when I pushed my way into Ruslan's cramped office and saw Amber, Stitch and Brittany's fucking daughter, standing in Ruslan's arms, I hesitated—too shocked to react—for a moment.

Amber's wide, ice-blue eyes passed over her audience then narrowed as she glared at us. The fuck? Stitch's daughter and Ruslan? What the fuck was going on?

Ruslan kept one arm around Amber and barked something in Russian to the guard who was hovering in the doorway. The guard

CHAPTER 2

mumbled something back in Russian then beat a hasty retreat.

They could've been an advertisement for a perfume ad or something. With Ruslan's suave three-piece suit and unshaven model looks against Amber's slender blond gorgeousness, they were the perfect couple. Aside from the fact that Ruslan was the scariest guy in the whole damn Bratva. Hell, probably the whole damn city. What the fuck was Amber doing with that asshole?

Ruslan ducked his head and kissed the top her head, staring at us the whole time. "I'm sorry we were interrupted, *moya zvezda*. I will deal with Viktor later, but I'm afraid my next meeting is here. I believe you know these . . . gentlemen?"

"That's not fucking funny, *malcik*." Axle leaned forward and pointed a finger at Ruslan. His voice was practically a growl as he continued. "I know who the fuck you're fucking, and it stops now. Amber is club property. No one fucks with True Brothers property."

Amber put her hands on her hips and turned her glare Axle's way. "Fuck you."

"What did you just say to me, princess?" Axle's voice went low and deep in that way of his when he was really, really pissed.

Oh shit. There was no way this was gonna end well.

"Fuck. You," she said slowly like she was talking to a toddler, only with cursing. "I'm not club property. I've *never* been fucking club property. You all can take your precious club and shove it up your asses."

Axle let out a strangled sound as he clenched his fists. A muscle flexed in his jaw when he finally spoke. "Bam, get her the hell out of here before I—"

I stepped forward, leaned my shoulder into Amber's stomach, and had her over my shoulder before she or Ruslan could mutter a protest.

Amber shrieked and banged her fists against my back. "Put me down, you goddamn behemoth."

Ruslan yelled something in Russian behind me, but I didn't pause in stride. I was halfway down the hall before the doors at the other end slammed open. There was more yelling in Russian, but three steps later I was out the back door and standing in the quiet parking lot. Well, quiet except for the yelling and creative cursing coming from Amber.

"Ooomph." I tightened my grip on her flailing legs when she managed to connect with my stomach. Crossing the parking lot, I eyed my bike with resignation. This was probably the only time I wished I'd brought a cage—my truck would've made getting this wildcat home a hell of a lot easier. Unable to avoid the inevitable, I stopped next to my bike and gently lowered the girl to her feet.

"Finally," she huffed. "What the fuck is wrong with you?"

"Me? You're shitting me, right?" I raised an eyebrow and crossed my arms. "You were in there dry-humping the craziest guy in the fucking Russian Mafia, and you think there's something wrong with *me*?"

"I wasn't dry-humping him," she muttered while her cheeks flamed red. It would've been endearing if she wasn't being such a pain in my ass. "Ruslan kissed me."

Like that made a fucking difference. "I didn't see you shoving him off of you."

"He's crazy." Amber shivered despite the warm August night. She crossed her arms over her chest in a stance similar to mine, but where I was pissed, she looked so small and vulnerable—like she was trying to protect herself. Until she opened her mouth and the sass poured out. "I was doing whatever I could to get the hell out of there."

"You shouldn't have been there in the first fucking place. Howl is not a goddamn college hangout. There's a reason why it's in the middle of fucking nowhere. You don't belong here."

"I had to be here. I wanted to know what happened to my dad and his killer. And you guys kept stonewalling me. Because men and their business were more important than fucking family."

"Bullshit. How'd you even know to come here in the first place?" What happened with Stitch and his killer was club business. No one outside of the club and the Bratva knew what went down. Or should've known. So how did Amber know to show up here to ask questions?

She shook her head and scowled but didn't say anything. I could respect the balls it took to come here on her own, but she was too young and inexperienced to play on the same level as Ruslan and his crew.

Which reminded me.

I narrowed my eyes at her. "Are you even old enough to be in a bar? Let me see your ID."

"Of course I am. I work in a casino." Amber patted her thighs before she looked up at me with another scowl. "But I don't have my ID. Ruslan's goon took my purse, along with my phone and house keys. I would've had them back and been on my way home but for you three and your fucking caveman routine. Now what am I gonna do?"

"Fuck," I muttered as I grabbed my phone out of my pocket. I tossed off a quick text to Tank. Lord knew Axle wasn't in a frame of mind to look at his phone right now.

Me: *R still has A's stuff. Grab it for her.*

Tank: *K*

Ever the eloquent guy. Although, given the fact that he was probably in the middle of a Mafia standoff, probably not a bad thing, either.

I jerked my chin in Amber's direction. "Tank will get your shit for you. Did you drive yourself out here or am I taking you home?"

She seemed calmer now, which was the only reason I was offering to let her drive herself. That and I don't ever have women on the back of my bike. Ever.

"I left my car at home and took an Uber. And even if I had my car, Ruslan has my keys so how would I even start it, Einstein?"

Fuck me. This was the night that kept on giving. "Fine. I'll take you home."

Given the way she was glaring at me, I didn't need to go into a spiel about what being on the back of my bike *didn't* mean. She wasn't my woman. Amber wasn't a club girl. She had no hopes or expectations with a guy like me.

This was the night from hell. As soon as I got this wildcat home, the better. I just wanted to crawl into my bed and get some fucking sleep already.

Amber's lip curled as she looked from me to my rough Indian motorcycle. My Indian had more scrapes than paint at the moment, but she still purred like a content cat when I started her up. I put all the spare money I had into maintaining her engine and making sure she ran like the well-oiled machine she was. One of these days I'd get around to making her look as good as she sounded.

I take that back. Judging from Amber's current expression, her only expectation was getting the hell away from me as soon as possible.

Which was fine by me.

After tossing my helmet to Amber, I swung a leg over and waited for her to climb on behind me. Then I cranked the ignition and let the vibrations from my bike wash over my soul. Nothing filled me with peace as much as sitting on my motorcycle. Even if it was to run to the other side of town with a hellcat on my back.

"You living with your mom in South Reno?"

"Yes." The word hissed from her lips like it pained her to either admit she was still living at home or accept a ride from me. Probably both. "Near Damonte Ranch."

I jerked my head in recognition. I'd been to Stitch's house a few times back when I was a prospect, but it'd been a while. We tore out of the parking lot, and a few moments later I was speeding down side streets. Since I didn't pack a loaner helmet and I'd given mine

CHAPTER 2

to Amber, I had to avoid the main roads and highways, which would hopefully let me avoid the cops. Although the way tonight was going, getting pulled over would be the nugget on top of this shit sundae.

It was different to have a chick on the back of my bike for once. The way she tightened her thighs around my hips when I accelerated. The way her body felt pressed against my back. I might've been wearing my leather vest, but I could still feel the warmth from her body. The way her fingers clutched at me when I took a corner too fast. I could almost imagine her clutching at me in a different setting. The way her scent enveloped me when I slowed at a stop sign. Something citrus and sweet. Almost like those orange cinnamon rolls my grandma would bake every Saturday.

Fuck. What was wrong with me? I was giving an annoying chick a ride home, not . . . whatever the hell this was. I wasn't made for happy times and families and fucking stability. I was the opposite of all that. And the sooner this wildcat got off my bike, the better.

The second half of the ride felt so much longer than the first. But finally, after a few eons, I pulled up to the house I remembered from my prospecting days.

Only it never looked like this while Stitch was alive.

The grass out front was dead and yellow—what there was left of it. Huge patches of dirt filled in the yard here and there. I doubted anyone had watered it in a year. And the house itself had seen better days. It looked like someone started scraping the old paint off, but only got halfway through before they quit. And the wood beneath was dingy and sun-bleached like it'd been exposed a while ago. Maybe a job from when Stitch was still alive?

But the thing that filled me with horror was the sight of Stitch's pride and joy—his Harley-Davidson Fat Boy—sitting on the side of the house with a huge puddle of dried and cakey oil beneath it. The leather seat was cracked and broken since it'd been left exposed to the elements, and a huge scrape marred the finish of his custom paint job. Like someone had purposefully scratched it.

I cut my engine, put my kickstand down, and waited for Amber to get off.

"Thanks for the ride," she said grudgingly. "Tank or whoever can just leave my stuff on the front step. No need to ring the bell or whatever."

"What the hell happened?" I waved a hand at her house and her dad's bike. "How did—"

"Are you fucking kidding me? What happened? *What happened?*" Amber's face turned a shade of red I'd never seen on a woman's face before. Her voice rose until she was screaming. "You and your goddamn club *happened*. My dad died because of your oh so sacred club business. What do you think happens when the person holding your family together dies? The family dies, too!"

Dogs barked in the distance and the lights next door turned on, but I couldn't look away from the pure anguish on Amber's face. It felt ridiculous to say, but I hadn't thought much of Stitch's family over the past year. I was the low man on the totem pole and hadn't known him very well. I think I'd met his wife once or twice at club functions, and maybe Amber once, too, but she wasn't the kinda girl I'd hang out with. I knew better than to sniff around a club princess—girls like Amber were off limits to guys like me—so I hadn't given much thought to how they were handling his death.

But clearly the answer was—not well. I looked at Stitch's pride and joy rotting on the side of the house. Not well at all.

Fuck, if this was what the outside looked like . . .

I swung off my bike and held a hand out to Amber. "Come on."

"What? No. *I'm* going inside. *You* can go to hell or back to your fucking clubhouse. I don't really care which. In fact, I'd be happy if we never saw each other again."

"You wouldn't be the first woman to tell me that today." I gave her

CHAPTER 2

my most charming smile. "But my grandma taught me to treat every woman like a lady. Which means I'm walking you to your door."

Amber rolled her eyes. "Whatever. It's ten feet. But just know you're not coming inside."

I shrugged a shoulder and didn't take offense when Amber ignored my offered hand and started up the driveway. The streetlight in front of their house cast enough light to let me enjoy the view. Her tight little jeans cupped her firm legs and ass, outlining them to perfection. And when she bent down to grab the key hidden under an empty flowerpot, I had to clench my fists. Because one, that was a ridiculous location for their key—so obvious, and anyone could grab it—and two, her ass looked so amazing when she crouched, I had to check myself.

As if she knew where my mind had wandered, Amber stood up and tossed a glare over her shoulder at me. I smirked back. Facing the door again, Amber unlocked it, then turned to face me. As she pushed the door slightly open, I caught an outline of something that made my heart drop.

"Here I am. Safe and sound. So you can—"

"Brittany?" I cut in, shoving my way past Amber and through the doorway. I stooped down next to a prone Brittany unconscious on the floor.

"Mom!" Amber shouted from somewhere behind me as I took Brittany's pulse.

She was alive. Her breathing was so slow and soundless I was afraid there for a second. Then I rolled Brittany onto her side and the pool of vomit beneath her filled me in on the story.

I sat back on my heels and turned to Amber. "She's just passed out."

"Yeah, I put that together myself, Sherlock," Amber muttered as she stomped into the kitchen then reappeared with a roll of paper towels, carpet cleaner, and a plastic bag. She dropped to her knees next to me and began mopping up the mess. "Thanks. I'll take it from here."

Given the slump in her shoulders and how quickly prepared she was to clean up, this wasn't the first time Amber had come home to her mom passed out in a pool of vomit. Fuck me, that was wrong. Amber should've been the one getting drunk at a college party and having someone else cleaning up *her* puke. She was what? Twenty-one? Twenty-two? Where was her brother, Jackson? He was a little older than Amber. Shouldn't he be here helping out his family? I knew he'd become a prospect for the club after his dad died, but this was his family. How could he not know what his mom and sister were going through?

Did any of the Brothers know what was going on here? Stitch had been one of us, and now his whole family was falling apart. Shit, someone somewhere dropped the ball.

I sighed and rubbed at my tired eyes. "I'll help you get her in her bed."

"That's okay. I've got it." Amber said as she gathered up the clumps of used paper towels.

Brittany let out a loud snore then rolled onto her back.

I looked from Amber's small frame to Brittany's more voluptuous and, well, larger body. "She outweighs you by what? Twenty? Thirty pounds? Just let me carry her into her bedroom, then I'll get out of your hair."

"I said I got it, all right?" Amber rocked back onto her heels and scowled up at me. "I don't need your help. I don't need anything from your club. You True Brothers have done enough for my family, don't you think? You guys only care about yourselves and fuck what comes after. Do you know not a single one of you has been here in months? Including my loser prospect brother? You guys only care about the club and your Brothers. Women like me and my mom don't matter. I've figured out how to get by on my own. So I got this. You can go back to your club and your drinking and your women and forget everything you saw here tonight. Your kind seem to be especially good at that."

Amber rolled her mom onto her side, and after some cajoling and a surprising amount of strength from someone so tiny, got Brittany to her feet. "Come on, Mom. Time for bed."

They stumbled down the hallway.

"I love you so much, Ambah." Brittany belched. "Is Jackson here? JACKSON? Where are you, boy-o?"

Amber sighed. "He doesn't live here, Mom. Remember? He moved out after… when he started prospecting for the *club*."

The rest of their conversation was muffled as they'd reached the bedroom. I stood silently and alone in the living room. The scent of vomit and floral carpet cleaner hung heavy in the air. Amber's words echoed in my head. No one had checked in on them in months? Including her brother?

Shit was gonna hit the fan. And after what I'd seen here tonight, it was months late in coming.

Chapter 3

Amber

Knock. Knock. Knock.

"Ugh," I groaned. I opened one eye and looked blearily at the clock on my nightstand. It was either six or eight o'clock in the morning. Either way it was way too early for some dipshit to be knocking on the front door so forcefully. Maybe if I ignored it, they'd go away. My head fell back onto my pillow, and I was just starting to get back into my dream about a Viking with long blond hair, a matching beard, and ridiculous muscles when the sound came again. But louder.

Pound. Pound. Pound.

"Fine!" I ripped the sheet off my body and climbed out of bed. Mr. Viking and his dirty lovemaking would have to wait.

I stumbled down the hall into the living room and the scent from last night slammed into my face. Lavender carpet solution tinged with vomit. I could still see the darker patch on the rug where I'd applied the cleaner. "Cleans and refreshes, my ass."

Pound. Pound. Pound.

"I'm coming. Keep your pants on." Reaching the front door, I pulled it open and swayed sleepily in the doorway. "What do you want?"

Needless to say I wasn't a morning person. Quite the opposite,

CHAPTER 3

actually. I needed at least an hour and two cups of coffee before I was somewhat presentable. But this asshole was persistent.

A man I'd never seen before stood buried beneath a mound of at least four dozen bloodred roses with a dozen or so white hydrangeas at the base. It was the largest floral display I'd ever seen. The blood froze in my veins as I stared at the ridiculously large arrangement. There was only one person I'd ever met who could afford to send it. Please let me be wrong. Oh God, please.

"I think you have the wrong address," I said weakly, hoping that was the case.

The man scowled at me from over the mass of flowers. "Amber Bennett?"

My heart did a freefall in my chest. *Oh God.* "Yes?"

"No mistake. Sign here."

"Who are they from?" I asked as I signed the clipboard he awkwardly juggled with the flowers. I already knew, but I hoped like hell I was wrong.

"Client information is confidential, but there should be a card." He nodded toward the tiny envelope facing me. "Are you going to take them or not? I have more deliveries to make today."

"Oh. Yes. Of course. So sorry." I grabbed the large vase from him. "Let me get my purse."

"No tips. The person ordering does the tipping," the man grumbled, then turned and walked away.

"Sorry, I've never gotten flowers before. Thank you!" I yelled at his back as he walked toward his box van.

He lifted a hand in my direction then climbed into his van.

I looked anywhere but at the extravagant floral arrangement as I closed the door behind me. They smelled amazing but felt like an albatross in my hands. Taking a deep breath, I set off for the kitchen then placed the vase on the high countertop. Unable to look anywhere else, I stared at the flowers in dismay. It felt like I was having an out-of-body experience. I dreaded opening the card because then I'd know. The longer I waited, the longer I could naively believe they were from someone, anyone, but *him*.

After what felt like forever, I finally got the nerve to grab the tiny envelope and rip it open.

Red for your luscious, plump lips
White to match your pure heart

There was no signature, but I didn't need one. There was only one man I'd kissed in the past month. Only one man who'd send flowers like this to me.

Ruslan. Bratva kingpin, scariest guy I'd ever met. Ruslan.

Shit, shit, shit.

What do I do? I didn't want to encourage him. But on the other hand, he was too scary to discourage, too. A man like that would not take rejection well. And I did kiss him back last night. Although in my defense, it was more of a reflex reaction than actual interest on my part. Not to mention the fact that he was really good at it.

But then I remembered what his eyes looked like when I'd pissed him off. Or the way I felt when he'd marched me down that hall, and I'd been sure he was going to off me. Ruslan was not a man to screw around with. I could very well end up in a small unmarked grave if I didn't handle this right.

Crap.

Why did I ever think it was a good idea to go to Howl alone? What the hell had I been thinking? I wasn't Nancy Drew. This kinda thing always ended bad. Like it had for my dad.

I was fed up with the runaround I'd been getting from my dad's club, and I had so much anger stored up. I wanted to do something about the shitstorm that my life had become. I was so frustrated with the lack of answers. All I knew was that my dad had been shot in a parking

CHAPTER 3

lot, and that the club had turned his killer over to the Bratva. That was it. I didn't even know the asshole's name or why he'd shot my dad. I'd been hoping Ruslan would tell me something, anything more than the tiny bit I knew.

But he hadn't.

Hell, Ruslan knew the party line better than anyone in my dad's club. So instead of answers it seemed that I'd picked up an ardent admirer instead. An ardent, scary admirer.

Regardless of how hot he was or how soft his lips were, I really shouldn't have kissed him back. Now he had the wrong idea about me. *Crap.*

"Who was at the door?" My mom grumbled as she lurched into the kitchen.

"I, uh, well . . ." It was too late to try to hide the flowers, but I couldn't very well tell my mom they came from a Bratva captain or whatever Bam had called Ruslan last night. I awkwardly stood in front of the flowers to hide them from my mom. Fortunately I didn't have to answer as her attention quickly turned to the lack of caffeine in her veins.

"You haven't made coffee yet? Who are you and what've you done with my daughter?"

"Haha, very funny, Mom." Every morning went like this. No matter what happened the night before, the next morning was a blank slate. We didn't talk about the booze or the vomit or the tears. And we *never* talked about my dad when Mom was sober. Instead we just danced around the herd of elephants in the room and pretended like everything was normal, that my mom wouldn't start drinking before noon, that my dad wasn't dead, or that the whole thing wasn't slowly killing us all.

Mom moved painfully around the kitchen in that way of hers that told me she had a killer headache—another thing we didn't talk about.

She was reaching for the can of coffee next to me when I heard her gasp.

"Holy mother of God, where did those come from?"

I closed my eyes and did something I hadn't had to do since I was sixteen. I lied. "I don't know. That's who was at the door. Delivery guy."

"Well, there's a card, isn't there? What does it say?"

Oh Lord, shoot me now. "It's not signed."

A huge grin swept across my mom's face. Quickly followed by a wince that we both ignored. "You have a secret admirer? You've been holding out on me. What's going on? Who do you think it is? Spill everything!"

"Mom, I haven't had any coffee yet. I can't even—"

"Say no more. Coffee coming in two minutes. *Then* you're telling me everything."

I couldn't wait.

I felt like crap for lying to my mom, but what could I do? I sure as hell wasn't gonna tell her that I'd caught the attention of a scary Russian Mafia guy while I was investigating what'd happened to Dad and his killer last year. That would violate so many of our unspoken rules regarding what we didn't speak about: Dad's business, Dad's death, *Dad*. Not to mention the scary Russian guy. Yeah, I was better off not confiding in my mom.

Instead I did a little verbal dancing and made up an excuse about not knowing who it was. Could've been a coworker, maybe a guy I'd gone to high school with; I didn't know. Then I made up another lie about a spin class I was late for and got the hell outta there. If I stayed any longer, I'd probably drown in my sea of lies.

Which was how I ended up at the Mackay Mocha House. I didn't feel like working out, and this was the only other place I could think of to go to and kill some time.

CHAPTER 3

I pulled out my phone and texted my best friend, Sydney.

Me: *You at work?*

She didn't reply. Either she was working or nowhere near her phone. Either way I was still all alone with no sounding board. I didn't have to be at work until the afternoon shift, so I had a lot of time to burn. Once I left the house I didn't like to go back. Watching my mom drink all day long on the couch got depressing for everyone. I really wish I knew what to do, but how do you confront your parent about *her* behavior? It was so backward. Hell, the whole thing was backward, since I was the one taking care of her now. I knew I should do something, but what?

A prickling sensation swept over my spine. The hair on the back of my neck tingled. I turned and looked, but nothing seemed out of the ordinary. A few guys talked in a booth across the room. Baristas busily made drinks for the drive-thru and in-house customers. A couple of people stood in line, waiting to order. But no one was looking my way. And there was no one I recognized.

My phone buzzed in my hand.

Unknown: *What time is your shift tonight?*

Yeah, okay. That wasn't freaky at all. My pulse pounded as I reread the text. Who the hell was it from? I knew better than to reply, but that didn't mean I wasn't freaking out. I hunched over my phone as my heart raced like I was being chased by Freddy Kruger.

Unknown: *Amber? You there?*

Whoever it was knew my name. Not totally shocking, given that they were texting me, but it still didn't make me feel good. Just the opposite, actually. My stomach clenched as I read the messages again. Who was texting me?

My phone buzzed again.

Sydney: *Not working today. Sleeping. What's up?*

Me: *OMG OMG OMG. I don't even know where to start.*

Sydney: *Okay calm down. Breathe.*
Me: *Can I come over? This is just too much to text.*
Sydney: *Fine. But you know the deal.*
Me: *Yeah, yeah. I know. Bring coffee.*

I got up from my table and grabbed my stuff. The back of my neck tingled again. Looking around, I still couldn't identify the source. Maybe I was crazy.

A few minutes later, I was in my car, two cups resting in the cup holders, and on my way to Sydney's. My phone chimed a few times in my purse, but my car was too old for Bluetooth so I didn't know who was texting. Hopefully it wasn't Sydney canceling on me. I needed to talk to someone.

Once I finally pulled up to her apartment complex, I parked my car, then dug through my purse for my phone.

Unknown: *This is Bam.*
Unknown: *Hope I didn't freak you out.*
Unknown: *Hello?*

A huge shuddering sigh left me. Not Ruslan. That was a relief.

Me: *Why do you want to know when I'm working?*
Bam: *Can't you just answer the question? Why do you have to be difficult?*
Me: *Not being difficult. Just don't see how it's any concern of yours.*
Bam: *I gotta get back to work. Just text me the time.*
Me: *Yeah no. Got enough to deal with without encouraging a stalker.*
Bam: *That's sweet you think I'm stalking you. I guess I'll have to figure it out myself. See you tonight.*

A ridiculous smile stretched across my face. Bam. Huh. Then I shook my head. I couldn't think that way about one of them. They were the enemy, after all. Regardless of how hot he looked last night when he wasn't annoying the crap out of me. I blamed my euphoria on my relief that it hadn't been Ruslan texting me. It had nothing whatsoever

CHAPTER 3

to do with Bam's blond good looks or how muscular and commanding he'd been last night. That part had been annoying. Mostly.

And had nothing to do with my hot dream about Vikings last night. I blamed the History Channel for that—despite the fact I hadn't seen the show in months. Bam's wild, long blond hair and beard had nothing to do with my sudden Viking obsession.

Maybe if I said it enough, I'd start to believe it.

Shoving my phone in my purse, I grabbed our coffee and made my way to Sydney's door. Once upon a time I thought I'd get to live in an apartment like this with her while we both went to college, worked part-time jobs, and had boys chasing us. How could so much go wrong in only a year?

I'd busted my ass during my gap year, saving enough money to afford to go to an awesome college. When all my friends were enjoying their freshman year, I'd been working three jobs and living at home. But then it'd been my turn. My first year was a blast—classes and boys and living on my own—I'd loved every minute of it.

But then my dad died and there wasn't anywhere I wanted to be but with my mom. So I withdrew from college and moved back home. Now all that money I'd saved for school was going toward the mortgage, taking care of my mom, and tons of other bills I didn't know my parents paid. The paltry life insurance payout had taken care of the credit card bills. My college fund was slowly getting eaten up by all the rest.

Meanwhile my bestie, Sydney, had dropped out of college and enrolled in beauty school. Now she was an adult with a career and an apartment of her own while I was still living at home and scraping by, working as a cocktail waitress at the Mother Lode Hotel/Casino.

Living the dream.

I trudged up the stairs to the third floor, then down the long hallway to her door. Despite the trek, it was a lovely building, built just a few years ago, so all the fixtures still looked nice. But I knew better than to wait for the elevator. Sydney and I got stuck in it on move-in day. We never used it again. Two hours was an eternity when you were trapped in an elevator.

Reaching her apartment, I kicked at her door with my foot.

A moment later, the door ripped open and Sydney stood framed in the doorway. "What the hell was that? You sounded like a cop knocking on one of those cop shows."

"My hands are full. I had to use my foot."

"You know you could've just called me."

"Seriously, Syd? My hands are full."

"Oh yeah. Right."

I waited a beat then rolled my eyes. "Are you gonna let me in?"

"What? Oh sure. Come on in. Which is mine?"

I held out her coffee as I walked through the doorway. Sydney took it, and I stepped into her living area. I was at home her in place, probably more so than my own. Here, at least, I never had to clean up anybody else's messes.

"What's going on?" Sydney asked as she sat on one end of her couch and I took up the other.

"I don't even know where to start. So much has happened since we talked last week."

"What's the thing that's freaking you out the most?" Sydney sat back and took a slug from her drink.

"I think I have two guys interested in me, and they're both . . . unsuitable." It wasn't the right word, but it was the closest I could come up with.

"Two? Two guys?" Sydney gave a little squeal. "You haven't dated anyone in forever, and now you have two guys after you? What the hell did I miss in the last week?"

"Apparently a lot. You also missed the part where I said they're both

CHAPTER 3

unsuitable."

"Are they old?"

"No."

"Are they ugly?"

"No."

"Then what's the problem?"

"One is in the Mafia, and the other is in my dad's motorcycle club."

Sydney sat back with wide eyes then whispered, "The Mafia?"

I gave her a brief rundown of what'd happened last night, including how gorgeous and scary Ruslan looked and acted, Bam's resemblance to a Viking god, the roses this morning from Ruslan, and the flirty texts from Bam.

"Wait, do I know Bam? He doesn't sound familiar."

"No, he just got his patch. He was a prospect when my dad was . . . still in the club." I finished lamely.

"But he looks like a Viking god? Why aren't you all over that? I would be."

"Because he's just another asshole biker who thinks he runs the world. He picked me up and carried me out of the club last night, Syd."

Sydney gave an exaggerated shiver. "Sounds yummy. I'd love to be with a guy strong enough to pick me up. Now that's a man. Not a little boy who needs permission to stay out late because he's still living with his mommy."

I gave Sydney a what-the-eff look.

She raised her palms. "That's not what I meant. It's different with you. You moved back to help out. You're there to help your family, not the other way around. You are awesome."

I hitched a shoulder and looked away. "Sometimes it doesn't feel that way."

Sydney knew more than most about what was going on at my home. I didn't specifically tell her how bad things with my mom were, but I think she'd filled in the blanks on her own. And she'd been over a few times when my mom was wasted, so Sydney had no doubt put two and two together. She knew my mom was struggling with my dad's death, and she'd watched how I struggled keep everything together.

And being my best friend, she knew when I didn't want to talk about something.

"How do you know the flowers are from Ruslan and not Bam?" She raised her eyebrows as she took a drink from her cup before continuing. "You said the card wasn't signed."

"No, but that thing it said about my lips—I only kissed Ruslan last night. Not Bam."

"You kissed a Mafia kingpin? Holy shit, Amber. You kinda left that part out."

I buried my face in my hands and moaned. "I know. Mostly because I can't think about it. He's scary, Sydney. The people in his own club are scared of him. You should've seen how everyone flinched when he walked by. He gets this look in his eyes when he goes blank. It scares the crap out of me. What am I gonna do?"

"You know what you have to do."

I looked at my best friend in horror. "No. Not that. Anything but that."

"Exactly that. Viking god to the rescue." Sydney put her coffee cup down on the end table, then turned to me with excitement shining in her eyes. "You should tell him tonight. You know he's going to show up sometime during your shift."

"Not if I don't tell him what time I'm working tonight," I muttered.

"Like that's gonna stop him. Guys like Bam get shit done. He's not gonna let a little thing like your stubbornness get in his way."

"Yay," I returned flatly. I looked at Sydney like I thought she was crazy. Because I did. Bam was not someone to get excited about. He'd proved last night that he was as bad as all the rest of the guys in the

CHAPTER 3

MC. The only thing that mattered to them was club business. I might as well have been an ant beneath his boot. At best he might want in my pants, but that was it. Men like my dad were a dying breed. Literally.

Sydney continued doggedly like she hadn't heard my disinterest. "Okay, we need a plan. What are you going to wear to work tonight?"

I blinked. "My uniform?"

"No, to work *before* you change into your uniform? Because whatever it is, it should be something Bam wants to see crumpled up on the floor next to his bed. Hot. Naughty. Maybe a little scandalous even?"

"I am not sleeping with him, Syd. Get that out of your head right now."

"Well, maybe not yet, but I wouldn't judge you if you did. He totally sounds worth it to break our two-week agreement."

Once we'd started college, Sydney and I agreed that we wouldn't sleep with any guy we'd known less than two weeks. We'd thought that was plenty of time to be able to tell if he was a sleaze and instead worthy of our time. To be honest, I'd kinda forgot about our pact. It'd been so long since I was around eligible guys I hadn't given it any thought. Besides, it wasn't like the pact had exactly worked out well for Sydney. It'd taken her months to figure out the last two guys she'd dated were tools. Long after the two-week timeline and their subsequent hooking up.

"Technically I've known Bam over a year. Almost two."

Sydney squealed and clapped her hands. "Even better. We have to find the perfect outfit. Something that says 'I'm available but not easy. I want you, but I'm gonna make you work for it'. Oh! I have the perfect thing. Come on!"

"I'm not sleeping with him, Syd!" I protested as she grabbed my hand.

"Oh, I can guarantee there won't be any sleeping going on tonight."

I shook my head in resignation as she all but dragged me down the small hallway and into her bedroom. I knew better than to fight Sydney when she got all excited like this. But despite what she thought, I wouldn't be sleeping with Bam tonight or ever. Ruslan, either, for what it was worth.

What happened to all the regular, normal guys? Why wasn't one of *them* interested in me? Couldn't I catch one tiny, little break? *Ugh.*

Chapter 4

Bam

It took me all of one phone call to find out when Amber was working. Well, one phone call and a text. Zag's wife used to work at the Mother Lode Hotel/Casino, so she was my in. A few phone calls on her end, and she had Amber's schedule. Although what she meant about "enjoy the view," I couldn't figure out. I was probably spending the next six to eight hours watching a reservations desk. Not exactly titillating stuff, and Jessica wasn't exactly known to be a snarky chick. But that was how I came to be sitting on my bike on the fourth floor of the employee parking garage of the hotel at three-thirty in the afternoon.

Although as I watched Amber exit her ancient car and walk toward the stairs, work wasn't the time we needed to be watching her. Judging by her outfit, Amber had plans *after* work. She wore a flowy red number with threads of gold and silver shining through it. Her dress clung to her shoulders and breasts before flowing down her body and ending just above her knees. And her shoes—I bit back a groan—sky-high black stilettos that if she were anyone else, I would be imagining them pressing into my mattress.

But I couldn't. She was Stitch's daughter. The ultimate untouchable woman—an MC princess. I'd only just gotten my patch. There was no way the beat down would be worth it. Because that would be the minimum price if I stuck my dick anywhere near Amber.

No, thank you.

But clearly she was prepared for another dick tonight. Ruslan's, maybe?

Fuck. I had to put an end to that. Ruslan was a fucking lowlife crime lord and a lunatic as well. No way was I letting Amber anywhere near that son of a bitch. Not in this lifetime.

I was ten steps behind her when Amber surprised me. Instead of stopping at the bank of elevators, she kept going straight past them to the rough-looking staircase. Considering her shoes and the fact we were on the fourth floor, that was the last thing I'd expected. I had to jog to catch up to her so I wouldn't freak her out in the stairwell. With my luck she'd trip and fall the whole way down.

"Amber, wait up!" I shouted.

She froze and after a beat she swung around on those killer shoes. I about swallowed my tongue. Her calves looked fucking fantastic as her dress swayed with her body. I got a peek of slender thighs before her dress fell back into place. Damn. I took a breath, then looked up at her face. Judging by the glare, she wasn't exactly pleased to see me. A second later when she spoke, I knew for sure.

"Really? Are you *actually* stalking me now?"

"Don't flatter yourself. We reported back to Reb all the shit that went down last night, and he wants eyes on you while you're in public."

"So you've been following me all day?" Amber slumped slightly, like all the tension had left her body.

Weird. "No. I called Zag's wife. She texted me your schedule for the week. I just got off work and been waiting for you to show up. She told me you always park on the fourth floor of the parking garage, so here I am."

Her shoulders went rigid. "Wait, so you *haven't* been following me all day?"

"No. Why? Something happen?"

Amber crossed her arms over her chest as she shook her head. "No."

I didn't believe her, but she clearly had trust issues so I wasn't gonna push it. "Expect it in the future. We're a little late getting the troops rounded up today, but someone will be tailing you until we have an understanding with Ruslan. Things got a little . . . difficult with him after you and I left last night."

Amber's mouth twitched. "That's a sweet way to put how you *bodily carried me* out of the club last night."

"You say potato . . ."

"Ha ha." Amber rolled her eyes. "I gotta get to work. Are we done here?"

"Yup."

"Fantastic." Amber whirled around on her heels again and made for the stairs.

I was a step behind her when she stopped and glared at me. "Really?"

"What?"

"You're really going to follow me to work?"

"Boss's orders."

"And you do anything the great and powerful Reb tells you to do."

I shrugged like I didn't care, but her words really pissed me off. I wasn't some mindless grunt. I was a voting member of the True Brothers Motorcycle Club. I'd die for any of my Brothers, and they for me. It wasn't a dictatorship. We were family.

And that was the entire reason I was following Amber. By extension, she was family, too.

I didn't bother to explain or justify myself. She was gonna think what she wanted to. I had to make sure shit got done right and no one screwed with club property.

Amber leaned against the banister and rolled her eyes. "You know, we have security at the Mother Lode. It's a casino, so it's pretty good security. They spent money on it and everything. They're not going to let you follow me around all shift."

"Really?" I turned around and surveyed the parking garage. "Because from where I'm standing I don't see shit for security. No one stopped me and my bike from riding straight up to the fourth floor of the employee only structure. I haven't seen a single security guard on the property since I got here. And I've been waiting a while."

"I meant in the casino, but there are cameras here." Amber pointed to the cameras aimed at the elevators.

I raised my eyebrows. "Cameras only prove something happened if they're pointed in the right direction. They do fuck-all in the moment when shit is going down. If you're lucky, you might get a guard noticing it and heading out here in ten minutes. After what went down with Zag's woman, we're not taking any chances with you."

A few years back Zag's old lady saw a rogue member of our crew dealing drugs in this very parking garage. She reported it, and a few weeks later the asshole threatened her and roughed her up in the same parking garage *again*. Our club knew the security at Mother Lode was lax. We'd learned the lesson the hard way, and were closing the gaps to keep Amber safe. No matter how much she protested.

I rocked back on my heels. "Speaking of which, we should take the elevator. It's faster and safer. The sooner you're out of the parking garage, the better."

"Sorry." Amber shook her head but didn't look the least bit apologetic. "I don't do elevators."

"You don't do elevators? What the fuck does that mean?"

Amber shrugged then started down the stairs. Her delicate shoes tapping on each step on her way down. "I got stuck in an elevator a few months back. Haven't been in one since."

We'd have to work on that. I fucking hated stairs. But after releasing a heavy sigh, I clunked my way after her. We didn't say a word as we walked down four flights of stairs. Amber was puffing slightly when we reached the main level. I wasn't, but my ankles ached a bit. Motorcycle boots weren't exactly built for stairs.

"So, who's the dress for?"

Amber whirled around, and her face turned a sweet shade of red with her blush. Then she glared at me. "None of your business."

"If it's Ruslan, it *is* my business."

Amber took off down the sidewalk. She was about five feet away when she tossed her hair over her shoulder and snarked, "Wouldn't you like to know?"

"I wouldn't like to know." I caught up to her and grabbed her arm, making her stop in her tracks. "I need to know. Ruslan isn't the kinda guy you can just screw around with. He's dangerous, Amber. Really dangerous."

"Well, you would know, wouldn't you? Oh wait, that's right—you can't tell me. I'm just a silly girl, and you're a big, bad biker with all the answers." Amber shook my hand off her arm with a glare. "Fuck you. You can take your little warning and your guard duty and shove it. I don't need you, and I don't need any of your Brothers watching me. I can take care of myself. I've had enough practice over the last year."

I knew I wasn't going to change her mind, so I let it go for now as I followed her across the dimly lit crosswalk. She stopped at the door marked "Employees Only" and had to use a badge to unlock it. Holding the door open, she turned to me. "Well, this is where I leave you, slick. See? Employees only."

I had to laugh as she let the door slam shut in my face. Did she really think it was that easy to lose me?

Ten minutes later, Amber came out of the employee locker room and jerked to a stop. "Really? How did you get back here? It's supposed to be employees only."

I shrugged as I surveyed her in her uniform and wished she could've spent more time in the little red number she wore earlier. At least it would've covered more.

"What the fuck are you wearing?" There was no way any of the guys knew what Amber had been up to since Stitch died. No way in hell would Reb ever let her work here wearing *that*.

Clad in a black and gold corset thing, Amber's small but shapely breasts were on display. A tiny gold skirt skimmed the top of her thighs and showed off the black garter encircling her right thigh. Judging by the black lace headband and ridiculous feather plume on the side of her head, they were going for an 1800s saloon girl motif. From my point of view so much skin was on display, she could've been the star of any skin mag. Or my fantasies. I had no problem imagining her wearing exactly that as she stretched out on my bed, curling her finger at me as she invited me to—

"My uniform. Sorry, did you think I was a candy striper or something? Here in the real world it's not all rainbows and lollipops. I have to work to keep a roof over my family's head, and that means I have to dress *like this* to earn a living. So if you don't like it, you can take your fake concern about my well-being and shove it where the sun doesn't shine." Amber shook her head at me in disgust, her feather brushing against the side of her head. "I have to get on the floor."

She stomped down the hallway in an impressive show of attitude and legs. Dumb fuck that I was, I let her go. I was still so shell-shocked. Sweet little Amber was a cocktail waitress. Suddenly Jessica's cryptic warning made sense. After a beat, I followed her at a distance down the hallway and onto the casino floor. It'd been hard enough to sneak into the back hall. I didn't need someone alerting security.

This was gonna be a long fucking night.

Three hours later, and I was still fighting a boner every time she bounced by me in her sky-high black heels with that ridiculous feather

CHAPTER 4

bobbing along. Thank God the bar I was sitting at covered what was becoming an increasingly uncomfortable problem.

My phone buzzed with an incoming call. I shifted on the stiff bar stool to grab it as I watched Amber make small talk with the bartender as he filled her order. Amber looked my way and rolled her eyes at me. I lifted two fingers in salute; then, after looking at the display on my phone, I answered. "Hey, Tank."

"How goes guard duty?"

"Oh, fucking fantastic. You know I think I missed my true calling in life. This is what I was meant to do," I replied sarcastically.

"I think Reb and his house would disagree with you."

I shook my head. "A guy gets knocked out *one time* while he's on duty, and you guys never let me forget it."

"Twice, actually. Remember the fire last year at the shop?"

"I didn't get knocked out that time. I just didn't see anyone starting a fire."

Tank's booming laugh filled my ears. "Why the hell did Reb put you on guard duty again? Does he *want* Ruslan to grab Amber?"

"Fuck you, man. If you don't want me guarding her, I'd be more than happy to go home and crawl into my bed. Just give me the word. Some of us have got to work tomorrow."

"I'm just screwing with you, Bam. Unclench. We know you've learned from your past mistakes. In fact there's no one I'd trust more with my own family."

"Like that's a ringing endorsement. You barely talk to your sister, and your mom doesn't even live here."

"Don't forget Nicole," Tank replied, referring to his girlfriend of more than a year.

"If I have to watch Nicole, I expect hazard pay." Judging by the silence on his end of the phone, that might've been a step too far. "Was there a reason for this call, or are you just checking to make sure I'm awake?"

Tank's sigh was loud and long. "Just wondering if you need a reliever. Nicole is over at Brittany's house. I guess the girls are having an intervention. I got nothing going on, so I can come take your place if you need to get some sleep."

I swallowed my tongue as I watched Amber prance away, her tiny skirt swinging precariously. She stopped next to an elderly guy sitting at a slot machine. After placing his drink down on the console, she accepted a bill from him with a smile that was almost magical—all white teeth and sparkling eyes. But for her scandalous outfit, I could practically hear the romantic comedy soundtrack swelling in the background. She never smiled at me like that. All I got were sneers and eye rolls. What would it be like to have Amber look at me with those tender, soft eyes?

"Bam? You still there?"

I jerked back to the present. "What? Yeah."

"Hey, man, I can be there in, like, twenty if you need a break. It's no problem."

"No. No. I'm fine. I just thought I saw something," I finished lamely. For some reason I didn't share the info of Amber's actual profession with Tank. It wasn't like we could do anything about it right now. And the thought of him sitting here watching Amber prancing around in her barely-there uniform made me oddly territorial. Tank might've had a girlfriend of his own, but I sure as shit didn't want him anywhere near Amber when she was dressed like this. Brothers be damned. "We're all good here. I'll stay with Amber and make sure she gets home all right. I've got this."

"If you're sure . . ."

Amber finished with her guest, and her gaze flicked up to meet mine. Her slight smile slipped off her face when she bit her lip. She tilted her head while her eyes flicked down my body before meeting mine once

CHAPTER 4

more. I held my breath as we stared at each other. Then she blinked and shook her head slightly, the moment gone.

"Yeah, man. I'm sure." There was no place I'd rather be.

About an hour later, I regretted my decision to stay. I was just starting to wonder if Amber was ever gonna take a break when someone in my peripheral caught my attention. My heart beat in a steady rhythm as I braced myself for the coming confrontation. But it wasn't Ruslan or one of his goons bearing down on me with a glint in their eye.

It was my mother, Evelyn.

"I don't know why I was surprised when my friend called me to say I wouldn't believe who was camped out at the bar at the Mother Lode Casino." She stopped in front of me with her hands on her hips and sneered at me. "I always knew you wouldn't amount to much. And here you are, drinking alone in a casino on a Thursday night, proving me right."

I settled my hands on my stomach as I didn't bother to get up and greet the woman. Giving her a smirk that I knew would annoy the fuck outta her, I tilted my head back and said, "Nice to see you, too, Ma."

"How many times have I told you? Don't call me that. It's unflattering and makes us sound like backwoods hillbillies." She finger-combed her shoulder-length bottle-blond hair. Little had changed with her both in appearance and in attitude since she'd kicked me out of her house ten years ago. She might've only been in her fifties, but life had been surprisingly kind to her. But then maybe that was part of the deal when you sold your soul to Satan.

I shrugged and didn't rise to her bait. My gaze moved past her to where Amber stood at another slot machine talking to a guest. Her eyes flickered to mine, then to my mom, before turning back to her customer. I had no idea what she was thinking, since her expression didn't change. My gaze did another sweep of the mostly vacant casino floor before Evelyn spoke again.

"I'm contesting the will."

Now she had my full attention. "Why the fuck would you do that?"

"Because there is no way in hell that my own mother would leave me out of her will. Clearly you did something to her."

"No, it wasn't what I did. It was what you did, *and* didn't do. She saw the way you treated me when I was little. She watched you kick me outta your house when I was in high school. She saw how you did fuck-all for her when she was sick last year. You only have one person to blame, and it isn't me."

Evelyn just shook her head and plowed on. "I also heard you hooked up with those bikers Maverick hung out with." She paused and nodded toward my jacket. "I see that disappointing news was right, too. Did you guys intimidate her? Tie her up and make her change the will?"

I had to laugh at that. "You've been watching too much TV."

"You did something. I'm going to find out and prove it in court, so you'll be left with nothing."

"If you had put half of this effort into being a decent daughter or mother, Grandma wouldn't have left you outta her will." I'd watched the way Grandma deteriorated over the last year while I'd taken her—by myself—to countless appointments. Meanwhile her own daughter came to visit a grand total of two times. The bitch had even argued with Grandma about something stupid right after a brutal chemo appointment. Then, after the second visit, Grandma suddenly couldn't find her favorite pearl necklace. She'd never said outright that my mom had taken it, but we both knew.

Grandma hadn't left me much, but I was going to fight like hell to make sure this woman never saw a fucking dime.

"You were a miserable little shit, and you know it. I did you a favor by kicking you out."

CHAPTER 4

I smiled in agreement. "Yes, you did. Because I didn't have to live with you and all the fucking dirtbags you brought home. So thank you."

She huffed in irritation. "You think you're so smart. But I know you. Whatever you did to trick my mother into leaving everything to you, I'm going to figure it out. Then I'm going to nail your balls to the wall."

"You know, we really don't do this enough. Maybe next time we can get together at your house? Have dinner and catch up? I've really missed these talks." I held my beer up. "Should I order you one, Ma?"

"You . . . You . . ." Evelyn broke off with a screech as she glared at me. "I don't have time for your bullshit. Next time you hear from me, it'll be through my attorney."

I jerked my chin at her, then smiled.

Which really seemed to piss her off. She shrieked again and stomped off.

"Love you, too," I yelled at her back, but she didn't acknowledge me.

I turned to face the casino again and found most of the people looking at me with wide eyes. But not Amber. Her brow wrinkled, Amber shook her head, then looked away.

I had to smile at that. But only for a second. Crossing my arms over my chest, I leaned back against the bar and glared at everyone else who dared to meet my gaze.

Except Amber.

Three hours later, and I was sure I was a masochist. It was the only explanation I could come up with to explain why I'd turned down Tank's offer. I was bone-deep exhausted. After working construction all day and then sitting for hours on that uncomfortable-as-hell bar stool, all I wanted was my fucking bed. Once I saw Amber home I'd only have maybe five hours to sleep before I had to get up for work.

I'd long abandoned the bar stool since I was in danger of falling asleep and falling off. I'd taken up a position across the casino, holding the wall up while trying not to fall asleep on my feet. I'd had enough experience of being on guard duty during my prospecting days, but apparently I was woefully out of practice.

We were closing in on midnight, and the casino was surprisingly empty for a Thursday night. A few diehards still sat at the machines, spending their hard-earned money, but I definitely stood out as I wandered the casino floor and watched Amber work from afar. And yet in all my time here I hadn't once been approached by security. Even after my sparring match with my mom. Apparently management didn't give a shit that a menacing biker had nowhere else to be on a Thursday night. The Mother Lode had a real crack security team.

I did get to watch a lot of Amber's interactions during my hours and hours in the casino. She was bubbly and sweet with everyone around her—guests, coworkers, everyone she met got a sweet smile and her full attention. Most were polite in return. Only one guy got a little handsy, but before I could close the distance between us, Amber had stepped away and said something that made the guy laugh and lift his hands in innocent surrender. She smiled charmingly at him, then walked away.

So far it appeared that I was the only one who received her squinty glares and pissed-off attitude.

Unlike my previous guard duty details where I sat around and thought about the weekend or shit with my family, this time all I could think about was her. What made her laugh? What did she like to do for fun? What did she look like naked? Were her nipples the same soft shade of pink as her lips?

It was the latter turn of my thoughts that had me adjusting my pants and hoping like hell no one noticed the sudden bulge.

I watched Amber walk around the superhero slots and slowly make her way toward me. Despite her approach, I didn't move from my slouch against the wall.

CHAPTER 4

When she was ten feet away, she raised her eyebrows and spoke. "Aren't you sufficiently convinced of my safety yet?"

"Kitten, I've been here almost seven hours watching you, and no one seems to give a shit. That's not safe. That's fucked up."

Amber crossed her arms over her chest and rolled her eyes. "That would be because I alerted security to your presence and told them you were okay. As long as you don't cause any problems, they're happy to leave you be."

"Huh." I shoved my hands in my front pants pockets and cocked my head. "Nice to know you've finally come around."

"I haven't. And don't call me kitten."

I had to smile at her show of attitude despite how tired she looked. "I'm open to suggestions."

Amber's lips quirked, but she didn't raise to my bait. "I worked through my break so I get to go home early. Bye."

"Thanks for letting me know. Makes it much easier to follow you if you tell me where we're going. I'll meet you outside the locker room."

Shaking her head, she turned toward the casino and walked away.

The view of her going was just as enchanting as the view of her walking toward me. Despite spending seven hours watching her prance around in that tiny outfit, I wasn't sick of the sight. Actually, I wouldn't mind viewing it for another seven years. With a sigh, I pushed off the wall and dogged her steps. In less than an hour I'd finally be in the place I'd been fantasizing about all night.

Unfortunately for me, I'd be all alone.

Chapter 5

Amber

I felt a bit conflicted as I stood in front of my locker and reached for the dress that Sydney had begged me to wear tonight. For the first time since I took this job, I'd felt confident and . . . well, sexy, as I walked around the casino floor in my tiny uniform. Usually I had all these voices in my head telling me I wasn't tall enough or that I didn't fill out the top of my bustier enough to warrant the kind of tips the other girls got. But tonight, I could feel Bam's eyes on me the entire night. And the few (okay, more than a few) times I peeked in his direction, his hooded gaze made me feel alive. Hot and bothered, actually, if I were honest with myself. Confident, even.

And when that one guy got a little handsy, the menace emanating from Bam was intense. I knew I had to handle the situation quickly before there was bloodshed. He was ready to go to battle—for *me*.

But the conflicted part came in toward the end of the night when there was that weird confrontation with Bam and one of his girls. They were obviously arguing but had been quiet enough that I couldn't make out the words. Right up until Bam sarcastically shouted "Love you," as the woman walked away.

Dick.

CHAPTER 5

Okay, I might've been a bit curious as to what that'd been about. Who was she? A jealous ex? But then why did he shout *love you?* Maybe she ended things and he was heartbroken about it?

And maybe I'd be going to college next semester. Both were just as likely to be true.

But seriously, was that who his type was? She looked older than him. Was he into chasing cougars? Even given the age difference, she was gorgeous. And tall and built and everything I wasn't.

So, I felt especially silly when I left the locker room in the dress my bestie had chosen for me to seduce Bam with. She'd been so certain that he was *the one,* and that my reaction to him was different. Special. Now I knew better. If that was the type of woman Bam wanted, I'd never had a chance.

Not that I wanted one, of course.

Bam's eyes ran the length of my body before meeting mine. There was a flat, soulless quality that hadn't been there before. His voice was barely a rumble when he finally spoke. "You know you never told me where you're going after work. Who are you meeting up with?"

"No one." I took off down the hallway toward the parking garage with Bam hot on my heels. At least he'd dropped the talk about my horrible uniform. But then I imagine after seven hours of watching me prance around in it, the uniform had lost its zing.

"Yeah, you said that. I didn't believe you before, and I sure as hell don't believe you now. Who are you meeting tonight?"

I'd reached the double doors at the end of the hallway, so I turned around to face Bam. A quick glance over his shoulder told me we were alone for the moment, so I let him have it. "No one, okay? There's no one. I work crap hours at a job I don't particularly like—the outfit is ridiculous, my feet hurt, and the tips suck—then I go home and pick up the pieces of my family. I don't have time to meet anyone, so there's no one in my life."

"Then why the dress?"

"My best friend, Sydney, thought . . . You know what? It doesn't matter. I'm going home, and that's all you need to know." I turned around and waved my key card at the sensor.

"You're only, what? Twenty-one? Two? You got plenty of time to meet someone."

I really hated the sensor on this side of the door. It always took forever for me to find the sweet spot that activated it. I continued to wave my card at the obnoxious thing. "Well, you would know."

"What the hell are you talking about?"

"The blonde? From earlier? It was obvious that she wasn't happy with your . . . services." I glared at the sensor and barely suppressed the urge to give it a roundhouse kick. Stupid machine. "You know what? I give up. Let's go out through the casino and walk around."

""The blonde from earlier?" The one at the bar?" Bam's eyebrows met his hairline. "You mean my mom?"

I froze. His mom? That woman with all the hair and dirty sneers was his mother? I slowly turned around to face him. He did that annoying thing where he raised only one eyebrow.

"I thought . . ."

"Yeah, I know." An undercurrent of laughter tinged his words.

"It's just . . . She was all . . . And you were all . . ."

He smirked then nodded slightly.

I sighed. "I'm sorry. I assumed, and I guess I shouldn't."

"I'm not gonna deny that I have been known to have some slutty ways, but no one has ever complained about my . . . *services*." He paused while he took in my flushed cheeks before continuing. "But that—tonight at the bar—was a whole different shitshow."

I looked down at the floor. "I have some experience with family shitshows."

"I remember." Bam's voice was just as soft as mine. "But at least you

CHAPTER 5

know your family's dysfunction is rooted in love. Your mom fell apart because she couldn't handle moving on from your dad. That is . . . a special, intense kind of love. The kind we all dream of having one day."

I shook my head. "Not me. No love could be worth the pain my mom is going through. It's stupid and painful and . . . and just not worth it."

Bam laughed quietly, and I couldn't *not* look at him when he made that sound. It was soft and sweet and so damn tender. The same as the expression in his eyes. "Good luck with that, kitten. Because there is no way a girl like you will be able to get through life without making every damn man you meet feel like that about you."

My heart melted. That was singularly the nicest, most romantic thing a guy had ever said to me. And it came from Bam. Maybe I had to rethink my whole stance on no bikers. I stared into his soft, sweet expression and couldn't come up with a single thing to say. Instead I stupidly whispered, "Wow. That is the most romantic thing I think I've ever heard."

Bam's eyes immediately lost that tender look and went blank. I mentally cursed myself. Why did I say that? Why?

"Come on." Bam grabbed my key card out of my hand, then waved it at the door. It clicked open after the first pass, and Bam pushed the door open. "I gotta get some sleep tonight. Work starts stupid early for me."

I followed silently at Bam's side as we walked to the employee parking structure. He'd opened up to me in a way I doubted he did with anyone else, and I had to go and ruin it. There was a reason why I was still so inexperienced at twenty-one, and it had nothing to do with my religious beliefs. Self-confidence issues combined with my foot-in-mouth disease had me woefully unprepared for the likes of Bam. Not that anything was going to happen with us. Despite the intense attraction I felt between us, he was still an arrogant biker. And that was one self-imposed line I wasn't going to cross in this lifetime. If there was one thing I'd learned from watching my mom fall apart, it was that men like Bam were never around to deal with the fallout. That was left to the girlfriends and family members.

I was better off alone.

Bam didn't pause at the elevators once we reached the parking garage. He led the way to the stairwell, and we climbed four flights of stairs, my panting breath and the clunk of our steps the only sounds to break the quiet night. But when we reached the landing, it was my gasp that pierced the ringing silence.

Because there was a brand-new Cadillac Escalade parked in the spot where my ancient Camry should've been. And leaning against the gleaming black paint was Ruslan.

Fuck me.

He stood upright with a grin when he saw me enter the parking level. His eyes danced down my dress to my legs before resting on my face. I had no doubt that he—unlike Bam—approved of my choice of outfit. Okay, technically Sydney's. But his smile quickly slipped off his face when Bam's hulking form popped out of the shadows behind me.

"And here I thought you had better taste, *moya zvezda*." Ruslan's drawl belied the tension lining his body.

"I, uh, I'm sorry?" I walked toward him, unable to wrap my brain around the fact that Ruslan was here, but my car wasn't. Our footsteps echoed in the garage as Bam walked a little bit in front of me. I stopped a few feet away from Ruslan with Bam close to my side.

Ruslan nodded toward Bam's silent figure next to me. "The company you keep doesn't bode well for you. Guys like him . . ." He broke off and shook his head ruefully. "Guys like him are not worthy of you."

"Guys like him? You mean like my father? The only man I've ever

CHAPTER 5

loved? The man who sacrificed his life to keep my mom and her friends safe? You mean a man like that?" I said it in reflex. I didn't have time to wrap my mind around the fact that I was *defending* Bam. All I wanted to do was take these damn shoes off and collapse in my comfortable bed. After I picked up the pieces of my mom, of course. But I couldn't do any of that because this crazy guy had done something to my car. "I don't have time for this. It's late, I'm tired, and my feet are aching from being on them all day. Where is my car?"

Ruslan spread his hand out in front of him. "Right here."

"Cut the bullshit, *malcik*." Bam's quietly menacing voice rang through the structure. "Where is her car?"

"Towed to a lot for those less fortunate, as a charitable donation. It was unacceptable for someone like you, Amber, to be driving such an appalling vehicle. And not very safe, either."

My heart dropped. "You can't do that. You can't just give away something that's not yours. How am I going to get to work? I need my car!"

"No, *moya zvezda*. You need *a* car. Which is why I've purchased a new one for you." Ruslan tipped his head toward the gleaming black Escalade. "Come. Let's take it out for a spin."

"Oh fuck no." Bam snorted. "She's not getting inside your car."

"It's not *my* car. It's my gift to her." Ruslan crossed his arms over his chest. "And I don't believe anyone here asked for your opinion, *dyebil*."

He bought me a car? That was crazy. He bought me a car. The sentence circled nonstop in my head as the two men stared each other down. It felt like at any moment a full-out brawl would break out. Meanwhile all I could think was that Ruslan had bought me a car. *A car.*

"I . . . It's too much. The flowers were lovely, and I had every intention of thanking you, but I can't accept a car. I mean, we hardly know each other. You can't just buy me a car."

"Flowers? What flowers?" Bam demanded.

At the same time Ruslan replied, "I'm glad you enjoyed them, *moya zvezda*. I hope you will enjoy this car just as much."

He was certifiable. Who does that?

"What. Flowers." Bam's voice rang with his intensity.

"Um." I paused and crossed my arms over my chest. "Early this morning Ruslan sent me a lovely . . . bouquet isn't quite the right word . . . arrangement? Of flowers. Red roses and white hydrangeas. They take up, like, half of the kitchen and are really . . . pretty." I finished lamely. I couldn't stop. My mouth kept going even as my brain screamed for me to shut up. I could tell by the menace emanating from Bam that each word pissed him off more and more, and yet I kept going. "No one has ever sent me flowers before."

Ruslan's eyes gleamed at that last bit. I could tell he was pleased that he'd been my first. Bam growled a low ominous sound that made a wave of goose bumps prickle the back of my neck.

"Go to my bike, kitten." That growl sound came again when I didn't immediately jump and do Bam's bidding. "Now!"

I jumped when he bit out the last word and all but ran to his motorcycle a few rows away from where I'd parked. I tossed a glance over my shoulder and watched as Bam took a few steps closer to Ruslan. I couldn't hear what they were saying to each other, but in a matter of moments Ruslan ripped open the driver's door of the Escalade and climbed inside. The roar of its powerful engine vibrated through the parking garage, and a few seconds later Ruslan left in a squeal of tires, taking a route that wasn't anywhere near me. Bam had obviously embarrassed him. And my refusal of his "gift" hadn't helped, either. But a car? Really? In what universe was that an acceptable gift for someone you'd known less than a day?

Thank God Bam had been here with me. I don't know how I would've handled that on my own. Ruslan was clearly certifiably

CHAPTER 5

insane. He went from flowers to a car. Who does that?

Now that he was gone, my adrenaline leached out of me, and the enormity of the situation sank in. I had an admirer. And not a sweet, pass-you-notes-in-class kind, either. What would he do next?

"Your car—not that fucking SUV Ruslan drove—will be in front of your house tomorrow morning." Bam stopped in front of me. The muscle in his cheek flexed as he paused. "If he sends you anything—and I mean fucking *anything*, even if it's a goddamn piece of gum—you will tell me. Immediately. No more fucking around."

I bit my bottom lip and nodded tightly. He was pissed, and I didn't want to say something stupid—again—and add to his anger. And honestly I was more than a little scared about the whole thing. I had a Russian mafioso after me. *Me*.

I tried to fight the wave of shivers that racked my body. I closed my eyes against the storm, but a few tears leaked out of my eyes. I was just so fucking scared.

"Ah, kitten. It's gonna be okay."

My eyes were still closed so I didn't see it, but a moment later I felt the comforting warmth of Bam's body as his arms closed around me. I rested my cheek on the firm muscle of his chest. A soothing scent of leather and bergamot enveloped me. I felt something touch the top of my head.

"I am going to do everything I can to make sure that sick fuck stays away from you. I promise." Bam's voice was quiet as he made his vow. In that instant I felt as safe as I ever had. After a few breaths, the shudders eased, and I just enjoyed the sensation of having a man's arms wrapped around me. I wished it wouldn't end.

Bam would keep me safe. I believed him.

"Okay," I whispered back.

He squeezed me one more time then took a step away. Despite the summer heat, I immediately missed his warmth.

"You okay?"

I nodded silently as I wrapped my arms around my torso.

"Good." He grunted at me, then tossed his leg over his bike and climbed on. Unhooking his helmet off the handlebars, he all but tossed it at me. "Take my helmet. I'll drive you home tonight."

I gnawed at my bottom lip as I struggled with the helmet. Tonight had turned out so weird. I couldn't wrap my head around it. Bam had had me off-kilter all shift, then Ruslan appeared with that car, and then I actually compared Bam to my father.

And that hug.

If I didn't know better, I'd think I was the one drinking tonight. Either that or I was still asleep. None of it made sense.

I climbed on behind Bam as best I could, given that I was wearing a dress and heels, then wrapped my arms around his waist. Trying not to notice how good he felt in my arms and between my legs, I closed my eyes. Again, I felt as conflicted as I had when I stood in the locker room only minutes ago. He started the engine, and my words were lost beneath the rumble of his bike.

"*Breathe, Amber. Just breathe.*"

Chapter 6

Bam

Nothing like waking to a fresh blast of cat asshole in your face first thing in the morning.

"Get off me, Pixie," I grumbled as I rolled over and blinked blearily at my alarm clock: 4:22. I still had roughly half an hour before I had to get up. Stupid cat.

Meanwhile Pixie took the opportunity to burrow into my pillow behind me as a *pffbbbbt* sounded in the same vicinity.

"Son of a bitch!" I bounded off the bed and glared down at my grandma's bitchy and gassy purebred Persian. "Fine. Take the damn bed."

I grabbed the pillow she wasn't burrowed into and stomped down the hall, muttering to myself. "Maybe there's one thing I won't fight my mom over when she contests that damn will."

It would serve that bitchy cat right to have to live with my mother. Persians might be known for their sweet dispositions, but that one had always had it out for me, ever since I moved in with my grandma. I don't know why I still kept the damn thing around.

Tossing my pillow onto my couch, I grabbed my cell phone off the coffee table, then reclined on the couch as I thumbed through my texts.

There was no way I'd be able to sleep now. I was up. Goddamn cat.

Hatchet, 2:30 A.M.: *All's fine at Stitch's place. Car delivered before two. Passed the keys onto the next watch. Wanna get a beer tonight?*

I knew he was probably still sleeping off guard duty, but I fired a text back.

Me: *Fuck yeah. This has been the week from hell. Meet up at the clubhouse after my shift at 3? Or are you working tonight?*

Hatchet worked as a line cook at a Mode Lode restaurant. He'd started there just washing dishes, but had worked his way up the ladder to prep cook and now line cook. Our own little Gordon Ramsay. Or at least that was one of the suggestions Axle had when they were tossing around road names for Hatchet.

He didn't immediately reply so I moved on.

Reb: *Need to talk. Call when you're up.*

Fuck, that couldn't be good. Despite the early hour I toggled through my contacts and called the club president back.

"What?" Reb groaned.

"It's Bam Bam."

"Yeah?"

I waited a beat, but when Reb didn't say anything more I clued him in. "You wanted me to call you when I woke up."

"Fuck. I did? Hang on a second."

I heard a feminine voice murmuring in the background and some rustling. A few moments later, Reb came back on the line.

"It's four in the morning? Fuck, man, I thought you'd call at, like, six at the earliest."

"You know I work construction, right? We're like farmers—up with the sun. At least that's what my foreman says. He's an annoyingly cheerful fucker." I don't know why I kept talking. Reb unnerved me like no one else. The chapter president had so much power over my life. I finally felt like I'd found my home with the True Brothers MC,

CHAPTER 6

and I didn't want anything to fuck that up. Although if I kept talking, I might do that all on my own.

"Christ, you're a cheerful fuck, too. You've been hiding that from us all this time?"

"No, sir." I swallowed and kept my damn mouth shut. Like I'd done for months while I was a prospect.

Reb snorted. "Right. Anyhow, I want to know what happened last night. With Amber. And Ruslan."

Last night I'd sent Reb a quick text telling him that R showed up with a new car for A, but didn't go into detail. When he didn't reply, I figured he was asleep or busy with club business. I'd passed on the intel to Hatchet since he was on watch duty, then I got my ass into bed.

I quickly filled Reb in on everything that went down in the parking garage last night, including Ruslan's Escalade present and the flowers he'd sent that morning.

"Fuck me. The last thing we need right now is to tangle with the fucking Bratva. We already have enough enemies to keep us busy for the rest of the decade." Reb sighed heavily. "She didn't tell anyone about the flowers?"

"No, sir. And given the escalation of his gifts, I'd say we have a huge problem on our hands."

"Shit, I think you're right. She has a huge problem on her hands."

"Err, no, sir. I think *we* do."

Reb was silent for a long moment. "So it's like that, is it?"

"Like what? Amber is family. Her and her mom are still considered club property, with all the rights and protection that entails. She's one of us. Isn't she?"

"Denial, denial, denial. You can play it like that, son, but it's gonna bite you in the ass sooner or later."

"Huh? I don't know what that means." Reb must've been working on little to no sleep because he wasn't making any fucking sense.

"Nothing, kid. You'll figure it out once you pull your head outta your ass. Hopefully before the guys get wind of it. But you're right. *We* have a problem on our hands."

"Any suggestions on how we should handle it?"

"I'll have another talk with Ruslan, maybe bring his daddy in on it, too. I'm gonna have you keep eyes on Amber when you're not working and are available."

"I can do that. But, um . . . speaking of eyes . . . do you know what she's doing at the Mother Lode?"

"Jessica got her the job, so she's working at the hotel reception desk." When I didn't immediately reply, Reb sighed. "Isn't she?"

"No, sir. She's a cocktail waitress."

"Fuck me. So they've got her prancing around in one of those tiny skirts and serving drinks to lonely gamblers?" Reb's voice rose a bit more with every word until he was practically shouting. "What the fuck?"

"I got the impression that Amber's the sole provider now. Brittany isn't firing on all cylinders. And what the fuck is with Jackson? Where's he? His whole family is falling apart, and he's not doing a damn thing."

Reb was quiet for a minute after my little impassioned speech. Then he murmured to himself. "So much fucking denial."

"What's that, sir?" My pulse thrummed in my ears, and my chest felt tight. He wasn't talking about what I thought he was talking about, was he? Fuck me. I wanted to babble something in my defense about how I wouldn't ever cross a fucking line like that, but what if I didn't need to? I didn't want him to know I was having thoughts about Amber. So instead I kept my mouth shut.

"Nothing, kid. You seem to have a lot to say about how Jackson is handling this mess."

"I happen to know something about moving on after you lose a huge

CHAPTER 6

part of your family. And Jackson is apparently too fucked up over losing his dad to pay attention to his mom and his sister." Silence reigned on the line, and like a dipshit, I rushed to fill it. "I'm just speaking on Amber's defense. Sir. I don't like that she has to work at a job like that, but she's doing all she can for her family. And Jackson—"

"Isn't." Reb sighed as he finished my sentence for me. "I get your point. I'll talk to him."

"If it's all right with you, I'd like to talk to him. I have some experience with this kinda thing."

"Fine. Let him know that it's not coming from only you. The whole club is behind Stitch's family, and it's high time Jackson started pulling his weight. Brittany's ultimatum be damned."

Before I could ask about that last cryptic comment, Reb continued.

"I'm gonna head back to bed. Let me know how your talk with Jackson goes. Later."

"Later," I echoed, then tossed my cell onto my coffee table.

Pixie meowed as she prowled down the hall toward me. A moment later she was rubbing against the couch and purring loudly. I reached down and gave her a rub behind the ear.

"All right. All right. I'll get you some breakfast."

She might be the most fucking annoying cat ever, but she was the last living link I had to my grandma. When I closed my eyes, I could almost hear her crooning to Pixie. That soft, mellow voice that let me know I wasn't alone—even if she was talking to the cat and not me.

Damn, I missed her.

"Come on, Bitchy. Let's get you fed. You woke me up early enough I can swing by Denny's before my shift starts."

Later that afternoon, I leaned against the clubhouse bar as I waited for Tank to fill my beer order. All the guys took turns behind the bar—usually it was the prospects' job, but it was still a bit early for them to be on shift. Most were still working their day jobs. For me, it was the end of my workday/week. Others like Tank, who worked as a bouncer at our secretly owned nightclub, had a few hours to kill before their workday even started. I had yet to find out where Jackson worked.

"You on guard duty tonight?" Tank asked as he pushed a Sierra Nevada Pale Ale toward me.

"No, thank fuck." I took a long drink from my beer. "Between the meeting at Howl a few days ago and my shift at Mother Lode last night, I am burned the fuck out. I need a little R and R."

Tank chuckled. "Amber hand you your balls? She's her mother's daughter, that one."

"I'll take your word for it. She's got a chip on her shoulder the size of fucking Lake Tahoe. I never thought an MC princess could hate bikers as much as that one does."

"Everyone handles grief differently." Tank leaned against the back of the bar and took a long drink of his beer. "And Stitch was the best of all of us. Anyone who comes after him with that girl will have big shoes to fill. She was a daddy's girl."

Axle pulled out the stool next to me and snorted. "You can't replace a man like Stitch." Rubbing a hand over his face, he contemplated the display of beer taps like they weren't the same fucking kegs we'd always had. "Believe me, I've tried."

Before I could wrap my brain around that, Tank pushed away from the bar back and grabbed a glass for Axle. "Coors? Or are you feeling wild?"

"Coors," Axle replied. "It's a bit early for wild."

I cleared my throat. "Speaking of Stitch's family, have you guys seen Jackson lately?"

"He's across the street at the shop." Axle replied as he tipped his head in thanks at Tank for the beer.

I picked up my mug and drained the rest of my beer. Tank and Axle

CHAPTER 6

talked quietly in the background as I set my glass down on the bar and stood. "Thanks for the beer, man."

"See ya, Bam," Tank said.

Axle shouted at my back as I walked toward the back door. "You coming back for round two?"

"Hell yeah. Gotta take care of some business first. I'll be back in a few," I replied.

"Going to let the prairie dog out of its cage." Axle nodded solemnly. "Got you."

Rolling my eyes, I didn't bother to correct Axle's assumption of toilet humor. With a wave behind me, I left the clubhouse and made my way across the gated parking lot to the club-owned motorcycle shop across the street. It'd taken a year, but we'd managed to rebuild the business that our rivals, the Wild Riders MC, torched during Reb's wedding last year. My gut clenched every time I looked at the building. I had been the one on watch when it went up in flames. I was the one who missed the signs and didn't notice the fire until it was too late. I was the one who let my Brothers down.

It'd been hard to face the club after the fire. But if anything, Reb had blamed himself. With every club member attending the wedding, there hadn't been enough prospects to guard everything. I'd been tasked with watching both the clubhouse *and* the motorcycle shop across the street. When the fire started, I was around the back side of the clubhouse rousting a few cats that'd been clunking around in the dumpster. Meanwhile a Wild Rider had been hosing down our shop with gasoline and lighting the match.

We'd get our revenge. It'd taken us months to plan, but we were a few weeks away from stage one of the eye-for-an-eye plan. They fucked with our business, we were gonna fuck them right back, but in a way they'd never forget.

I walked through the big roller door at Dirty Side Down Mechanics.

It was probably my imagination, but a tang of smoke mixed with the engine oil and metal odor. Looking around, you'd never know that the building had been a smoldering shell only a year ago. Aside from the freshly painted walls, everything looked exactly the same. Club insignias mixed with motorcycle brand posters on the walls; Reb's pride and joy—a fully rebuilt 1962 Indian Motorcycle—was displayed on a rack on the far wall; and as always, tools were scattered everywhere.

"Hey Bam, you need something?" Zag asked from behind one of the five motorcycle lifts.

"I'm looking for Jackson. Axle said he was here?"

"Yeah." Zag tossed a socket wrench aside then wiped at the grease on his hands with a rag. "I got him in the back, cleaning the john."

"Don't we have a cleaning service for that?" In all my time as a prospect for the club, I never once had to clean a bathroom. Guard duty, bartending, gofer, and a few other embarrassing jobs I'd rather not remember, but toilets? No.

Zag smiled mockingly at me. "Gotta haze the newbies. You remember how it goes. Everyone gets their own special little task. Jackson is really good with a toothbrush. Whereas you had that amazing falsetto to serenade us with."

I tilted my chin, but didn't respond to that little dig. "I need a minute with him."

"Have at it. Those toilets aren't going anywhere."

Shaking my head, I walked to the back hallway and found the door to the men's restroom propped open and Jackson down on his hands and knees with a toothbrush in his hand and a can of Comet at his side. Fuck me, I was suddenly glad none of those embarrassing jobs I'd been given as a prospect included this shit. The bathroom might've only been a few months old, but the stains were already visible. And disgusting.

CHAPTER 6

"Jackson. I need to see you out back. Now."

Jackson's head wiped up at my barking command. Relief etched his features. "Thank you, Jesus. Prayers really do come true."

I bared my teeth at him in an expression nowhere near a smile. "The piss stains will be here waiting for you when we're done."

Jackson's shoulders slumped, and I caught the edge of his grimace as he pushed away from the patch of scrubbed floor and rose to his feet. At least he was smart enough to keep his thoughts to himself.

I led the way out the back door, and Jackson followed silently behind me. Stopping a few feet from the door, I rested my shoulders against the brick wall of the shop and surveyed the prospect in front of me. Physically, Jackson was only a few years younger than me, but judging by the annoyed expression on his face, he was eons behind me in maturity. This was a punk who'd never had to wonder where he was going to sleep tonight, and I doubted he'd ever had to dodge the fist of his mom's annoyed boyfriend. Up until a year ago, Jackson had a mostly functional and loving family. And it would all fall apart if he didn't step up soon.

"We need to have a little talk about your sister, Amber."

Jackson lost the annoyed-little-boy expression as he narrowed his eyes. His lips curled with his sneer. "What the fuck do you know about my sister?"

It was phrased like a question— except with the way he bit out the words, it was anything but.

"I know that she's been wiping up your mama's vomit and carrying her to bed night after night, with no help from you." That hadn't been how I'd planned to start this conversation, but the way this prospect was looking at me—like I wasn't worthy to speak Amber's name—pissed me off like nothing else. "While you've been having a fun time whoring around and playing prospect, your sister is the only thing keeping your mom together. Amber should be going to college and having someone else clean up her puke, not working as a fucking cocktail waitress, letting old men grope her for tips, and then going home to mop up your mama's mess. What the fuck is wrong with you?"

"She's doing *what*?"

"Taking care of your mother. Something I thought maybe you should lend a hand with."

"Not that shit. I know all about my mom's drama. I wanna know about what you said before—Amber's working as a cocktail waitress? Since when?"

I wasn't really happy with her job, either. It'd been hard as hell to watch her prance around in that tiny skirt and not carry her out of the fucking casino and into my bed. But that wasn't what this little powwow was supposed to be about. "Maybe if you took care of your fucking family, you'd know what the hell is going on at home."

Jackson huffed out an annoyed breath and looked away.

I sighed. "Look, man. I came at you hard, and that wasn't how I wanted to handle this. But I've seen the shit that your sister is dealing with, and she needs some help. If you're having a hard time balancing work, your family, and your prospect duties, then speak up. We don't know you need help if you don't ask."

"You don't know what it's like. I can't just . . ." Jackson groaned and punched the wall. "It sucks. It fucking sucks."

Jackson's immature reaction pissed me off. Like my life was all club girls and whiskey with no worries about anything. Christ, he was so young and stupid and immature. Was there ever a time in my life when I got to be a whiny little bitch like Jackson? Just thinking about it pissed me off even more.

"I know more than you think." I took a deep breath to calm myself down, then unloaded something that'd been bottled up for a long time. "Life wasn't exactly easy for me growing up. But it got a hell of a lot

CHAPTER 6

better once I moved in with my grandma. She was the only person in my life since my dad died who gave a fuck about me. She cared. But then last year, while I was a prospect, she got sick. I was taking her to appointments while working a full-time job and prospecting for the club, and things fell through the cracks. If I could go back, I'd do so much shit differently. I'd spread myself so thin that I wasn't there for her, and I wasn't there for my Brothers. I came really close to fucking it all up."

Jack inclined his head as he rocked back on his heels, but he still wouldn't look at me. Or say anything.

"You're skirting the edge, too. I know what it's like to lose the center of your family. But you're fortunate in that you have a sister and a mom who care about you. I'd kill to have that. But you know, apparently violence doesn't solve everything." I paused. "Hey, that was a joke, Jackson." He laughed weakly at my piss-poor attempt at humor. "This isn't coming from just me. Everyone is concerned about what's going on with your family. We don't want to see you fuck it all up because you're spread too thin. Take some time and take care of your family. We'll still be here."

Jackson shoved his hands into his front pockets, but still didn't say anything.

"Think about it, okay? If you need anything, give me a call."

Jackson nodded tightly. I sighed and gave him a soft punch on the shoulder, then left. I'd done what I could. Hopefully he wasn't a stubborn shit and could see the truth in what I'd said.

Amber didn't need all the weight of the world on her slender shoulders.

Chapter 7

Amber

"So how are things with your mom? She still going to meetings or whatever?" Bam asked as we walked down the hall, away from the locker room.

It was Saturday night. I'd just spent the last six hours at work with Bam's eyes burning a hole in my back. And my front. With every shift I was becoming more and more aware of him. I'd thought this guard duty thing wouldn't be so intrusive—that the guys would just be background noise—and that was true for everyone *but Bam*. When Bam was on watch duty, I knew where he was all the time. I could feel his eyes on me. With Hatchet or Sig, I had no clue.

I really didn't want to think about what that meant.

"I don't know. We don't talk about it." I shrugged.

"Really? I thought your family was close." Bam held his hand out for my employee pass so he could open the impossible outer door that I always struggled with.

I handed it over and tried not to be pissed when the door immediately clicked open for him. "That's just the way my family is. We didn't talk about things when she was drinking. We're not talking about things now that she's not drinking. And it was like that when my dad was with us, too. He'd disappear for days sometimes, and my mom would just say he was taking care of business. Then he'd come back, and it'd be like he never left. I guess you could say we're pros at avoidance."

Bam handed my pass back to me as he held the door open. "Huh."

"I always thought she'd give me a big speech about quitting drinking and how she was sorry for what she put me through. But she didn't. She hasn't." I gave him a weak smile. "Whatever. It's okay. I see a difference, though. She's not in a puddle of puke when I get home, the house is clean, and she's not hungover in the mornings. So that's good. I'm glad she's getting help. She disappears every night at a certain time, so I assume she's going to meetings and getting help. I hope she is."

Bam nodded as we started up the four flights of stairs in the parking garage. It'd only taken him a week to give up on pressuring me to use the elevators. Now he just headed for the stairs like it was a given. "Maybe she doesn't want the pressure. It's hard to do when it's just you and your demons. It's probably a hell of a lot tougher when you don't want to let your family down."

"I guess. That makes sense. I just wish I knew what snapped her out of it. What was the thing that pushed her over the edge and made her realize that she didn't want to do this anymore? I kinda feel like I should've seen it. Maybe it was something I could've said or did or . . . I don't know. Something."

"You can't do that to yourself, kitten." Bam grabbed my arm and stopped me somewhere between the second and third floor. His eyes were serious as he stared down at me. "Your mom's drinking is not on you. You took care of her and the bills and probably more shit than I know about. You stepped up. Be good with that."

His pride in me had me ducking my head. To be honest, I wasn't used to direct praise. Or at least I'd lost that in the year since my dad had been gone and my mom had fallen apart. I didn't know what to say, where to look, so instead I just bobbed my head and bit my lip, avoiding his eyes the whole time.

Bam huffed an irritated breath. "Kitten, look at me."

I tipped my head back and took in his long blond hair, his scruffy beard, and the serious expression in his gray eyes. God, why did he have to be so gorgeous? He looked so much like that actor in the Thor movies. The one I'd spent so much time fantasizing about when I was a teenager. Now his carbon copy stood in front of me, taking in all of me, and all I could do was gawk back at him like a ninny.

"You stepped up and took care of your family. That's pretty awesome. Trust me when I say not everyone would've done the same. I know more than most about that shit."

I wanted to ask him about it, find out more about this intense—and gorgeous—man, but I didn't want his walls to come slamming back down. So instead I bobbed my head like a chicken and whispered, "Thanks."

Bam's eyes sparkled and the side of his mouth hitched with a slight smile. "When's the last time you went out and just had a good time? Had a few drinks and a few laughs?"

I ducked my head again as I thought about my answer. "Does coffee with my best friend last week count?"

"Did you guys go out or stay in?"

"In."

"Then no." Bam chuckled softly. "That doesn't count."

I didn't want him to think I was a total friendless fool which is when the babbling started. "We were supposed to go out tonight. Sydney wanted to hit up a couple of bars, maybe sing some karaoke, but she texted me and canceled before my shift started. I guess she's got a summer cold or something. Caught it from one of her clients. She does hair at Plumb Beauty Salon. And I'm going to stop talking now."

CHAPTER 7

My face hot, I pivoted away from Bam and resumed climbing the stairs. Sometimes my mouth just ran away from me. Case in point. And I swear I didn't make any of that up—Sydney and I had plans that she'd canceled—but why did I have to spew it all out like that at Bam? If anything, it sounded made-up, given the way he'd asked me about my downtime, like I never let go and had fun. I had fun. It'd just been a while.

"I take it that means you're free tonight?" Bam's laughing voice echoed in the concrete stairwell.

The combination of my suddenly free Saturday night, not to mention the fact that I was never scheduled to work Saturday night—a sure sign I was horrible at my job since weekend nights had the best tips, or so I'd been told—and the laughter in Bam's voice made me burn with embarrassment. Suddenly it felt like I was failing at everything. I worked the day shift as a cocktail waitress. My mom got sober without me. My brother, Jackson, was taking my mom out to dinner tonight—just the two of them. Aside from Sidney, my friends had all but disappeared since they were busy with college crap. And now Bam was laughing at me. Literally.

I whirled around on the step above him and glared straight into his eyes. "I don't know. Maybe I'll give Ruslan a call and see if he's interested in going out."

It was impulsive and petty and totally not true. I'd never willingly call Ruslan. Despite his model good looks, the man was completely unhinged and more than a little scary—petrifying, really. But I wanted to score a point with Bam, and judging by his scowl I definitely did.

"You think that shit's funny?" he bit out.

I scowled back at him. "I wasn't trying to be funny. I just wanted to point out that I'm not some pathetic loser. Ruslan at least seems to think I'm worthy of spending time with him."

"I wasn't making fun of you, Amber. I was gonna ask you if you want to go get a drink and hang out, but now I'm thinking not. You obviously have some growing up to do." He gave me a look of absolute disgust, then shouldered past me and continued to climb the stairs.

I felt about two inches tall. His disgust was obvious, and the fact that he'd used my name instead of that silly nickname he'd given me filled me with regret. I'd struck a low blow, and for what? It didn't make me look good or feel good. And I'd hurt Bam. He'd been on the cusp of reaching out to me, and I'd slapped him down.

He was right. Maybe I did have some growing up to do because that was immature as hell.

I followed silently behind him as we climbed the stairs. We reached the fourth floor without speaking a word to each other, so when Bam finally spoke, his voice sounded louder than before.

"I'll follow you. Are you going straight to your house, or do you need to stop somewhere on the way?"

I heard his question. I was sure the two floors beneath us could hear his booming voice, but I couldn't answer. I was too busy staring at my car.

"Amber?" Bam turned with a huff when I didn't answer.

My body started to shake, and Bam's annoyance morphed to confusion, then quickly became that chilling angry-biker expression I'd seen at Howl. His hand went to the back of his waistband, and he turned to block me from the rest of the parking garage level. I caught a flash of metal beneath Bam's leather vest, and my blood chilled. He had a gun.

"Stay here," Bam murmured before he slowly walked toward my car.

I wanted to be snarky about his lack of watchdog skills, but I couldn't form any words. Next to my car was a vase with a dozen or so bloodred roses. I didn't have to look at the card to know who they were from. Ruslan. Again.

Bam surveyed the parking level, making sure we were alone, then

CHAPTER 7

stomped to my car. He grabbed the paper pinned under the windshield wiper, and his lips moved as he read the message. A beat later, he balled up the paper then threw it with an angry roar.

"Son of a bitch!"

I wrapped my arms around my waist and tried to calm the shudders shaking my body. This was my fault. I shouldn't have poked my big nose where it didn't belong. I shouldn't have flirted with Ruslan under the guise of getting answers about my father's killer.

And I really shouldn't be keeping secrets from Bam.

For the past week, Ruslan had been leaving pictures of my father's tortured and disfigured killer on my back step. Every morning I woke up to a new gruesome photo of how they'd maimed the asshole. I knew I should've told Bam when the first one appeared, but I liked finally having some answers. And the dark side of me really liked seeing the bastard suffer.

But I should've told Bam. If I had, he would've been able to end this weird courting-stalking thing Ruslan was doing. I hadn't, and now apparently Ruslan thought he had a chance with me. *God, what do I do?*

"Reb," Bam barked into his cell. "Yeah. He left a fucking dozen red roses at her car and a note about how he handpicked every fucking one to match her lips or some fucking thing . . . No. No! He needs to get a fucking clue. This is bullshit. You need to send a message now."

Bam looked up and locked eyes with me. I could see all the anger and frustration in his eyes. If he reacted this way about a few flowers, I was afraid to see how he'd take my collection of photos of my dad's tortured killer. So, like a coward, I said nothing.

"I want to be there, but someone should stay with Amber. No, I'll do it . . . Shut up. Later."

With my arms still wrapped around my waist, I took a few steps toward Bam. "You know, I don't think you're supposed to tell your president to shut up. It's part of the bylaws or something."

Bam didn't even acknowledge my weak attempt at humor. "It's gonna be okay, kitten. Reb and a few guys are going to pay a visit to Ruslan and his daddy and make sure they all understand that you are club property and are off limits. You got nothing to worry about."

I nodded slowly then cleared my throat. "What, uh, what did the note say?"

I was paranoid that it mentioned something about his other gifts, and I really didn't want to explain it all to Bam, given his current mood.

"It doesn't matter, kitten. After tonight, you won't have to deal with Ruslan or his bullshit again. Reb will make sure of it." Bam shoved his hands into the front pockets of his jeans and tilted his head. "How about we go get that drink after all? Maybe play a few rounds of pool and get your mind off all this bullshit. How does that sound?"

"I, uh, sure. I guess. I could use a drink."

Bam's lips lifted in his trademark half grin. "All right. Let's go."

I tossed a look at the vase of roses next to my car. I didn't really want to pick them up. Somehow it seemed like a betrayal of Bam to touch them in front of him, but I'd need to move them to get into my car.

Bam noticed my indecision. He tossed an arm around my shoulders and gently led me toward his motorcycle. "Let's take my bike. I'll get one of the prospects to clean this up and take your car back to your house. Tonight we drink."

And that was how for the third time since we met, I found myself clinging to Bam's back as he sped through the Reno streets.

But unlike the two earlier times, I wasn't angry or scared. This time I just held on and enjoyed the feel of Bam's large body between my thighs. This time I wrapped my arms around his waist and rested my cheek against his back. It felt . . . right. All my anger about bikers and their business and their part in my father's death fell away. It was just

CHAPTER 7

me and Bam and his bike.

When we pulled into the parking lot for the Mineshaft Bar, I swung off his bike and tried not to stare at the obvious bulge behind Bam's fly. I fiddled with his helmet he'd lent me and spent way too much time taking it off, as he shook out his pant leg, then fiddled with the leather bags on the side of his bike. I passed his helmet to him with a slight smile, but he avoided my eyes as he hung the helmet off the handlebars.

My body burned when he grabbed my hand and tugged me toward the front door. His hand felt rough and calloused in mine. I was dying to know if the hand-holding meant something or if he was just impatient and didn't want to wait for me, but I didn't know how to ask without sounding like a needy girl.

Judging by the way the bouncer looked from Bam to our joined hands, then avoided looking at me altogether, I had a feeling it wasn't just a casual gesture. Bam had claimed me.

I didn't get a chance to think about it, though, because after exchanging chin lifts with the bouncer, Bam pushed open the door and tugged me inside the bar. It felt like that moment in the movies when the record scratch sound rang through the bar and everyone turned to look at the door. There was no record scratch, but everyone was looking at us. Across the room I could see Tank and Hatchet and a few of the other guys from the club leaning against the bar with beer mugs in their hands and their wide eyes pointed our way.

Needless to say, I felt a little conspicuous. Like that dream where you show up to class and everyone's staring at you and then you realize you're naked. Like that. I even took a quick peek down to make sure I was wearing clothes.

Bam apparently didn't see anything out of the ordinary. He tugged my hand as he took off for the bar, practically pulling me the entire way. I gave a few weak smiles here and there as I recognized a few faces from my dad's club.

I'd never been to the Mineshaft. I'd heard enough stories about it when I was a kid, and knew better than to try to hang out here when I was a teenager. It was a club hangout and a smart kid didn't try to score booze at her dad's bar. They'd have taken away my fake ID in a heartbeat. Overprotective alphaholes. But it was your typical dive bar with neon beer signs, scuffed wooden floors, and exposed brick walls. Where Ruslan's nightclub, Howl, had been slick and classy with its brick walls and chandeliers, the Mineshaft was not. This bar was rough, worn, and not the kinda place me and my friends ever would've hung out in. And yet somehow it still felt comfortable.

I smiled at Tank and Hatchet and Zag when we reached the bar. The guys nodded at us, then eyed Bam's iron grip on my right hand. I looked up at Bam and caught the glare he sent the guys' way before he casually dropped my hand to wipe his hand down his beard. I rolled my eyes and leaned against the bar. Before the guys could really jab Bam, an ancient bartender popped up out of nowhere with his cliché rag and wiped down the bar.

"Hey guys. What'll it be?"

"I'll have a shot of Patrón," I answered. "And a glass of water, please."

Bam quirked an eyebrow. "A Sierra Nevada Pale Ale for me."

I shook my head. "Really, Bam? You're going to make me do a shot of tequila all by myself?"

"I'm not doing a body shot, if that's what you're getting at." Bam narrowed his eyes at me, then tossed a glare over my shoulder at the guys.

"Wow. Okay. Never mind." I pulled out a bar stool and avoided everyone's eyes as I sat down and waited for my shot.

"Make that five shots of Patrón," Hatchet called over my head to the ancient bartender before giving me a smile. "We'll have a little toast to your dad. Although Patrón is more your mom's kinda booze than his.

CHAPTER 7

Errr, I mean not anymore, clearly. But before. You know, when she would party with the club back in the day."

I laughed and reached for the shot closest to me. "It's okay, Hatchet. I know what you meant."

"Good." Hatchet passed out the remaining shots then lifted his own. "To Stitch. The best damn biker—"

"And father," I tossed in.

"And father this town has ever seen. You are missed, buddy. Every damn day."

"To Stitch," the entire bar around us echoed.

My eyes burned with unshed tears before I even downed my shot. I gulped the fiery liquor so I had an excuse, then surreptitiously wiped at my eyes.

"Did I ever tell you about the Giants game I went to with Stitch a few years back?" Tank asked after he'd slammed his empty shot glass down on the bar. "They actually have a little jail in the stadium, because your dad wouldn't get rid of his—"

"Switchblade," I finished for him.

"He told you that one, huh?" Tank grinned.

"Nope. He did the same thing when we went to a theme park in California when I was little. Although that time my mom pitched the biggest fit you'd ever seen and made him go back and leave his knife in the glove box of his pickup. I think we went on three rides before he showed up again."

"Probably found a bar to take the edge off first." Tank laughed. "Those parks give me the heebie-jeebies."

"That sounds like something Stitch would say." Hatchet laughed.

"He was a great guy," Bam rumbled next to me. "Did he ever tell you about the time he showed up at the hospital when my grandma was having surgery?"

I shook my head.

Bam ducked his head and ran a hand through his hair, avoiding everyone's eyes. "It was a shit time. She'd just been diagnosed, and I was driving back and forth from Tahoe to here, apprenticing at the union, and prospecting at the club, and pretty much fucking it all up. I hadn't told any of the guys what was going on, but somehow Stitch found out. Both him and Maverick walked into the waiting room of the hospital and sat next to me. They didn't say shit about my grandma or why I was there; they just started shooting the shit like we were here having a beer, and kept my mind off my grandma. I never got a chance to thank him. A week later, he was . . ." Bam trailed off and cleared his throat. "Anyway, it was nice of him. That's the kinda guy your dad was. You were lucky to have him."

My eyes sheened with tears, I smiled at Bam. "I really was. Thank you."

Bam smiled back at me, and I felt a heavy sensation in my chest. We stayed there for a second and just stared into each other's eyes until Tank slapped Bam on the back, breaking our spell.

"He was an awesome guy. Did I tell you about the time back when I was a prospect and Stitch . . ." Tank droned on, but I wasn't listening. I couldn't look away from the sheen in Bam's eyes even as he tilted his head and downed half of his beer in a few gulps.

I was seeing Bam in a whole new light. He wasn't just a loudmouthed biker who had to get his way, or one who put club business before everything. He'd taken care of his grandma while she was sick. And was taking care of me now. He cared, and was a pretty fantastic guy himself.

I wanted to think that there was more between us than club duty, but I was afraid I might be projecting. Did Bam feel the same way as I did? Did he want me, too? Or was I just a job to him? I couldn't forget how I'd felt when I'd bared my feelings to my high school crush, and he'd just shrugged and walked away. I didn't want to put myself in that situation again. It'd been painful and embarrassing and just soul-crushing.

So, I didn't say anything.

The rest of the night I laughed with Tank and the guys. We drank shots of tequila and whiskey and told stories about my dad. We played pool and hung out, and it felt right. It felt like home.

And I tried not to let my heart shine in my eyes when I looked at Bam.

Because in the back of my mind, the secret that I was keeping from the guys burned a hole in my soul. I knew somehow, someway it was going to come back and bite me on the ass. But not tonight.

Tonight I was one of the guys, and I enjoyed every minute.

Chapter 8

Bam

I pulled up to Amber's house and let my bike idle for a second. When Amber didn't bound through the front door as she usually did, I killed the engine, put the kickstand down, then swung off my bike. Amber was almost always waiting for me on her front step, or out of the house seconds after I pulled up. Something wasn't right. I pulled my helmet off and left it on the seat, then went to her front door.

I pounded on the door and tried to get a glimpse of the inside through the curtains, but couldn't see shit. I was debating whether to force my way in when the door swung open. Amber stood in the doorway and gave me an apologetic look.

"I am so sorry. My mom's gone all happy homemaker on me and made me eat lunch before my shift, so I'm running late. I'll just be two seconds." She ran off before I could say anything.

I stood there on her front step like a tool. Do I go inside? Should I go back to my bike? Shaking my head at my sudden teenage angst, I reached forward to close the door when Amber popped back into the living room and took my breath away. Before, she'd been wearing a loose tee and sweatpants. Now she had on skintight jeans and a sparkly top that clung to her body and let me know just what she had

CHAPTER 8

going on underneath. Christ, she was hot. Suddenly I had the urge to palm her breasts and feel the bite of those sequins against her soft chest. I wanted to know what she had on underneath it. I wanted to taste what was underneath that.

While I was busy trying not to swallow my tongue, Amber grabbed a few things next to the door as she shouted, "Bye Mom! My ride's here!"

"'Kay, honey! Have a good shift!" Brittany shouted back from somewhere inside the house.

Meanwhile I was still standing in the doorway with my mouth open. Amber shot me a strange look, so I spun around and stomped off to my motorcycle without waiting for her. I grabbed my helmet and shoved it onto my head—like it would somehow shield me from my sudden dirty thoughts about her. I zipped open my saddlebag and grabbed my spare helmet. Without looking Amber's way, I shoved the helmet in her direction, then got on my bike. I knew I was acting like a moody fuck, but I really wasn't happy with the turn my thoughts had taken. So, like a man, I was taking my frustration out by ignoring her. I could feel Amber's confused gaze on me, but I fiddled with my keychain and ignored her probing eyes. A beat after Amber swung on behind me, I revved the engine and peeled out of her driveway.

Not that my current situation was any better. Instead of staring at Amber's tight body, I was now feeling it pressed against my back. When I took a corner too fast, her arms tightened around me and her body pressed even closer to mine. It was torture. I tried to shift and get my hardening cock under control, but I couldn't move much. And every time I moved, Amber shifted with me, reminding me of her tight body and those gorgeous sparkling breasts. Son of a bitch. I couldn't decide whether this was the trip that wouldn't end or the one I didn't want to end.

Finally, I roared up the parking garage ramp and slowly wound my way to the fourth floor. It was more a force of habit that had me going to the same floor Amber always parked on. We'd decided after the flowers incident that it would be easier for us to just cart her around instead of shadowing her ancient car. This way Ruslan wouldn't have additional access to her, and we would always have her with us. I'd been prepared for Amber to pitch a fit when I told her, but she'd accepted the change in her guard duty with no fuss. She'd just smiled slightly and said, "Okay."

I pulled my bike up to a spot near the stairwell and killed the engine. Waiting for Amber to get off, I willed my body to behave. I really didn't want her giving me shit because I had a boner.

"What's got your panties in a wad?" Amber asked after she got off my bike and pulled her helmet off.

I took off my helmet and lifted a shoulder. "Nothing. I'm fine."

Amber's forehead wrinkled as she gave me a dubious look. But after a beat, she handed me her helmet and then silently led us down the four flights of stairs. When we reached the ground level without a word spoken between us, Amber folded her arms across her chest and squared up to me. "Really. What's going on? Has Ruslan . . . done something you're pissed about?"

"No. Nothing's going on. Come on, let's get you to the locker room."

"Have *I* pissed you off?"

"What? No, you're fine. Come on, let's go." Not waiting for her, I took off toward the employee entrance and after a beat, Amber followed.

I know I was being a moody douche, but I couldn't get the image of Amber wearing that sparkly top and nothing else out of my head. She was undeniably gorgeous—I'd thought it when I first saw her two years ago—and if anything she'd only gotten more gorgeous. It didn't help that I was practically spending all my free time with her. Watching her prance around in that so-called uniform, listening to

CHAPTER 8

her talk so kindly with every customer, seeing her go out of her way to do whatever she can for the people around her.

Fuck. I had to stop thinking about her like that. This was a job. She was Stitch's daughter, an MC princess, and way too naïve for a bastard like me.

That state of mind was easier said than done, though. As I sat at the bar and watched Amber prance around in that damn excuse for a uniform, my rage bubbled to the surface every time a guy would get near her. I watched Amber with the intensity of a lion eyeing its prey. I wanted to pounce on her like one, too, but I couldn't. This was a job.

She came up to the bar and I watched, spellbound, as her breasts jiggled as she set her tray down. "One Jack and Coke, a tequila sunrise, and two Buds."

She cleared her throat, and I jerked my gaze up from her chest to find her staring back at me with a disgruntled frown. "What is your deal tonight?"

"Nothing. What's your deal?" I replied like a pissed-off teenager.

Amber just rolled her eyes and cocked a hip as she waited for the bartender to fill her order.

I heaved a sigh. I knew I should apologize for being such a surly asshole, but I was damned if I could come up with a plausible excuse for how I was acting. I sure as shit couldn't tell her that I wanted her, and it was pissing me off. So instead I said nothing, just glowered in her direction as she took off with her loaded tray of drinks.

Amber ignored me and smiled charmingly at her customers. She had delivered her last drink—the Jack and Coke—and was reaching for the tip when it happened. The guy jerked the bill out of her reach, grabbed her around the waist, and pulled her onto his lap. I was off my bar stool and across the casino floor in seconds.

"No. Let go of me," Amber bit out.

I grabbed her arm and jerked her out of the asshole's lap. Amber teetered unsteadily on her heels next to me. I didn't even think about it: I hauled back and punched him on the jaw with all my strength.

"You don't ever put your fucking hands on her! Do you fucking hear me?" I cocked back to punch him again when Amber put her hand on my arm.

"Bam! No!"

"No? He had his fucking hands on you. Are you telling me you wanted to be in this asshole's lap?" I gestured to the frat boy punk who was currently cowering in front of me.

"Of course not. Don't be a moron. But you need to get your shit under control. Security is gonna be here any second."

Sure enough, two burly guys in security uniforms hustled their way toward us. I shook my head. I knew it was my reaction to the situation that had them all running this way. They didn't give a shit about what had happened to Amber. And they proved it when the first one opened his mouth.

"We got a problem here, gentlemen?" Thing 1 asked when they reached us.

"Fuck yeah, we do," Frat boy prick wailed. "That asshole punched me. I want to press charges."

"Fine by me." I crossed my arms over my chest to keep me from punching him in the face again. "Amber here will press charges for harassment, because she sure as shit didn't want you touching her."

Frat boy prick's lip curled. "That's bullshit. She was begging for it, prancing around in that skirt, smiling at me, and asking me what I wanted all breathlessly."

"Because that's my job, asshole." Amber's brow wrinkled. "I'm a cocktail waitress, not a hooker."

"My bad." Frat boy prick laughed, holding up his hands. "But you could see where I got confused. I mean, this is Nevada, after all, right?"

"Prostitution isn't legal in Washoe County, sir," Thing 1 replied.

CHAPTER 8

"Would you please come with us?"

It apparently wasn't a request as he grabbed Frat boy prick's arm and hoisted him out of his seat. Thing 1 "escorted" Frat boy prick across the casino floor as Thing 2 held back.

"You okay, Amber? Do you want to press charges against him?"

"No. I just want to get back to work." Amber crossed her arms over her chest and hugged her elbows.

"You know that's not how we handle situations like this. You gotta go back and talk to someone in HR, then fill out some paperwork. It might be best if your, er, friend came with you."

Amber nodded tightly then fell in line as Thing 2 led the way to the back offices. Every bit of her body language said "leave me alone."

But I couldn't.

I put my hand on her shoulder and didn't let her shrug me off. Instead, I grabbed her hand and pulled her to a stop next to me. Thing 2 stopped as well but hovered respectfully out of hearing distance.

I dropped her hand and shoved mine in my pockets. "I'm not going to apologize for defending you."

"Well, you should. I could've handled it. I've spent months here handling assholes like him, and no one ever got hurt."

I shrugged. "He deserved it. And that's what I'm here for."

"No. You're here because I was stupid and got some Mafia asshole interested in me. You're here to keep Ruslan and his goons away from me. You're not here to protect me from my life. What happened to the whole I'm-a-shadow-you'll-never-know-I'm-here routine?"

"It went out the window when that prick put his hands on you. He needed to be taught a lesson. No one disrespects True Brothers property."

"Well, congratulations. This True Brothers property probably just lost her job." Amber looked at me with such disgust that I flinched.

"Kitten, I didn't—"

"No. Don't call me that. And just . . . just don't fucking talk to me. Okay?" Not waiting for my reply, Amber turned on her heel and stomped off toward Thing 2, leaving me following silently behind them.

How I went from knight in shining armor to asshole in the wrong I couldn't wrap my brain around.

I spent the next hour brooding in the corner of the break room while Amber talked to an HR manager, then filled out a binder's worth of paperwork. She didn't look my way once. Not even when the HR prat asked about me. I couldn't hear Amber's reply, but I could feel the judgement in the prat's eyes every time he looked at me. Not that I gave a shit. I was used to it, actually. But I couldn't be the reason that Amber lost her job. I might hate the fact that she worked here, but she needed this job—her family needed her to keep this job.

So I swallowed my pride and approached the HR prat as he was leaving.

"Sir? Can I have a moment?"

"We don't need a statement from you. Surveillance verified your story. Amber has given me your contact info in case the gentleman is foolish enough to actually press charges. So if there's anything else . . ."

"Yes, sir. I just wanted to apologize for my part in what happened. And I hope that my actions won't affect Ms. Bennett's job." I had gotten plenty of practice in the art of apologizing during my time as a teen punk. I just treated this guy the same as I would any impartial judge—I lied. Except for the part about Amber's job.

"If that's your idea of a threat, you should know that we have cameras in here as well."

I blinked. "That was my idea of an apology. I said I'm sorry."

He took a step back as my anger gave my words an edge I didn't want.

Nodding cautiously, he continued to step away. "Right. I accept. All forgiven. If that's it, I have some work to get back to."

He fled out the door before I could reply.

"You really need to work on your apologies." Amber snorted, her head still bent over her paperwork.

"What? I said I was sorry."

"Maybe practice in front of a mirror next time."

"What's that supposed to mean?"

Amber shook her head, then looked up at me with a slight smile. "All that." She waved a hand in my general direction. "It's a little scary when it's pointed at someone like him."

"Doesn't seem to scare you."

Amber bit her lip then dropped her gaze to her paperwork again. "I'm used to it. Mostly."

"Didn't seem to scare that frat boy prick much, either."

Amber snorted again. "Really? He pissed his pants—literally—or didn't you notice?"

I shrugged. "I don't usually look at guys' crotches."

Amber rolled her eyes and bent over her paperwork again.

"I am sorry, though. Really."

She looked up at me with her ice-blue eyes and my heart stuttered.

It took me a second to remember what we were talking about. I cleared my throat roughly. "I don't want to be the reason that you lose your job. I know how important it is to your family."

Amber nodded slowly. "Thank you."

I nodded back and rocked back on my heels. I felt foolish suddenly. And I didn't know what to say to break the seriousness of the moment.

Amber gave me another slight smile. "If it helps, I don't think I'm in danger of losing my job. The HR guy went to great lengths to explain their sexual harassment policies. I think they're spooked that I'll want to sue or something."

"That's, uh, that's good news. The keeping your job part, not the lawsuit."

"Yeah."

"So how about I take you out for dinner as an apology?"

"Oh, you don't have to."

"But I want to. So how about it? Steak dinner on me?"

Amber smiled. "Sounds like a date."

But it wasn't a date.

I had to remind myself of that again and again throughout dinner. Despite how gorgeous Amber looked in her sparkly top or how she made me smile every time she laughed. This was just dinner between two friends because I didn't go on dates and Amber was too good for a bastard like me.

Chapter 9

Amber

"Oh my god." I turned my head and puked into the bushes next to my back door. I couldn't get the image out of my head. Closing my eyes didn't help. I could remember what it looked like, and *ugh*. I puked again.

I heaved until there was nothing left to come up. And then I heaved some more.

I'd lulled myself into a false sense of security over the past two weeks. Jackson had actually stepped up and was helping out around the house. He even gave me some money to help cover the power bill. I still had a True Brother MC member shadowing me at all times, mostly Bam Bam when I was on shift. And Ruslan had calmed down to a certain degree. He hadn't bought me another car or sent me more flowers, but his gifts had taken a turn. Instead of romancing me the old-fashioned way with flowers and chocolates and cars, he started sending me little mementos of my father's killer.

Mostly framed photos depicting how they'd tortured him.

Only these weren't little Polaroid jobs. They were blown up into huge poster-size works of art and framed like they should've been hung in a museum or something. But the subject matter wasn't something that would appeal to the masses. Or me, frankly. I might've talked a big game, but I didn't have the stomach for this. And I certainly didn't have the stomach for what I'd just found on my back step.

A liquid filled jar containing what I think—judging by what a few of the posters depicted—was the tongue of my father's killer.

I heaved again.

I didn't want to look at it again, let alone touch it. But I had to, because I didn't want my mom to see it. She'd been doing so much better since the little intervention that her friends from the club gave her while I was at work. Mom had been going to some meetings at night, and I hadn't seen her drink in weeks. I didn't want to be the thing that sent her off the rails again.

Steeling myself, I grabbed the bottle off the step and tore through the house. I could hear my mom moving around in the kitchen so I took off upstairs to my room. I opened my closet—where I'd been stashing my collection of maiming art— grabbed an old backpack, and carefully set the bottle inside it. My hand crinkled against a note. I'd forgotten to read it once I'd caught sight of the horror show inside the jar. After carefully pulling the note off the jar without looking at the contents, I zipped up the bag, then read the note.

I've showered you with flowers, chocolates, and a car. I've shown you what I'm willing to do for those I love. I'm getting tired of waiting, moya zvezda.

—R

I swayed unsteadily on my feet. That sounded so ominous . . . and delusional. Ruslan didn't torture that guy because he loved me—my dad's killer was his enemy who had information. It had nothing to do with me at the time.

Suddenly I really regretted not telling Bam about the pictures.

To be honest, I'd kinda liked the first one. I had the proof I'd wanted that the scumbag had suffered. And I felt like finally, *finally* someone

CHAPTER 9

was listening to me. He'd heard what I wanted, and he'd delivered, unlike Rebel or Tank or Bam. But then the pictures got . . . disturbing. They portrayed things I'd never imagined in all my years of watching horror movies and crime shows.

But I still didn't tell Bam.

We'd finally found this unspoken understanding where he didn't give me shit about my job, and I didn't give him shit about being a Brother. And honestly, I was starting to like him. He was sweet in his grumpy, pain-in-the-ass way. And it didn't hurt that he was hot as hell. With his blond gruffy beard and longish hair, he still reminded me of Thor. I continued to have confusing dreams about Vikings and blond gods of thunder. Not that he'd ever made a move on me. He was frustratingly nice. Even if his eyes lingered on me from time to time, nothing came of it. And I was fine with that. Really.

But it would all end once I told him about Ruslan's . . . gifts.

Fuck me.

"Amber? Do you want breakfast, honey?"

That was the other weird thing. With her newfound sobriety, my mom had morphed into some crazy fifties housewife, always making meals and cleaning. I think maybe she was working through her grief and guilt over what'd happened in the last year. If I didn't watch it, I'd be packing on the weight in no time, given all her baking lately.

"No, thanks!" I yelled down the stairs. "I'm meeting Sydney at the coffeehouse."

"Okay, honey. Love you!"

"Love you, too, Mom."

I darted over to my dresser and changed out of my pajama shorts and tank and into a pair of yoga pants and a T-shirt. Grabbing my phone, I fired off a quick text to Bam.

Me: *I need to talk. Where can we meet up?*

He didn't immediately text back, and I paced a hole in the floor while

I quietly freaked out. I ran into the hall bathroom and washed my face then brushed my teeth, all the while watching my silent phone. I was just about to floss out of pure boredom when my phone finally pinged.

Bam: *I'm home but I can meet you anywhere you want.*

Thank God. I immediately typed out a response.

Me: *I'll come to your place. I don't want anyone eavesdropping on us.*

We'd swung by his apartment last week to grab a spare helmet. After Ruslan's last floral delivery, Bam had been giving me a ride to work, and I wasn't exactly complaining. Being wrapped around a strong man on the back of his bike was a feeling like nothing else. Even if it was under the guise of guard duty and not because he had feelings for me.

Bam: *That's hella cryptic. I'll put a pot of coffee on.*

Me: *I'll hit the Mackay Mocha drive-thru and bring you a cup. See you in 15.*

At least that way, what I told my mom wasn't a total lie.

Crap, I really had a problem. I needed to stop lying to everyone. What was wrong with me? I sighed as I grabbed the backpack I'd hidden the jar of tongue in. Holding it carefully, I walked downstairs and grabbed my purse and keys. The first step was admitting you had a problem, right? I'd heard my mom say as much in the past few days.

Nothing like starting with the biggest and scariest lie of them all. Bam was the forgiving kinda guy, right?

Twenty minutes later, I knocked on the door to Bam's apartment, a drink holder with two large coffees in my other hand. I hadn't known what to order the big guy, but I figured I couldn't go wrong with large and black. He struck me as a no-froufrou-kinda-drink guy.

My heart raced as I waited for him to open the door. I didn't need the pick-me-up from my large mocha latte with whipped cream, but I'd ordered it anyway. At this rate, I'd be vibrating like a hummingbird in ten minutes.

CHAPTER 9

The door ripped open and a disheveled *and shirtless* Bam stood in the doorframe. "Coffee. Thank fuck."

He grabbed my coffee out of the holder and took two large gulps before I could unstick my tongue from the shock of seeing so much of him. He was simply magnificent. Large and muscular and just so damn perfect. He could've easily modeled for any fitness magazine, or hell, even underwear. If anything, the large avenging angel tattooed on his right peck, curving onto his shoulder and continuing down his arm, only highlighted just how muscular he was. My dreams were gonna be hot tonight.

Bam groaned much like I imagined him groaning during sex. "This is delicious. What the hell did they put in it?"

"That's my drink, thank you very much." I grabbed the cup from him, then ducked into his apartment, hoping he didn't notice my bright red cheeks. "I got you a plain ol' black coffee."

Bam accepted the offered coffee and took a drink. "Ugh, yours was better."

I had to laugh at that. Just when I thought I had him figured out. "Noted. I'll order you a mocha latte next time."

"So, what's going on?" Bam took another drink then made a face. "This needs sugar."

He took off for the small kitchenette next to the door while I stood there uncertain of what to do next. To be honest, I wanted to delay my confession as long as possible. I knew he wouldn't be happy, and I'd already seen a pissed-off Bam. I sure as hell didn't want that anger pointed in my direction. Instead I deflected, and like a goofus, said, "You have a nice place."

Bam looked at me like I was insane. "This place is a shithole. Your house is nice."

"I live with my mom. It's not exactly *my* house. I still sleep in the same room I had when I was five. I'd give anything to have my own place like this." I didn't know what Bam was complaining about. He had a tiny kitchenette with all the appliances a twenty-something needed—a microwave, a refrigerator, and an itty-bitty stove. A high countertop with a couple of bar stools. Across the smallish space was a worn sofa, a battered coffee table, and a large, flat-screen TV. I couldn't see from here, but judging from the three closed doors down the small hallway, he had at least one bedroom, a bathroom, and probably ample closet space. What more would a single guy need? This place was the embodiment of my living-on-my-own fantasy. What was he complaining about?

"I know shit hasn't exactly been a bed of roses at your house since Stitch passed, but come on. Do you know what I'd give to be in your shoes? To have a family that actually gave a fuck? To be able to sleep in the same room for what? Fifteen years? That's the fucking fairy tale, kitten. This"—Bam waved his arms, gesturing at his apartment—"this is just fucking sad. The carpet is older than dirt, the super doesn't give a shit about the ants living in my kitchen, and the fucker next door thinks he's the next Charlie Watts. I'd give anything to be in your shoes."

I nodded soberly at his reality check. "I know. I know I'm fortunate to have the family I have left. It's just . . ." And for some reason—maybe it was the tender look in his eyes or the way he'd opened up to me—I unloaded something that I hadn't told anyone but Sydney. "This was supposed to be my time, you know? I know it sounds selfish as hell, but I'm only twenty-one. I should be going to college and living on my own. That's all I really want."

"I'm sorry, kitten." Bam braced his arms on the counter and leaned toward me, the expression on his face intense. "And you should know that I'm doing everything in my power to make that happen for you. Hopefully, if things go right, you should be able to go back to school soon. If not next semester, then the one after."

CHAPTER 9

Wow. He'd said it with such fervor I felt his passion down to my toes. This was a man who cared. He gave a shit about me. I swayed toward him, aching to feel his lips on mine.

Mmrrrroww. The cutest, fluffiest white and gray striped Persian cat came strolling down the hallway, leaving the far door slightly ajar.

My jaw dropped. "You have a cat?"

This big, tough, burly biker had a cat? And the cutest, fluffiest cat I'd ever seen.

Bam huffed an annoyed breath. "Pixie was my Grandma's. I inherited her."

"Awww, she's so cute." I dropped down on my knees and beckoned her toward me. "Here, kitty, kitty. Come here, Pixie."

"She doesn't really like peop . . ." Bam trailed off as Pixie butted her head against me.

I held the back of my hand out and let her delicately sniff my fingers before I rubbed them against that spot behind her ear that had her purring in no time.

"I'll be damned," Bam murmured to himself.

I looked up at him as I continued to rub Pixie. He had the most flummoxed expression I'd ever seen. After a moment, he shook his head and muttered, "Uh, you had something you wanted to talk about?"

I closed my eyes as I mentally cursed. I guess I couldn't hide my head in the sand forever. I gave Pixie one last pat, then pushed myself up to my feet. "Yeah. The talking thing. Right."

Bam raised an eyebrow but didn't say anything.

"Can we sit down, maybe?" I gestured toward his sofa. I hoped that maybe he'd be less intimidating in a seated position.

Bam hitched a shoulder, then grabbed his newly sweetened coffee. "Sure."

I followed him over to the worn leather sofa and took a seat on the end, tucking my backpack with its horrible contents under the coffee table. Bam sat on the opposite end, leaving a cushion between us. He set his coffee down on the table next to mine, then twisted until he faced me, his left leg bent and inches from me.

I was wrong. He was still intimidating, now probably because he was so close to me. If I reached out, I could touch him. I think I liked it better when we still had the countertop between us.

"There was something you wanted to talk about?" Bam prompted me.

"Uh, yeah." I took a deep breath and had to look away to say it. "I haven't been honest with you the last few weeks."

Even though I wasn't looked at him, I could feel the tension emanating from him, belying his casual body language. "About what?"

I took another deep breath and said his name as I exhaled. "Ruslan."

"You're seeing that fucker?" Bam shot up to his feet and paced agitatedly across the room.

"Bam, that's not—"

"He's a demented fucking lunatic, Amber!" Bam's voice rose with every word until he was shouting at me. "WHAT THE FUCK ARE YOU THINKING?"

"You need to calm down. I'm not—" I broke off with a cry as he drove his fist through the wall. I covered my head with my hands like the blow had been at me. "Oh my god. What are you—"

But Bam wouldn't let me finish as he turned and pointed a now bloody and drywall-covered finger at me. "It's not happening. No way in fuck am I letting you waste yourself on that fucking piece of trash. DO YOU HEAR ME?"

"I'M NOT SEEING HIM!" I shouted back at Bam. We both stared at each other, our chests heaving with our breaths. Mine out of fear and anxiety. His out of anger and frustration.

"What?" His hands dropped to his sides as he stared blankly at me. "But you said—"

CHAPTER 9

"I said that I hadn't been honest with you about Ruslan. That doesn't mean I've been seeing him." I shuddered. The thought was so disgusting it made bile tickle the back of my throat. "I know he's a psychotic SOB. *Believe me*, I know."

Bam's eyes hardened at that piece of information. "What the hell does that mean? He can't have been hanging around you—we have eyes on you or your house at all times. Has he been calling you? That's it, isn't it? I'm gonna—"

"Oh my god. Would you calm the fuck down? Here. Sit. Please."

I waited until he sat back down on the couch, although it didn't seem to calm him any. His knee bounced, displaying his nerves. But I continued anyway.

"When the first one came, I thought I could handle it. Honestly I was glad to see it. I liked that he had listened to me, that he heard what I wanted, but then . . ." I blew out an unsteady breath. "But then they kept coming. And each one was more deranged than the last, and I just couldn't . . ." Tears sheened my eyes as I remembered the posters and the ugliness they portrayed. Yes, I'd wanted revenge, but it turned out that, at the end of the day, I didn't have the stomach for it. I was weak.

So fucking weak.

I covered my face with my hands and sobbed. I couldn't take it anymore. Between my dad dying, my mom falling apart, my brother disappearing, and now my crazy-ass stalker, I just couldn't take it anymore. Why did everything have to be so fucked up? Why couldn't I catch just one break? Just one. Was that too much to ask?

Chapter 10

Bam

I sat there, lost as fuck, as Amber sobbed beside me. I had no idea what she was talking about. Air left me in ragged breaths as I tried to get my anger under control. Just the thought of Amber with that fucker filled me with colossal rage. To go from that to watching her sob on the couch next to me . . . I couldn't handle the roller-coaster. I needed a fucking minute to get my shit under control.

Amber did this hiccupping sob that I felt in my heart. The last time I heard that sound was just after my grandma died, and I sat all alone in her house. I never wanted to hear Amber make that sound ever again. Putting my arm around her shoulders, I pulled her to me.

"It's gonna be okay, kitten," I murmured to her. "I swear to God, whatever's going on, we can handle it. It's gonna be okay."

Amber burrowed into my chest as her sobs slowly subsided. She kept one hand over her eyes, like she was embarrassed to look at me. Finally, after a few minutes, she scrubbed at her eyes with her wrist then gave a sad laugh. "I'm sorry. It's just been building for a while. And then when that tongue showed up this morning, I—"

"Tongue? What fucking tongue?"

"Okay, I'll tell you, but only if you promise to stay calm and not go

CHAPTER 10

all Hulk on me again. Okay?"

I nodded tightly.

Amber's body shuddered as she let out a breath. Then she tilted her head up and the soft, wounded look in her eyes tore me up. "About a day or two after our weird encounter with him at the parking garage, Ruslan started sending me these photos. Huge, blown-up photos the size of a poster, but framed like something you'd see in a gallery. He left them on the back step late at night, where you guys couldn't see."

Shit, this didn't sound good. "What were the photos of?"

"My father's killer. Being tortured."

I muttered a curse under my breath.

"The first one wasn't so bad. Just him hanging from some chains, looking bloody. But then they got more . . . intense after that."

"Why didn't you tell us, Amber? We could've taken care of it. Fuck, we could've at least made sure that you didn't have to see that."

Amber pushed away from me with a glare. "I *wanted* to see that. That's all I've wanted since my dad died. I asked and asked and asked. But you all wouldn't listen to me. You guys thought it was more important to protect your *"club business"* and leave me and my family out of the loop. That's why I went hunting for answers. Because you assholes wouldn't give them to me."

"And how did that work out for you? Did you feel better when you saw what that fucking monster did to your father's killer?"

"Yes. Okay? *Yes!* I wanted to know that he felt pain. That the end wasn't easy for him. That they made him suffer." Her chest heaved as she gave her impassioned little speech. After a moment, the hitch came back in her breathing, and she shook her head. "Or I thought I did. I thought I could handle it. But seeing with my own eyes what they did to him . . . made me sick. I can't—I can't go to sleep. Every time I close my eyes, I see one of those ugly photos. It's haunting me, Bam. And I can't take it anymore."

I couldn't deny that I wasn't pissed that she'd hid this from me, and yet everything inside me wanted to protect her so she wouldn't have that soft, wounded look in her eyes ever again. Putting my arms around her shoulders, I pulled her toward me until she rested against my chest with a sigh. I also couldn't deny that it felt so fucking good to hold her in my arms.

But then something she'd said earlier niggled at the back of mind. "Wait, you said something about a tongue."

Amber nodded against my chest. Pulling away, she reached under the coffee table and grabbed a backpack then set it down on the coffee table with a clunk. "Yeah. This morning there was a jar on my back step with what looked like a tongue suspended in liquid inside." Her voice got softer with every word until I had to duck my head to hear her. She buried her head in my chest again as she whispered. "And there was a note."

I clenched my jaw as rage flashed through my bloodstream. It took everything inside me not to vent it and pound the wall again—or go looking for Ruslan—but I didn't want to scare Amber, and I needed more intel before we went after that fucker. "What did the note say?"

"It's in the bag. It says something about how he's given me so many gifts, and how he's shown me what he's willing to do for those he loves." She clenched her arms around my body like she had to draw from my strength as she whispered. "And that he's getting tired of waiting."

Fuck.

I closed my eyes and mentally said every curse word I could think of. I'd been around him enough to know that an impatient Ruslan was a scary fucking Ruslan. I couldn't let her go *anywhere* until we had this shit with Ruslan locked the fuck down.

"Okay, I'm not gonna lie. That's not good."

Amber chuckled morosely against my chest at my lame joke. "You

CHAPTER 10

don't have to tell me that. I kinda got the picture when he sent me a freaking tongue."

"Yeah. That'll do it." I brushed my hand over her soft blond hair and sighed. "But I promise I'm gonna take care of it. When I'm through with that deranged fucker, he's not gonna remember your name, let alone send you any more fucked-up gifts. I promise you he'll be out of your life for good."

Amber pulled back slightly until she could look up at me. Whatever she saw in my expression must've convinced her because she smiled slightly. "Thank you."

I nodded tightly as I stared into her ice-blue eyes. Christ, she was enchanting. Even scared out of her mind over Ruslan, she was still gorgeous. And sweet. And soft.

And too good for an SOB like me.

Even knowing all that, I didn't resist when she swayed toward me and gave me the softest, sweetest kiss I'd had in my entire life. She kept her eyes and her mouth chastely closed as she pressed her lips against mine.

I groaned low in my throat as just the hint of promise in her kiss, in her body pressed against me, stirred the animal inside me. My hands wrapped around her arms, and I pulled her even closer to me as I took control of the kiss. My mouth commanded hers to open to me and when it did, my tongue darted out to learn and taste every part of her.

It felt like eons later when I lifted my head. Both of us were breathing ragged as I stared into her lust-darkened eyes.

I wanted her. I wanted her more than anything else in my life at that moment, or fuck, ever . . . Christ, why did she have to be so gorgeous? And sweet?

My phone on the end table pinged with an incoming text message. The sound alone reminded me of why I couldn't have Amber. I owed my Brothers everything, especially Reb and Maverick. I just couldn't betray those guys by making a move on Stitch's daughter. True Brothers didn't work that way.

No matter how much I wanted to.

"That was a mistake," I gritted out, my voice hoarse. I stood, grabbed my phone off the table, and read the text. Anything to avoid looking at Amber's wounded eyes.

Maverick: *Wanna come over for Sunday dinner? The wife is cookin.*

Christ, that was the knife in the belly I didn't need right then. Maverick had been my sponsor in the club when I was a prospect and the closest thing I had to a father, ever. For the first fifteen years of my life we'd lived next door to Maverick and he'd let me hang out at his place and help him out in his garage tinkering with his truck and motorcycles. He'd been my hero for more years than I could remember. Right up until I moved to Tahoe to live with my grandma. Hell, he was the reason I went to trade school and became a welder. Maverick was a welder, too. While I was growing up, he'd been my example of what a man was.

He didn't know it, but I was already letting him down.

I quickly typed back.

Me: *Can't. Got club business to take care of. Give Sarah my thanks tho.*

"I'm just gonna go." Amber muttered as she stood and grabbed her purse. "I can crash at my friend Sydney's house. I doubt Ruslan knows to look for me there."

"I know to look for you there. If you're not at work or home or that damn coffee house, you're at your friend's. It's not safe. You're staying here." I still didn't look at her while I fired off another text, to Hatchet this time.

Me: *Need you at my place ASAP. Shit is hitting the fan.*

Despite working at the restaurant the night before, Hatchet was still awake as the three little dots beneath my text let me know he was typing a reply.

CHAPTER 10

Hatchet: *On my way*

"Hatchet's gonna come over and keep you company. Do you know him?" I looked up from my phone and found Amber standing next to my kitchen counter with her arms wrapped around her waist, her eyes suspiciously wet as she avoided my gaze.

I'd hurt her.

I felt lower than a snake's belly at that moment. This beautiful, amazing woman deserved so much better than me. If I wasn't fucking things up one way, I was screwing them up another. It seemed like I couldn't do anything right when it came to Amber.

"Listen, kitten, I'm sorry if—"

"No, please. I really don't want to hear your little speech about how I got the wrong idea and how I'm a great girl, blah, blah, blah. I don't think my ego could take it right now." She chuckled huskily as she searched through her purse. "I'd really rather go hang out with Sydney, or maybe Jessica? At least her husband's in the club. Zag's house would be safe, right?"

"Jessica also has a kid. I don't want to worry her or little Harley right now. You'll be fine here with Hatchet."

"But—"

"Look, I'm not debating this with you. You're staying here, and that's the end of it. If you don't wanna talk about the kiss, that's fine, too. But just know this." I stared intently at her so she'd know I was fucking serious. "It might've been a mistake, but it was still the best fucking kiss of my life. And I'd do it again in a heartbeat if I wasn't me, and you weren't who you are."

"I-I-I . . . I'm confused. What does that mean? If you liked it, why was it a mistake? I'm just a girl; I'm no one important."

I shook my head. "That's where you're wrong, Amber. You're so fucking important that you deserve much more than what someone like me can give you. But you'll find it. And when you do, he'll be smart enough not to let you slip through his fingers."

Amber opened her mouth, but I wasn't sure I wanted to hear whatever she had to say to that, so I cut her off.

"Where are the pictures that Ruslan sent you?"

Amber ducked her head and crossed her arms over her chest, hugging her elbows. "I, uh, hid them in my bedroom closet, so my mom wouldn't see them."

"I'm gonna go get dressed. Do you mind feeding Pixie for me? Her food is in the cupboard over there. Thanks."

"No problem," Amber said softly to my back as I walked down the hall toward my bedroom.

I couldn't stand there one more minute and see the pain and confusion that I put in her eyes. Thank God I had Ruslan to take out all my frustrations on. That sick fuck had a world of pain coming his way. He just didn't know it yet.

"Wait, wait, wait a minute. She's been getting gifts from this fucker, and no one thought to fucking bring me in on this?" Tank's usually calm and quiet disposition exploded as he pounded his fist on the bar. "That's a load of bullshit, and you all know it. Stitch was my sponsor, he was my best fucking friend. If something is going on with his family, I best be in the loop from here on out. You got me?"

I'd come to the clubhouse with Amber's horror show of a backpack in hand to fill Reb in on the situation with Amber and her stalker. He'd called Tank and Axle in, and Maverick had wandered in to lend a hand after my text exchange with him about shit going down. I'd already said my piece, so I tucked my hands in my back pockets and didn't respond to Tank's explosion. Calls like that weren't my job, they were Reb's, and judging by his expression, he wasn't happy to be called out on it.

Reb rested his elbows on the bar top and leaned toward Tank. "You got a problem with how I'm running things, we can talk after. But right now, that shit is not helping. Do you wanna be part of the takedown at Howl tonight, or do you wanna run your fucking mouth?"

Wow. My eyes widened as I took in the extremely pissed-off expression on Reb's face. I'd only been around the club for two years, and we'd had our share of rumbles with rival clubs, but I don't think I'd ever seen Rebel as pissed off as he was today.

"I'll be there." Tank sat back on his bar stool and crossed his arms over his chest, clearly still pissed off.

Join the fucking club.

"I will, too," I said, finally speaking up for the first time since I'd laid all the facts out for the guys.

Reb shook his head. "I'd rather have you with Amber, making sure she's protected."

"I got Hatchet watching her in my apartment and Sig in the parking lot watching my building. She's covered. This is my job, and I'm gonna be there."

Reb stared intently at me for a long minute, but I didn't budge as I stared right back at him. Finally he nodded. "All right, Bam. You're with us. I got a few calls to make while I round up a few other guys. I'll send Jackson to pick up the fucking torture porn Amber's hiding in her closet. We don't need Brittany seeing that shit. You guys stick close. I won't go hunting for you if you're not here when we ride out."

Reb nodded to a silent Axle and Maverick as he took off for his office. I pushed away from the wall I'd been holding up and crossed behind the bar to grab a bottle of water from the minifridge hidden underneath. "Anyone else want one?"

The guys shook their heads while Tank had moved his glare from Reb's retreating back to my blank face. I cracked open the lid on my water, then took a good, long drink.

"Seriously? You don't have a fucking thing to say to me?" Tank growled.

I shrugged. "I reported everything to Reb."

"Oh, me and Reb are gonna have it out. After I straighten shit out with Ruslan."

I slammed the water bottle on the bar and water sloshed out. Not that I gave a shit. I jabbed a finger at Tank. "I'll be the one to straighten shit out with Ruslan. That fucker is mine."

Tank smirked. "You've had fucking weeks to straighten shit out with Ruslan. You haven't got the first clue how to handle this, kid. You need to leave the tough business to the big boys. At least until your testicles drop."

"You don't know the first fucking thing about the shit I've already handled with that fucker. He showed up to her work two weeks ago and freaked her out in the parking lot—had her fucking car towed because he wanted her to drive a goddamn Escalade that he picked out. When I kicked him out of that parking garage, she was fucking trembling in fear. She shook so hard I was afraid she wouldn't be able to stay on the back of my bike. Now I find out he's been sending her gory pictures for weeks? And today a fucking *tongue*? Along with a threat? That's bullshit. He fucked with the wrong girl. If anyone's giving this asshole a long-deserved beat down, it's me." I leaned toward Tank and thumped my chest. "He's mine."

If anything, my little speech just pissed off Tank even more. "That's the way it is, huh?"

"What the hell are you talking about?"

Tank stood, his bar stool careening off behind him as he prowled toward me. "I don't know who the fuck you think you are, but you do not fuck with club property. Brothers don't do that shit."

I didn't back down when Tank stopped only inches from me. "I don't know what got your panties in a twist, but I'm not fucking anyone."

"Yeah." Axle snorted somewhere behind Tank. "None of the girls will give him the time of day since he dropped Destiny on the fucking

CHAPTER 10

ground."

"It was a fucking accident, Axle." I glared at him. "Reb barked for me, and I jumped. It was a fucking reflex thing; I forgot she was on my lap for a second. Christ, you're never gonna let that go, are you?"

Axle laughed. "Destiny's the one who's not gonna let it go. Neither will her friends. Hope you like your right hand, Bam, 'cause the girls aren't gonna give you the time of day for a long fucking time."

"I'm not talking about them," Tank bit out. "I'm talking about Amber. If you think we're gonna sit here and let you screw around with a Brother's daughter, you're about to be the one to get a well-deserved beat down."

"Speak for yourself," Maverick rumbled. "Personally I have no problem with Bam and Amber hooking up. They're kids. Let 'em have their fun."

Tank didn't look away from me as he answered Mav. "Amber is not someone you have fun with. She's a good girl. Too good for anyone here."

"I think you should let Amber decide that," Maverick retorted. "Because good girl or not, she's an adult. Let her make her own decisions."

"Mind your own business, old man." Tank's lip curled.

"Whoa! That's bullshit and you know it." I glared at Tank. No one, and I mean no one, ever talked to Maverick like that when I was around. "You spout all this shit about respect, but you got none of it in you. Mav has been a member here probably longer than you've been alive, so you show him some fucking respect. But if you need a little lesson in respect, I'd be more than happy to teach you."

"Anytime, anyplace, Bam," Tank sneered.

"Ho! As much fun as this little standoff has been, boys, we've got bigger fish to fry today." Axle stood up and shoved his way between me and Tank, keeping a hand on both of our chests. "I think one beat down a day is our max. Now I'm gonna need you two to shake hands and promise not to tell Daddy about our little dustup here. Reb has enough on his hands without worrying about you two knuckleheads."

Tank grunted something I couldn't make out, then grudgingly held out his hand. I really didn't want to—he'd been such an ass—but after a beat, I reluctantly shook his hand. Then Tank muttered something about calling to check on Brittany, and retreated to the officer bedrooms on the other end of the clubhouse.

"Try not to take it personally, Bam." Axle patted me on the back after Tank left. "Stitch's death hit him hard, and I think he's blaming himself for not noticing how Brittany fell apart afterward. It's hard to watch the people you care about implode. No matter how many times you offer to help." He said that last part almost to himself.

Axle was usually such a cheerful fucker that his melancholy expression was out of character. But it was gone before I could even think of saying something. He clapped me on the back one more time, then smiled. "But seriously, if you fuck around with Amber, Tank won't be the only one who has a problem with it. *Capiche?*"

"Fuck me, I'm not screwing her." I tried not to think about that hot kiss earlier in my apartment. Or how she'd looked wearing those soft black yoga pants as she stretched out on my couch just before I left. Or how she'd felt wrapped around me when I took her home last night on the back of my bike.

I might not be fucking her, but if I wasn't careful *I* would be the one who was screwed.

"As long as we're all clear." Axle bared his teeth in a smile that looked like anything but. "I'm gonna check on Reb and make sure we're ready to ride tonight. I don't know about you, but I'm in the mood to kick a little ass."

Axle took off in the direction of Reb's office, leaving me alone at the bar with Maverick.

CHAPTER 10

Mav snorted into his coffee. "You really know how to make shit complicated, kid."

"You have no idea." Between the problems with Amber, our coming meetup with Ruslan, and the threats from both Tank and Axle, my day had taken a nosedive.

"But Tank is full of shit. If I had a daughter, I'd be happier than a two-peckered puppy if you became my son-in-law. I'm proud as can be with how you turned out, Hunter Kincaid. You've come a long way from that scrawny, silent teenager who dogged my steps back when you lived in my neighborhood. I watched you handle taking care of your grandma last year while prospecting with the club *and* holding down a full-time job. You're just the kinda guy anyone here would want dating their daughter."

I ducked my head as I felt my face heat. I couldn't say anything to that. I wasn't exactly used to people singing my praises. Really, my grandma was the only person in my life who'd seemed to give a shit, and she was gone now. But hearing all that from Mav? I suddenly felt like I could do anything.

Except apparently reply to his compliments.

But Mav didn't need me to say anything. He tipped his coffee cup at me and continued. "You just gotta decide if she's worth the aggravation from her family. Because that's what this is—her family putting their big fucking noses where they don't belong." Maverick paused as he looked away with a little laugh. "That reminds me of the time back when I first started dating Sarah. Did I ever tell you about that?"

I shook my head while I walked around the bar to take a seat next to my old friend. Apparently we had some time to kill, so I settled in to hear a story about Maverick hooking up with Sarah back in the day.

Chapter 11

Still Bam

There was nothing on this earth like riding in a pack of bikes with my Brothers. We roared down the interstate toward Howl in a thundering herd with Reb at point, me in the middle with Axle, Tank, and Maverick, while our road captain, Bumper, took up the rear. Cars and trucks moved out of our way because they knew we owned the road.

My euphoria didn't last long. Before I knew it, we rolled into the parking lot at Howl, which was unsurprisingly quiet for a Sunday afternoon. My eyes scanned the deserted lot as we parked our bikes next to the front door in a display of ownership. I counted two luxury cars and an SUV that was a dead ringer for the one Ruslan tried to give Amber weeks ago.

I swung off my bike and grabbed Amber's backpack and my Ruger 9mm from my saddlebag. Setting the tongue jar down on my seat, I checked the magazine and the slide on my handgun then shoved the pistol into the small of my back where I could reach it later if need be. The other guys did the same as we converged on our meeting points. I carried Ruslan's "gift" in my hands. We'd all been given our assignments back at the clubhouse. Maverick and Bumper took off for the rear exits. The rest of us waited until they were in position, and then we pushed through the front door.

The club was empty and silent as we walked inside. We knew we wouldn't have the benefit of surprise, since the place was wired with surveillance cameras from the street out front to the parking lot and everywhere inside. So instead of storming the building looking for Ruslan, we stood just inside the entrance doors and waited.

Not even a minute later, the doors on the other side of the room opened and two huge guys wearing suits approached.

"We closed." The guy on the left muttered in heavily accented English. I recognized him from our last visit.

"Like we give a shit," I retorted. I knew Axle was supposed to be the one to talk, since he'd established a rapport with the Bratva, but I couldn't stand passively by. It'd been my job to keep Amber safe. "Get Ruslan. Now."

The chatty guy exchanged a look with his friend before the friend nodded and disappeared through the doors again. I could feel my Brothers shooting me looks, but no one said a word.

After a few moments, the doors slammed open again and Ruslan appeared. "This better be good. We open in two hours. I don't have time to deal with biker shit right now."

"Are you fucking kidding me?" The words came out of my mouth before my brain even registered that I was talking. "You send a fucking tongue to our girl, and you think we're gonna take that shit lying down?" I threw the jar at Ruslan's feet. Glass shattered as the tongue flopped out and landed inches from his polished dress shoes.

Ruslan's men jolted at the explosion of glass, but it was the look in Ruslan's eyes that had my fingers itching to reach for my gun.

"She belongs to you?" Ruslan asked with dead eyes.

"She's club property." Axle growled. "Has been since she was born. And we don't appreciate bastards like you sending her threats. She's a fucking kid who deserves better than to be dragged into your world. And we're not leaving here until you get that through your thick head."

Ruslan crossed his arms over his chest and glared at us. "I didn't see a ring on her finger."

"Seriously?" Axle drawled. "You know how shit works in our world. We've claimed her. Fuck, we claimed her the day she was born. She's ours. Back. The hell. Off."

Ruslan smirked. "She's not wearing a ring. Seems to me like maybe we should let her decide. We're not talking about a child here. She's a woman who can make up her own mind."

"She did," I barked. "She came over to my place this morning terrified outta her fucking mind because of the crazy shit you sent her. She doesn't want to be with you. She's with me."

"I seriously doubt that she'd choose you when she could be with me," Ruslan scoffed. "And she asked for the gifts I sent her. She wanted to know what'd happened to her father's killer. I can't help it if you don't have the goods to keep her satisfied."

"BACK THE FUCK OFF!" I shouted as I whipped my pistol out from its hiding place and pointed it at that cocky fucker's head. "She's *my* girl. She fucking cried because she's scared of what you're gonna do. *You* did that to her. She's terrified of you. And if you don't back the fuck off, it'll be your brains painting the back wall over there. You get me now, *malchik*?"

"Whoa, whoa, whoa." Reb held up his hands as Ruslan's guards drew their guns in response to mine. "I think we all need to calm down here for a second. It sounds to me like we've got a little misunderstanding on our hands."

"You're gonna have a little blood on your hands if you don't calm your boy down." Ruslan sneered as he kept his hands in his front pockets. "I'm done with your insults and your fucking disrespect. If you punks don't leave now, it won't be my brains painting the walls."

CHAPTER 11

"I think you're mistaken," Reb drawled in the coldest voice I'd ever heard him use as I kept my gun trained on Ruslan. "I'm the one done with your fucking disrespect. We've asked you to back off, we've told you Amber is club property, and Bam here has fucking claimed her in front of you. We're the ones who are done. You've got exactly thirty seconds to call your dogs off and apologize for the fucking disrespect *you've shown me,* or you're gonna have a goddamn war on your hands."

Ruslan glared back at Reb, his brow low over his eyes. I held my breath as we waited to see what he'd do next. After five heartbeats, Ruslan gestured for his guys to lower their guns. I kept mine pointed at Ruslan's forehead.

"Bam," Reb barked. "Put it away."

It burned like hell, but like a good little soldier, I dropped my arm to my side, keeping my gun pointed at the floor. And not at Ruslan's head like I really fucking wanted.

Ruslan tilted his chin. "It wasn't my intention to be disrespectful. I know my father values the alliance we have, and I trust that it is still in place."

Reb jerked his head in a tight nod. "As long you stop harassing Amber. The kid has been through enough over the last year. I don't want her tied up in this shit. She no longer knows you exist. Got it?"

"You have my word that the harassment toward Ms. Bennett will end."

I narrowed my eyes over his choice of words. If he didn't believe he'd been harassing her in the first place . . . Fuck. Nothing was over with this fucker.

But his contrition seemed to pacify Reb as he nodded again. "Okay. We're done here."

I couldn't believe Reb was eating that line of bullshit. "Reb—"

"We're done." Reb barked. "Ruslan, let Ivan know that I'm good for the meet-up on Friday."

"I will tell him."

Reb waved a hand and the guys backed out the door. We might have a tenuous alliance, but none of us were stupid enough to turn our backs on those crazy fuckers.

I had a lot to say to Reb, and judging by the looks the guys were giving me, the feeling was mutual.

Axle started toward me. "If you think for a fucking second—"

"Ax." Reb barked. "Not here."

Axle sneered. "This can't fucking wait."

"The hell it can't," Reb retorted. "I'm not standing around here a second longer than we need to. Give Mav and Bump the all-clear. We'll take care of the rest of our business back at the clubhouse."

Axle shot me a disgusted glare, but he texted Mav and Bumper that the coast was clear. I could feel the stares of the other guys while we waited. But I didn't say anything. I just stood there with my arms crossed over my chest. Once the guys came around the side of the building, we got on our bikes and got the hell out of there.

The entire ride back to the clubhouse my mind kept repeating what I'd said to Ruslan in front of the whole fucking executive board of my club. I'd claimed Amber.

Claimed her.

What the fuck was I thinking? I couldn't really blame it on the heat of the moment because those words had to come from somewhere. Was that really how I felt about her? I mean she was hot. And sweet. And so fucking sassy it made my hands itch. Sometimes I just wanted to grab her and spank her ass until she admitted that she was mine.

What the fuck?

I let off the throttle a little as that last thought floored me. I wanted her. I wanted Amber to be mine.

Before I could wrap my brain around that new revelation, the guys in front of me pulled into the gated parking lot of the clubhouse. I

CHAPTER 11

pulled in alongside them, put the kickstand down, then swung off my bike, ready for anything they'd give me.

"Not here." Reb commanded. "We handle our business inside."

No one said a word, but Tank and Axle loomed behind me as we silently filed into the clubhouse and followed Reb down the hall to the meeting room. He took a position at the podium alongside Axle and Tank, while I stood in front of them, ignoring the chairs behind us.

I clenched my jaw as I waited for the ax to fall. And I didn't have to wait long.

Tank didn't wait for Reb to start. He leaned toward me and pointed a finger. "I said this morning, and I'll say it again: I don't know who the fuck you think you are, but you do not fuck with club property. We need to get some shit clear if you wanna keep on wearing that patch."

"Who keeps their patch isn't fucking up to you, Tank." Reb glared menacingly at his friend and board member. "This is my meeting. I'm holding the fucking reins. Back. Off."

Tank didn't look away from me, or I from him, but he tilted his head slightly and shut his mouth.

"Bam," Reb barked.

My eyes slid to him.

"Was that all heat-of-the-moment bullshit, or do you intend to claim Amber for yourself?" Reb leaned casually against the podium, but his intense stare belied his laid-back body language.

"I-I think—"

"You *think*?" Axle laughed harshly. "Are you fucking shitting me? This is serious fucking business. You can't just fucking *think* you want her. You gotta know, man. *If you think* we're gonna sit here and let you play fast and loose with Amber's fucking heart—with her goddamn reputation—you're a dumber fuck than I thought."

I nodded tightly. He was right. I needed to get my shit together.

Axle opened his mouth to continue, but Reb cut him off.

"We'll give you a day. Think about what you want. If you wanna claim Amber then, we'll listen to what you have to say."

"I don't care what he has to say," Tank retorted. "There's no way he's good enough to claim my best friend's little girl. What the fuck are you thinking, Reb?"

"I'm thinking that I'm the goddamn president, and this shit is up to me to handle. We'll discuss it tomorrow. Everyone's a little amped up from the fucking Mexican standoff we just had with the Russians. Once we calm down, we can talk about it then."

"Technically you need three sides for a Mexican standoff," Maverick cut in like it made a difference. Or anyone cared.

"I don't give a shit," Reb all but shouted. "You know what I mean. We're gonna wait for twenty-fucking-four hours *because I said so*. Now I'm gonna get me a beer and then find my woman. Meeting adjourned."

We all stood there silently when Reb stomped off toward the bar. The other guys sent me menacing looks as they tried to intimidate me. Which was kinda hard to do, given that I was inches taller than all of them except Tank and outweighed most by at least twenty pounds.

Tank used his height to his advantage as he loomed over me. "Don't think this is over, kid."

"I stopped being a kid long before you knew me, Tank," I sneered. "I can take whatever you're willing to dish out. Just let me know the time and place."

"I think here and now sounds good."

"Tank!" Reb barked from the doorway. "What the fuck did I say? Goddamn stubborn assholes. Tank, come grab a drink. Bam, maybe you need to go home and think through your options. Because if you're leaning the way I think you're leaning, you need to decide if it's worth all this hassle. If you claim Amber, these aren't the only people who'll have an opinion about it."

CHAPTER 11

Axle gave a harsh howl of laughter. "Fuck me, can I be there when you tell Brittany? I think that'll be more fun than the beat down I plan on giving you. She has a way of unmanning a man that'll make your balls crawl back inside your abdomen."

Gulp. Like I didn't have enough to worry about as it was.

Maverick clapped a hand on my shoulder. "Life sure has gotten more exciting since you got your patch, Bam. Mafia and tongues and threats to your balls. You sure know how to live."

I was beginning to have my doubts about that. Shaking my head, I sighed. "I'm gonna head home. Got a lot to think about."

"I'll follow you." Tank smiled menacingly at me. "Sounds like the girl needs a ride home."

"The *woman* can decide for herself. She came to me when she was in trouble, and I'll be the one to take her home when she's ready. You all need to back the fuck off. We clear?"

"Crystal. Give Amber my best." Tank muttered. "Let her know Uncle Tank is thinking of her."

"Me, too," Axle tossed in.

"Tank," Reb barked. "Drink. Now. You, too, Axle."

My teeth ground as I walked out of the building and to my bike. I'd fought like hell for the right to call those guys my Brothers. The fact that most of them were threatening me wasn't surprising. I'd stepped over a line. A huge line.

But it still pissed me off. They were treating me like a fucking kid. Like I was still a goddamn prospect. I'd bled for the club and earned the right to be called a fucking Brother.

Strapping my helmet on, my mind turned over the clusterfuck I'd gotten myself into. I'd claimed Amber in front of a Bratva brigadier and my fucking Brothers. I had a hard time understanding what the hell I'd been thinking, but one thing was clear: When someone—anyone—threatened the woman under my protection, I'd go after them until one of us was fucking dead or dying.

    Now I just had to tell Amber about the mess I'd made and that she was right in the fucking middle.

Chapter 12

Amber

"Oh my god, I can't take it anymore," I groaned as I threw a pillow at the man sitting on the couch next to me. "Give me the remote. Come on, please?"

I tried batting my eyes at Hatchet like a wounded puppy, but judging by the snort he made, it wasn't as effective as I'd hoped.

"I sat through more than half of *Legally Blonde* and didn't say a word. I think you can watch *Fight Club* with a little less bitching."

"Didn't say a word? You '*didn't say a word*'?" My voice rose in volume until I was shouting. "You wouldn't stop groaning and sighing until I handed over the remote halfway through. It was like watching a movie with a constipated basset hound."

"And I didn't say a word. Come on, Amber. That was the most vapid, boring movie I've seen in my entire life. If I could, I'd get that hour of my life back. Reese Witherspoon owes me that much."

"Then write her a letter. I'm sure she'd love to hear from you. But I'd rather you watch *Fight Club* with your bros because, speaking as someone who just got a tongue in a jar delivered to her, I'm over the violence. I can't watch another bare-knuckle fight and still keep my pizza down."

"Oh shit!" Hatchet grabbed the remote and turned the channel before handing the remote to me. "I wasn't thinking. Sorry, babe. Here, you pick something. I swear I'll keep my grouchy thoughts to myself. I think the second *Legally Blonde* movie is on HBO."

All his fumbling kindness made me smile. The guys were actually pretty sweet once you got past their grumpy, macho exteriors.

"Or you could meet in the middle and watch *Princess Bride*."

I jumped at the masculine voice coming from somewhere over my head.

Bam was home.

Adrenaline sang through my bloodstream, and I tried to scale back my excitement. Bam had checked my ego earlier today by calling our scorching kiss a mistake. But then came that amazing little speech that left me all kinds of confused. He liked me but didn't think he was worthy of me? I'd turned that over and over in my head the entire time he'd been gone. It was sweet and charming and the kind of thing I thought only happened in movies.

And also a big load of horse crap.

I wasn't anyone special. Heck, I worked as a cocktail waitress in a bustier and a garter belt, for crying out loud. If anyone could and did deserve better, it was Bam. Over the past two weeks I'd found him to be funny, protective, and so unbelievable hot it was criminal. He made me realize that my little no-bikers-ever rule was more than a little shortsighted. And maybe a reaction to my grief over losing my father. They were the kind of guys I'd been around my whole life. They were the kind of guys who banded together when stuff got tough. And as Bam had showed me over the past two weeks, he was the most protective, kindest, and hottest of the bunch. I wanted to give him a chance.

If only I could convince him that he was worthy of a chance. Unfortunately, I had no idea where to start. I really needed some

CHAPTER 12

brainstorming time with Sydney, but instead I watched mindless movie after mindless movie with Hatchet. I couldn't get away from him to call her, and every time I started a text he was looking over my shoulder, wanting to know what I was doing and who I was talking to. I'd have to figure out what the hell to say to Bam on my own.

My belly was a squirming mess of butterflies as I turned on the couch and smiled tentatively at him.

The expression he gave me in return was enigmatic. I had no idea what he was thinking. The guy could be a poker champion.

"Shit, I'm glad you're home, man." Hatchet stood up and grabbed his gun off the coffee table. "If I have to watch another chick flick here, I'm gonna be the one to go insane. How'd shit go with the Russians?"

Bam shoved his hands into his pockets as his eyes flickered to me, then rested on Hatchet. "About like you'd expect. Threats were made, guns were drawn, but I think he got the message. You taking off?"

"Yeah, if you're all good. I thought I'd swing by the clubhouse and see who's hanging out." Hatchet shoved his gun into the back of his waistband. A frown wrinkled his forehead as he looked between me and Bam. "I can give Amber a ride home if ya want. It's kinda on the way."

Between my jittery self, Hatchet's urgency toward leaving, and Bam's brooding hotness, no one was comfortable. Apparently, Hatchet was proficient at reading a room—the tension in the apartment was high, and my house was not remotely on the way to the clubhouse.

Bam turned and stared at me for a long moment. I still didn't know what was on his mind. Was he thinking about the Russians? Or what had happened in his apartment between us before he left? Either way, the expression on his face wasn't encouraging. His eyes were serious and not a hint of a smile curved his straight lips.

Wanting to get out before he not so subtly kicked me out, I stood up and brushed my sweaty palms on my pants. "I just need to grab my shoes, and we'll get out of your hair." I crouched down to search for my shoes under Bam's couch as I continued to babble. "Thanks again. I am sorry that I didn't tell you about . . . all this. But I swear I learned my lesson. If anyone ever sends me weird pictures or body parts again, I'll—"

I broke off in a gasp as someone grasped the back of my arm. Peeking over my shoulder, I saw Bam bent down over me with his hand on me.

"Which is why you're not going home with Hatchet. You and me need to have a little conversation and figure a few things out." Bam kept his hand on my arm as he helped me back up. "You can head on out, Hatchet," he said without taking his eyes off me. "I got her from here."

Hatchet growled something under his breath. "You sure about that, Brother?"

The intensity in Bam's gaze increased, but he still didn't look away from me. "I'm sure."

I had no idea what that meant, but judging from Hatchet's groan, it wasn't good. Still, after a beat, Hatchet said goodnight and let himself out of Bam's apartment.

Leaving the two of us alone and locked in a staring contest.

I didn't want to be the one to blink first, but I had no idea what I was still doing here or why we were locked in this intense stare-off. I bit my lip to hold the storm at bay, then lost as my babbling streamed out. "I really am sorry. I had no idea what I was getting into when I went to Howl that night. And I should've told you the second that first picture showed up. I'm so sor—"

Bam placed a finger on my lips. "I know. I believe you."

I nodded slightly with his finger still on my mouth. He didn't move, and I didn't, either. We just stood there, staring at each other in silence.

Finally, after what felt like forever, he slid his finger from my lips to my jaw and cupped my chin in his hand. Keeping his eyes locked with

CHAPTER 12

mine, he bent down slowly until his lips were a hairsbreadth above mine. After a beat, he closed the distance and kissed me.

He'd given me ample time to refuse, to demand to know what he was doing, or to back away. Instead I wrapped my arms around his back and held on as his lips took mine. His tongue prodded at the seal of my lips, and I parted them to his onslaught. I groaned softly as his tongue darted in and teased mine. My breath left me in shuddering gasps. The tease of his tongue and the soft slide of his lips against mine had my whole body tingling. I arched up against him and buried a hand in his long, thick, golden hair.

Bam grumbled something against my lips and pulled back only to rest his forehead against mine. His breath fanned hotly against my face. I wanted to ask him what had changed his mind—*if* he had changed his mind—but I couldn't form the words.

Bam stepped back and held out a hand. I didn't even need to think about it. My hand slid into his before it was fully outstretched.

Which seemed to concern Bam. He squinted at our joined hands, then tilted his head as he looked into my eyes. His voice was more of a rumble when he finally spoke. "You sure?"

I nodded confidently even as my stomach fluttered. "Yes."

"Well, all right then." A light gleamed in Bam's eyes, and before I could wonder at it, he used our joined hands to tug me to him. I jerked off balance, and he used the momentum as he ducked and put his shoulder into my belly. The room whirled around and my hair obscured my vision as I found myself hoisted over his shoulder.

"Bam! Oh my god. Put me down." I laughed, torn between glee at his lightheartedness and irritation at his high-handedness.

Bam just laughed as he walked down the hallway. I bounced against his shoulder, and the only view I had was of his fantastic rear flexing and the blurry outline of the carpet below. My hands had been gripping his sides, but after a beat I let them wander down to that perfectly plump, flexing ass. Christ, he was a work of art.

"Ack!" I shrieked as the room whirled around me for the second time, and I landed with a bounce on Bam's bed.

Bam stood at the foot of the bed and eyed me as he toed off his boots. I bit my lip and stared back for a second before I lost my nerve and turned my eyes to survey his room. It was surprisingly sparse. The walls were empty of any photos or posters. A single dresser stood opposite the bed with some loose change and a few crinkled receipts on top. One narrow closed door, no doubt leading to a closet, was on the next wall. And that was it. Literally nothing else aside from the bed I was lying on. And the bed was just as generic as the rest of the room. He had a dark blanket, dark sheets, and two pillows. No personality whatsoever. The only nice thing I could say about the bed was that it smelled like him. If I were honest, I'd admit that I really wanted to lie down and wallow in the scent. Leather, bergamot, and Bam. It was intoxicating. And heady.

And okay, I might just be a smidge nervous.

I'd taken so long looking at his room, I was afraid to meet Bam's eyes again. He had to know that I was freaking out. I think I was putting out such huge vibes that the people in the next apartment had to know that I was freaking out. But he didn't say anything or do anything to get my attention. I could see his outline in the corner of my eyes. He'd gotten his boots off, and that was it. He just stood there.

After a deep and shaky breath, I bit my lip and looked up at him. Bam stared back at me with that enigmatic expression again. I still didn't know what he was thinking, but, God, he looked so amazing. Gorgeous and built and just everything I ever thought I wanted in a guy. And he'd been right in front of me this whole time.

I could do this. I *wanted* to do this.

Finally Bam spoke, his voice soft in the mostly dark room. "Nothing has to happen tonight."

CHAPTER 12

I shook my head. "I'm just nervous. I want to be with you. I want you so, so much."

With that enigmatic expression like a shield hiding his thoughts from me, Bam surveyed me. "Do you understand what this means? What will happen if we sleep together tonight?"

"Um, I know all about the birds and the bees." I laughed nervously as I sat up. "We had that session in health class where we watched a video and everything."

A sparkle lit Bam's eyes as a small smile curved his mouth. "Good to know. I meant that this won't be a one-time thing. I can't sleep with you and not have it mean something."

"Wait a minute. Isn't that my line?"

Bam sat on the edge of the bed next to me as his shoulders shook with his low, husky laugh. "Fuck me. This is why I keep my mouth shut. I always fuck shit up."

"No, don't." I reached out toward him and clasped his hand in mine. "It's sweet that you have standards. I respect that."

"I don't have standards." Bam closed his eyes and bit out a curse. "I mean I have standards—clearly—but that's not what this is about. I just—Fuck, why is it so hard to get words out?"

"Sounds like you might be out of practice. You know, if you're not feeling it, we can always just cuddle."

"Christ, when did you get to be such a smart-ass?" Bam chuckled.

"I've always been a smart-ass. I was just hiding it behind my raging paranoia and rampant stupidity."

"Hey now, don't talk that way about my girl. If you keep that up, you and me are gonna have a problem."

My heart raced at the *his girl* reference. To be honest I hadn't really thought much beyond tonight. I had no idea Bam had those kinds of feelings about me. It was heady and exciting, and if I kept thinking about it, I might just self-combust. I ducked my head as I smiled.

"Okay. Good to know."

"It's just that . . ." Bam sighed as he stared as his hands like they might hold the answer. "You're not the kinda girl a guy like me can just screw around with. You deserve more. Honestly, you deserve better than a degenerate asshole like me, but I'm a greedy son of a bitch."

"Hey, don't you talk that way about my guy. If you keep that up, you and me are gonna have a problem."

Bam bumped his shoulder against mine. "Touché."

"So what you're saying is if we do this—sleep together tonight—we'll be . . . exclusive?"

"Exclusive. Together. You'll be my property. I'll stand up at the next club meeting and claim you as my woman. You all right with all that?"

"I-I-I I guess." I blew out an unsteady breath. "To be honest, I haven't given what happens tomorrow much thought. I'm still worrying about what happens next."

"You mean here." He jerked a thumb over his shoulder at the bed. "Between you and me?"

"Yeah, uh, there's something I need to tell you." I gulped. It felt like the words were stuck in my throat. I'd been waiting years for this moment. Was it a mistake to tell him? God, I'd never been so scared in my life.

I laughed nervously. Okay, that last thought was a little bit of hyperbole. All I had to do was think of what had brought me to Bam's apartment today in the first place to put this whole thing in perspective. Severed tongues were a hell of a lot scarier than confessing *this* to him.

"What's going on? Are you . . . okay?"

And now he thought I had an STD. I groaned and fell back on the bed as I covered my face with my hands. This was the day that just kept on giving. "No! I mean, yes, I'm okay. It's just . . . It's just I've never . . ."

"You've never been with a biker?" Bam blinked at me. "You know

CHAPTER 12

we're like other guys, right? Same equipment and everything. Nothing strange, although I know a few of the guys have piercings. We can talk about that later if you want."

"Oh my god." Was he seriously that thick, or was he just screwing with me? I peeked through my fingers. Bam stared back at me with that serious expression of his. Who could tell with that look? I groaned. "Really? Are you screwing with me? You don't know what I'm talking about?"

Bam's brow wrinkled. "I don't. Is everything . . . okay?"

I covered my face with my hands again and groaned. I felt like all of me was laid out for him to look at and inspect and judge. This was so very embarrassing. I never should've started this.

"Amber? Are you okay? I don't want you to feel pressured or anything. We could just talk or watch a movie or—"

"I've never done this before. Okay?" I cut in with a shout. "I'm a virgin."

Chapter 13

Still Amber

The words hung there between us and seemed to echo in my mind.

I'm a virgin. I'm a virgin. I'm a virgin.

And still Bam didn't say anything.

Peeking between my fingers, I found him staring at me with his mouth open and eyes wide in shock. After a beat, he closed his mouth and gave a soft laugh. "Very funny. So really, what is it? Do you have a bum knee or something? Maybe an extra toe?"

I pushed up until I was sitting up and glared at him. "You'd prefer I have an extra toe to me being a virgin? Seriously?"

"Wait, you're serious? Fuck me. Do you have any idea what this means?" Bam closed his eyes and muttered something under his breath. The only word I could make out was ass.

Good. At least he could see that he was behaving like one.

"Yes, it means that I haven't had sex with anyone before. Why, is that a deal breaker for you? You'd rather I'd been with tons and tons of guys? Well, I'm sorry. It's not like I've had the chance, ya know. I had my dad breathing down my neck all through high school. He had all the guys in my class petrified to even come near me. And then I was too busy working to meet anyone worth my time. The few guys I did

CHAPTER 13

meet were tools. But believe me, had I known that this was the way you were going to react, I would've slept with that skeevy guy who hit on me at work last week and solved the problem of my stupid, pesky virginity." I shook my head when Bam didn't say anything. With a sigh, I pushed myself off the bed and stood in front of him. "You know what? This was a mistake. I'm just gonna go."

"Kitten, don't." Bam grabbed my arm before I could take two steps. "I'm sorry, okay? It's just . . . You have no idea the pressure this puts on me. It was already going to be a big deal for the two of us to be together. But this?" Bam shook his head as he muttered to himself. "The guys aren't ever gonna let me live this down."

Only this time I was close enough to make out his words. I pushed him away. "You're gonna tell the guys? Are you fucking serious? Now I really am leaving."

"You mean they don't know?"

"Why would they know? Are you high? Because that's the only explanation I can come up with to explain this whole conversation."

"You're Stitch's little baby girl. They've watched over you your entire life. You do realize that I'm gonna get my ass handed to me by most—if not all—of the club once I claim you, right? You being a virgin is like the cherry on top of the ass-kicking cake."

My heart stuttered in my chest. They were going to jump him? Because of me? "W-w-why? Why would they do that?"

"Because you're Stitch's little baby girl. And according to Tank and Axle and Reb and I'm sure a whole bunch of others, you're too good to waste on a punk like me."

I closed the distance between us and reached up to brush his hair out of his eyes. Resting my hand on his cheek, I smiled into his gorgeous eyes. "You are the best thing to happen to me in over a year. I have never felt as safe as I did when you were following me through the parking garage at work or giving me a ride on your bike. And if those guys in the club can't see that you are a fantastic, caring, worthy man—" I shrugged. "Then fuck them."

During my little impassioned speech, Bam's eyes turned from frosty to soft with an inner heat. He turned his head and brushed his lips against my palm. "Why bother, when I'd much rather be fucking you?"

My heartbeat picked up as I felt a new pulse point throb between my thighs. But given the way we'd seesawed for the last few minutes, I wanted to make sure he wasn't having any doubts. He had so much on the line just by being with me. I looked up into his beautiful gray eyes and whispered, "Are you sure?"

"I think that's my line," Bam murmured back before he ducked his head and took my lips in the sweetest, gentlest kiss I'd ever experienced. Still cupping my face with one hand, his other hand slid along my back and pulled me to him, until my body was flush against his as he deepened the kiss.

Immediately I felt the hard, pulsing outline of his cock pressing against my belly. I went a little light-headed from the combination of sensations and the idea of that huge part of him pressing inside me later. Oh God, it'd never fit. Maybe I should've picked someone a little less . . . a little *less*. This was never going to work. What had I gotten myself into?

Bam pulled back, breaking our kiss. "Hey, you are way too inside your head if you're already this tense and tight." His hands moved to my shoulders, and he gently rubbed at the knots there. "What's going on?"

"I just . . . I don't know how this is all going to work. I mean you're all . . . and I'm just . . ." I released a shaky sigh and shook my head. "It's like I'm starting in the big leagues when I should be batting in double A."

Bam's lips quirked. "You are funny as fuck. And trust me, you've got nothing to worry about. It'll work, and you'll love every fucking moment. But we're not even there yet. How about we worry about it then?" He paused and waited for me to nod my agreement. "In the meantime, let's just enjoy the moment. Come on."

Bam grabbed my hand as he sat on the end of the bed. With a tug, he pulled me toward him until I stood between his spread thighs. I only had to tilt my head down a tad to meet his eyes. I bit my lip as I stared into his sparkling gray eyes. I should've known by the devious glint I saw there that Bam had a plan to distract me from my fears. He better get to it soon, because if anything, our current position just underlined how large he was everywhere.

"You still with me?" Bam asked as he fiddled with the bottom of my shirt.

I slowly nodded. I had some reservations, but I still wanted him. Especially when he looked at me like that.

"Good." Bam grunted as he grasped the bottom of my shirt in his hands and in one motion ripped it over my head and off my body.

"Bam!" I shrieked as I jumped back, covering my chest with my hands. It was at that moment that I realized I'd forgotten to put on a bra this morning. It happened when you had a small chest like mine. "Have you ever heard of seduction? You know, taking it slow?"

"What are you talking about, kitten? This is seduction." Bam grasped my ass in his palms and encouraged me to move a few inches forward until I had no choice but to straddle his legs.

My knees rested on the bed near his hips and our pants-covered groins kissed. Despite the warm tingling sensation coursing through my body, I tried to glare my displeasure at him. "Are you happy now?"

"Mmmm, move your hands a bit like this." Bam guided my hands so that instead of hiding my breasts, I was framing and lifting them toward him. "Perfect. *Now* I'm happy."

Before I had a chance to say something snarky in reply, Bam tipped his head and captured the tip of my breast in his mouth. Humming deeply, he played his tongue over my tingling, throbbing nipple. The feeling was out of this world. The interplay of his mouth combined with the vibration of his humming, and I lost it. My head dropped back with my groan. Bam's hair brushed against my chest while he suckled. I shivered as a wave of goose bumps spread over my body.

I wanted more. I wanted him. But I couldn't seem to articulate my demands. Instead I arched toward his mouth and moaned.

Bam kept teasing me. After a few moments, he pulled back and blew on my moistened nipple. I shuddered. His teeth flashed as he gently nibbled on the throbbing tip of my breast. I shivered when his hair brushed against me as he moved to my poor, neglected right nipple.

A few minutes later, I was lost to the sensations pulsing through my body, and I swayed on Bam's lap.

Not losing a beat, Bam grasped my back and pivoted until I fell back onto the bed with him looming above me. He moved to my other nipple, licking and stroking until I was panting along with him. My hands moved restlessly along his back, grasping him, silently urging him for more.

I slid my hands under his shirt, eager to feel his skin against mine. His back was warm and smooth, but the sensation of a few ridges had me curious. I made a mental note to check them out later as I groaned. Bam used his teeth to tease me while he ran them over the slight mounds of my breasts. He stopped on my nipple and rasped his teeth gently against my throbbing tip.

Somehow, while I was too occupied wallowing in the erotic sensation of Bam suckling my breast, he'd worked his hand under my yoga pants and inside the front of my panties. I gasped and jerked my hips.

"Settle, kitten. It's okay. I won't go faster than you're ready for," Bam murmured against my breast.

"I'm not . . . whatever, you just surprised me. When did you get inside my pants?"

CHAPTER 13

Bam laughed huskily. "It's a talent. Bet you didn't even notice when I took your bra off earlier."

"You did?" I frowned, trying to remember whether I'd been wearing one today when Bam burst into gales of laughter. It was easily the most lighthearted sound I'd ever heard him make. I was entranced by how gorgeous and buoyant he looked as his laughter softened the harsh lines of his face.

"Christ, you're cute. And gullible. That'll come in handy later."

I rolled my eyes, but didn't say anything. He could think what he wanted.

Bam raised an eyebrow. "How about we lose some of this clothing though?"

"Fine," I retorted. "Since you're behind in the getting-naked race, you go first."

Bam's lips quirked like he was biting a response back, but his hands went behind his neck as he pulled his shirt up and off his body, revealing an impressive display of muscles and tattoos. I had to lift a hand and check for drool. He was that hot. I'd never seen so many muscles outside of a gym in my life. He was built and bulging and . . . I sighed. Gorgeous. I wanted to trace all those ridges with my tongue. I wanted to lick every square inch of his body. He was just so perfect.

"Your turn, kitten."

I snapped my gaze back to Bam's face and my body burned at the glint in his eyes. In a few moments it'd be his eyes eating up me in all my pasty, scrawny glory. "Um, how about you go again? We're still even in the stripping wars. But I went first last time, so I think you should take off more."

I closed my eyes in embarrassment at the babbling that poured out of my mouth. Why couldn't I be smooth at this? Where was my brain when I needed it? On permanent vacation, apparently.

My eyes snapped open as I felt the bed heave with Bam's movement.

I found him standing next to the bed, his eyes locked on my face. And then with no ado, he unsnapped his jeans and shucked them down his legs. His tight, royal blue boxer briefs left little for him to hide behind. It was all there, outlined in all its large and anatomically correct glory.

I bit my lip as I couldn't help but stare. All my earlier fears rose up again. There was no way in hell that that thing would ever fit. *Oh God. Oh God.*

"Shit, that was probably a mistake," Bam muttered. "You're all back to wide eyes and biting your lip again. You really need to learn to relax, kitten."

"Easy for you to say. That thing isn't going to—" I waved in the direction of his boxer briefs and flinched when his cock moved. "Oh God."

Bam chuckled huskily. "Sorry, he's got a mind of his own."

I groaned and closed my eyes. I felt so silly and ridiculous and completely out of my depth. My whole body burned with my embarrassment.

"Aww, baby. Relax." Bam crawled up the bed, straddling me so he could nuzzle at my neck. "We won't get there until you're ready, and I know you're not right now. You have to have at least two orgasms before we get anywhere near that part of the show."

"Two orgasms?" I murmured back. I was having a hard time concentrating because Bam was doing this thing with his tongue. *Gah.* He traveled up my neck and nibbled on my earlobe. His breath was harsh as he panted against me. I let go of my fears and hung onto his back while goose bumps warred with throbbing erogenous zones.

"You have no idea how gorgeous you look sprawled out on my bed." Bam crooned into my ear. "All that blond hair and your swollen lips. I could spend a lifetime looking at you and not get my fill."

I melted into the mattress. He was so sweet and gorgeous and just so freaking swoony. I swear he could probably make me come with

CHAPTER 13

only his words when he whispered like that.

"But then you add these babies into the mix, and fuck me." Bam plumped my left breast in his hand while his thumb teased the aching tip. "They're just so fucking perfect."

Bam lost his eloquent words as he buried his face between my breasts. I laughed and threaded a hand through his hair and held him. After giving my slight cleavage a smacking kiss, he turned his head and captured one of my nipples between his lips. He tugged slightly then laved attention on my aching tip with his tongue. I groaned and held onto his hair a bit tighter. Bam hummed in the back of his throat as he nipped and licked my nipple. It only took a moment for me to feel an answering throb between my thighs.

I groaned and moved my legs restlessly. It was at that point I noticed that Bam had a hand between my legs. I'd been so lost in the sensations he was evoking in my body I hadn't noticed he'd moved. While he was using one hand to prop himself up next to me, his other was currently buried between my thighs. I opened my mouth to say something—no doubt biting and brilliant—when I broke off with a moan. His clever thumb had found that bundle of nerves between my legs. Between his lips and tongue on my breast and his hand between my legs, I couldn't hold a coherent thought. Instead I just lay there and felt.

Bam continued to gently tease my clit, stroking the edges with a soft touch. It was so different compared to when I was alone and touching myself. He got me closer to the edge so much faster. In moments I was climbing toward the pinnacle. I arched my hips toward his clever hand, silently urging him for more. Then he simultaneously bit my nipple as he flicked my clit, and I broke. Wave after wave of sexual release coursed through my body, and still Bam kept softly petting my clit. An aftershock shook through me, and I had to roll away to escape Bam's provoking touch.

In the distance I heard some rustling as Bam left me to my orgasm and did something else on the other side of the bed. To be honest, I didn't really care. Short of a building-wide fire, nothing was going to get my gelatinous body in motion. I couldn't move even if I wanted to.

Once my heartbeat lost its frantic pace, I managed to roll myself onto my back, and I stretched languidly.

Bam propped himself up on an elbow at my side and smiled down at me. "Ready for round two?"

Chapter 14

Still Amber

I snorted. "I'm ready for a nap, maybe. I don't think I have any more left in me."

"Oh, you have more. We've only skimmed the surface." Bam leaned down and brushed a gentle kiss against my lips. "But while you're all relaxed and agreeable, let's get rid of the rest of your clothes."

I blinked down at the lower half of my body and sure enough, I was still wearing my pants and panties. Bam hopped off the bed, his cock jutting straight out from his body. He was naked. My eyes slammed shut in mortification.

Until I felt a tugging at my heels.

Opening my eyes, I locked gazes with Bam—mine no doubt filled with chagrin while his sparkled with humor. In seconds he had my yoga pants and panties pulled off my legs and tossed somewhere over his shoulder. I didn't know because I couldn't look away from the new light in Bam's eyes. I was completely naked now, and Bam was free to look his fill. Which he did. My body burned as though I could feel his gaze as he raked his eyes up my body. They finally rested on my pussy, and I felt an answering throb between my legs.

Bam's eyes were hot as he crawled up the bed, pushing my legs apart so he could rest between them. "Fuck me, kitten. You are a goddamn work of art."

I groaned and buried my face in my hands. I jumped as I felt the soft caress along the seam of my pussy. "Bam, I don't know about this."

Bam groaned low in his throat. "Do you trust me?"

My hands fell away from my face, and I looked into his gentle eyes. "Yes. I trust you completely, Bam."

A fire flickered in his eyes and more than anything in that moment, I wanted to kiss him and reassure him that he was enough, and that I wanted to be with him.

"Then trust me enough with this. I'll take care of you." He paused and waited for my nod of acceptance, then he smiled deviously. "If it helps, you can always just lie back and think of France."

I opened my mouth to correct him, but could only sigh as his deft fingers teased the seam of my pussy. He ran a finger up and down, gathering moisture as he went. A second later his tongue joined the party, and I almost lost it. I bit back the giggle burning to get out and took a few deep breaths to relax. Every book I'd read and chick flick I'd seen made me think that this was an epic deal—some men couldn't be bothered to go down on their girl. The last thing I wanted to do was laugh at Bam and ruin the moment. Still my sense of giddiness was hard to shake. That might have something to do with the fact that this hot, gorgeous, caring guy was staring up at a place only my doctor had been before. I felt vulnerable and worried he wouldn't like it. That he wouldn't like me. I didn't want to let him down. I wanted to be enough for this amazing man.

Bam went slow. His tongue and fingers slowly relaxing me until I could only concentrate on the amazing emotions he was evoking inside me, and my giddiness and worries melted away. His fingers traced a path up and down, pausing at the apex to tease my clit, then wandering down to trace the opening of my vagina. Back and forth

CHAPTER 14

he went as my pulse picked up. Finally, on his next downstroke, his finger slowly pierced the opening of my pussy. I gasped as his thick digit pressed my tender flesh open. While his tongue continued to flicker against my clit, he slowly slid his finger in and out. In seconds, the combination of sensations had my pulse racing as I built toward my second orgasm. My breath left me in shuddering gasps while Bam teased me.

A few seconds later, I felt a new fullness as a second finger pressed inside me. I didn't like it. It felt like too much. Then Bam's tongue flickered against my clit just before I felt a sharp nip there. My muscles tightened, and I broke. My body shook uncontrollably as a volcano of sensation ripped through me. Blinding white light flashed beneath my eyelids, and I groaned. Bam continued to lick at my pussy until I had to roll away from him to escape the exquisite torture.

But I didn't get far because his fingers were still locked deep inside me.

His body hugged my back as he slowly slid his fingers out of me. Unable to control it, I felt my pussy grasp his digits, silently urging them to remain. Bam groaned against the back of my neck. I heard some more rustling behind me, but for the second time that night I was too lost in my bliss to focus on what Bam was doing.

I squealed in surprise as Bam rolled me none too gently onto my back, then loomed over me.

"If I don't get inside that sweet pussy, I'm gonna lose it." Bam muttered as he rolled a condom onto his large length.

There were plenty of places for me to look—anywhere but his large cock—but I couldn't help myself. It was right there out in the open, and in moments would be pushing itself inside me. His cock was every bit as large as the rest of him. And honestly, the first one I'd ever seen live and in person.

"Relax, kitten. We'll take it slow. Go at your pace." Bam murmured as he no doubt saw the fear in my eyes. "You were made to take me inside you. We'll fit. Now take a deep breath."

"Yeah, that's not going to work for me." I giggled nervously. "Do you think maybe we could just cuddle? Or I could jack you off? I'll let you come all over my breasts."

Bam's lips quirked with a half-smile. "We'll circle back to that one. I might've pictured that a time or two in the shower. But right now, I wanna feel your legs wrapped around me and your tight cunt grasping me."

Something about the husky way he said *that word* made my insides quiver in a completely yummy way. But I still felt apprehensive. His large, condom-covered cock bobbed threateningly in front of me. I bit my lip and whispered, "I don't know, Bam."

His hungry expression gentled as he reached out and brushed the hair off my forehead with a gentle hand. "It's going to be okay, kitten. We can wait if you're not ready." His smile looked a little pained. "There's plenty of other fantasies we can knock out in the meantime."

I shook my head determinedly. "No, I'm sorry. I want to be with you. It's just—can we go slow? You're just so . . . And I'm . . ."

Bam leaned down and gave me a soft, sweet kiss. Then he feathered a few pecks down my jaw to my neck and down my chest. In between kisses, he muttered. "You're not ready. There's nothing wrong with that. I told you I'm in this for the long haul. We'll wait until you are ready."

His large body covered me, but he kept his weight braced with his arms against the bed on either side of me. I was safe and protected and still so turned on. It didn't help that when he kissed his way down to my breasts, he groaned low in his throat like he'd found exactly what he was looking for and didn't want to leave. His cock throbbed hotly against my thigh, reminding me of Bam's earlier impatience. Despite the hunger he no doubt felt, he'd rather see to my needs—again—than

CHAPTER 14

try to sweet-talk me into sex.

I fought back tears. I couldn't let my fear control everything in my life. I'd let it rule me too much this last year. I was strong, and I wanted to do this. I wanted Bam. After one more shaky, deep breath, I reached down and grasped his hard, turgid length in my hand.

"Uh, Amber?" Bam asked as he released a shaky breath of his own.

"Hmmm?" His condom-covered cock was sticky, and I really wanted to feel the heat of his skin, find out if it was as soft and hard at the same time as I've always heard, but the latex covering prevented me from feeling it myself. Spreading my thighs open, I slowly guided him toward my opening.

"Whatcha doing?" Bam's voice rumbled above me.

"Having sex." I held my breath for a moment as the blunt tip of his cock nudged against my clit. That felt good, but wasn't the right spot. *Lower.* "That is unless you don't want to. I don't want to pressure you into anything you're not comfortable with."

"God, you're driving me crazy. Let me do that." Bam brushed my hand aside and replaced it with his own. "Are you sure, kitten? I don't want *you* to do anything you're not comfortable with. I wasn't joking. We can just cuddle or whatever."

"Oh my god! Are you serious? Will you just fuck me already?!" I all but screamed.

Bam laughed. "Yes, ma'am. Just checking."

"You've checked enough. I'm ready. Do you need me to sign something first?"

"Nah, I think we're good." Bam looked down at me with an intense expression. "Try to relax." He slowly pressed forward as he watched my face.

I winced, and Bam froze. "You try to relax when someone's trying to impale you with a battering ram."

"How'd you think I got my road name?"

"Are you seriously bringing up all the women you've banged *while* you're taking my virginity?"

It was Bam's turn to wince as he dropped down to his elbows above me. His face hovered a few inches above mine. "Sorry. Bad joke."

"You think?" I winced again as Bam's large cock pressed another inch deeper. "There is an end, right? I mean, it doesn't go on forever, does it?"

Bam laughed softly, and I could feel the vibrations through our joining. It wasn't unpleasant. For that split second, it didn't feel like he was trying to flay me alive.

"It's gonna be okay," Bam whispered softly just before his lips covered mine. He kissed me softly with only his lips at first. They moved over mine like he wanted to encourage something from me, but I didn't know what. Then he took the kiss deeper. His tongue teasingly darting into my mouth to dance with my tongue. He led me in a parry-and-thrust dance that had me breathless in moments. When I couldn't take it any longer, I turned my head slightly and took a ragged breath. Bam kissed the tip of my nose, then pushed himself up onto his palms in an impressive display of muscles and gleaming tattoos.

"You okay, baby?"

It took me a beat to realize that he was seated to the hilt inside me. He'd distracted me with his naughty kiss and pressed the rest of his impressive cock inside me. I gave a test wiggle, and Bam groaned. A smile pulled at my lips at his reaction, so I wiggled again.

"You're okay," Bam gruffly muttered before slowly pulling out until only the head of his cock was still inside me. It was my turn to groan.

A moment later, Bam pressed forward until our pelvises kissed. He bent his head down and kissed my lips. He continued to kiss me as he withdrew again. So slowly. Iiiiiinn and oooouut. The delicious slide of our bodies against each other, him inside of me, his chest brushing against mine, had my eyes rolling in the back of my head. It was heady

CHAPTER 14

and luscious—and if he kept going so slow we'd be here all night.

It was hard to complain about that. But still, I wanted to come, and given our orgasm tally, I was certain that Bam was dying for it, too.

Since it worked last time, I did another test wiggle. Only this time Bam froze, his cock halfway out.

"You okay, baby?"

I bit my lip and groaned, "Yes. Just faster, please. It feels so good."

That sexy-as-hell smirk curved his lips again. He picked up his slow, tortuous rhythm. "You know what they say about those who wait . . ."

Rolling my eyes, I lifted my legs and wrapped them around his hips. "You know what they say about those who finish . . . they get an orgasm and a while later start up round two."

"You're cute. You think you'll be in any shape for another go-around?"

"Parts of me might not, but there's more than one way to squeeze an orgasm out of you." My pussy clasped tight around Bam.

"Christ, baby." Bam rested his forehead against mine. "You're making it hard for me to go slow and be gentle."

I tilted my head and nipped at his bottom lip. "You're not listening to me. I don't want slow and gentle."

With a new light in his eyes, Bam pushed himself back up at the same time his hips pulled away from me. Before I had a chance to gasp, he set up a new, faster rhythm. My thighs squeezed reflexively around him, and Bam groaned. Bracing himself on one hand, Bam reached between our bodies with the other and found my clit. With a delicate touch, counter to his new brisk rhythm, he gently caressed me. My thighs quivered as sparks rained down behind my eyelids. I felt myself climbing toward that peak with every thrust of Bam's cock and flick of his finger.

Circle, circle, flick. Circle, circle, flick. I don't know how he was able to be so dexterous and keep pounding away. I'd have to ask him later.

Right now all I could concentrate on was my impending orgasm. I was almost there when Bam let out this sound somewhere between a groan and a roar. His hips picked up a faster rhythm, and three thrusts later I lost it. All my muscles tightened up and fireworks popped behind my eyelids. Pure bliss sang through my bloodstream.

Moments or hours later, I sank back into the mattress a limp noodle, unable to move or to think. Sometime during my endless orgasm, Bam must've come because he was frozen above me, his weight still supported by his large and strong arms.

I blearily blinked up at him and gave him a drunken smile. "Thank you."

"You're welcome, kitten." He slowly withdrew his cock and after a beat, sank it back inside me.

"You're not . . . you didn't . . ." I flushed as I tried and failed to find the words.

"Felt fucking amazing, you squeezing me so tight, but I didn't want to miss a moment of you coming in my bed with me inside you for the first time."

If it were possible, my body melted a bit more with his sweet words. I wrapped my arms around his shoulders and my legs around his hips as I held on and let him ride. His breath came out in choppy, uneven huffs. I tilted my head and nipped at his earlobe, breathing hotly into his ear as I made my first-ever attempt at dirty talk.

"That was so fucking hot. I don't think I've ever come as hard as that last time. Feeling your big, hard cock inside my body as I fell to pieces? Hot. You are the only man to ever be inside. You. And only you."

Bam was like a pile driver now, pounding inside my body. The wet slap of our flesh competed with the sound of our panting breaths. And I loved every second of it. The fact that *I* was the one who'd driven this hot, tough man into a mindless puddle of need was overwhelming.

CHAPTER 14

Awe-inspiring. Empowering.

I couldn't wait to do it again.

But first Bam had to come. I flexed my hands on his broad back and scraped my fingernails lightly down his flesh.

Bam let out a muted roar and thrust inside me one more time. He dropped his forehead down on mine and groaned fiercely. Unable to control my body, my pussy grasped reflexively around him as my nipples tingled. Bam groaned again, softer this time, then kissed the side of my mouth.

"You are gonna be the death of me, kitten."

"We wouldn't want that," I whispered back. "We've only just started having fun."

"Christ, I've created a monster."

Judging by the grin on Bam's face, I don't think he minded.

"Hold that thought. I gotta go take care of a few things." Bam grasped himself, then slowly withdrew from my body. After scuttling to the side of the bed, he swung off and disappeared out the door in an impressive show of muscles and adorable tush.

I wiggled in the bed with the biggest grin on my face as I ducked under the covers. That had been the singularly most amazing moment of my life. Bam was so sweet and tough and thoughtful. I don't know why I'd been running from him for so long. But that stopped as of today. There was no way I'd ever run from Bam again. I wanted to be with him. Understand what made him tick. See that soft anguished expression on his face when he orgasmed. Know that I was the one who'd made him feel that way. I couldn't wait to experience it all again.

"Not so fast, kitten."

I froze at Bam's commanding voice coming from the doorway. Had I done something wrong? What was going on?

"We gotta clean you up before we can go to sleep. Come with me."

It wasn't exactly a request, given his commanding voice and the way he swept me up into his arms and then over his shoulder.

"Bam! Oh my god! Put me down. You're gonna drop me!"

"Aww, kitten. Never. Not gonna let you go, now that I've got you." He smacked my bottom. "Now shut up and let me take care of you."

"Fine." I rolled my eyes and huffed, but I had a feeling Bam could hear the smile in my voice. He certainly couldn't see it on my face.

He slapped my butt again, and I squealed as he carried me out of the bedroom.

Chapter 15

Bam

The driving guitar rhythm of Metallica's *Enter Sandman*—and my ringtone—woke me the next morning. I rolled over to grab it, but my body stopped because I'd run into something. I opened my eyes and swiped at the hair in my face as I took in the object in my bed that I'd rolled into. Make that someone. Amber. My ringtone faded and a loud beep sounded. But I ignored it as the night before came back to me in flashes. The threats from my Brothers. The way Amber had looked, all barefoot and innocent in my apartment. The way her lips had tasted. The soft keening noise she'd made when she came. All of it.

Amber snuffled as she burrowed into the blankets, and I smiled. I didn't regret my decision. Whatever hell the guys unleashed on me later would be worth it. The fact that this amazing, giving, gorgeous woman had chosen me made me feel ten feet tall. I'd do whatever it took to be the man she thought I was.

"Enter Sandman" started up again and tore me from my thoughts of Amber and showers and sex. Reaching across her, I grabbed my phone and hit ignore before the sound could wake her. A beat later someone pounded on my front door. Maybe the hell from my Brothers was coming sooner than later. I pushed off the bed with a weary sigh and grabbed my crumpled pants from the floor at the foot of the bed.

"I know you're there, asshole." A muffled male voice boomed. "Open the damn door."

Christ. They seriously couldn't wait until I had a cup of coffee before they beat my ass down? I gently closed the bedroom door behind me and hoped that Amber slept through the coming onslaught. No need to worry her. In the hallway I hopped into my jeans, leaving the buttons undone. I didn't bother with a shirt. If this went the way I thought it'd go, I didn't want to get blood on my tee. That shit was hard to get out.

Pound. Pound. Pound. "Fucking open the door!"

I bypassed the peephole. I didn't recognize the asshole's voice, but there was little doubt as to how I knew him. It sure as hell wasn't my boss cursing at my door. Fuck, hopefully the guys gave me a second to call in to work first. I didn't want to pull a no-call no-show. I needed my fucking job.

"All right, let's get this over with," I muttered as I pulled the door open.

Only it wasn't an angry group of Brothers at my door, or even one. Instead, our club lawyer, Harry Hastings, stood in front of me with a disgruntled expression.

"Fuck, boy, don't you ever answer your damn phone?" He grumbled as he pushed me aside and strode into my apartment.

"What the hell is going on? Since when do attorneys make house calls?" I shut the door and turned to find Harry making himself at home on my sofa as he dug through his briefcase.

"Since you don't answer your damn phone. I've called you ten times in three days. You think maybe that means I want to talk to you about something?"

I didn't have any outstanding warrants, and I'd been so busy with

CHAPTER 15

Amber's shit, I hadn't given Harry's calls much thought. Apparently that'd been a mistake. I wasn't a stranger to warrants and arrests, although all of my crimes were petty in nature—shoplifting as a teen, a few assaults here and there—nothing to warrant a house call from our club attorney. Fuck me. That wasn't good.

I cleared my throat uncomfortably. "Sorry, man. There's a lot going on. Uh, what's the emergency?"

Harry slapped a stack of papers on my coffee table. "Your mother's attorney called my office last week and is threatening to file a petition to challenge your grandmother's will on the grounds of 'undue influence.' She's claiming that you—and I quote—'the thugs in his gang' forced your grandmother to sign over everything to you, thereby leaving her out of the will."

I rubbed at the back of my neck and scowled. "That's fucking bullshit."

"It's smart is what it is. Litigation takes time and money. This way she is only out the initial attorney's fees for making her threat and isn't delaying the probate process. *Yet.* We have one week to respond, and if it's not the way she wants, she's threatening to file an official petition."

"What are we facing then?"

"If she goes through with it? A typical will contest can cost between ten and fifteen thousand dollars in legal fees. A fight can easily take one to two years—or longer, especially if the case goes to trial. You have to decide whether the estate is large enough to justify the expense. It might be easier to placate your mother by giving her a part of the estate. With a little back-and-forth we can have this cleared up by the end of the week, and then probate can go forward with no fuss."

I shook my head. "Treatment ate up my grandma's savings. Aside from her house and a few odds and ends, there's not much to fight over. I've been paying the property tax out of my own pocket since before she even died. I don't know what the hell my mom's fighting for."

"You mean the property in Tahoe? How much is that worth today?"

"The casinos in Tahoe have cratered because of the reservation casinos popping up in California. Property values have plummeted. I doubt it'd bring more than two hundred thousand."

Harry raised an eyebrow. "Sounds like something worth fighting for to me."

"And I'll be damned if I let her have it. That bitch deserted me. She didn't give a fuck when her own mother was dying and having chemicals pumped into her to try to fight it off. I'm gonna see Grandma's final wishes through. That bitch gets nothing."

Harry sighed. "I kinda thought you'd say that. I'll contact her attorney and tell him that you're not budging. It might just be an idle threat on her part. Do you know if your mom has the money to go forward with the petition?"

"I think I've seen her a grand total of five times in the last year. Once she picked a fight with my grandma after chemo, once she stopped by to steal a necklace, then she made a scene at the funeral to fake cry over the casket, and she ran into me at the Mother Lode Casino a couple weeks back and threatened to sue over the will. So, four times. Judging by the theft, I'd say she doesn't have the money and is blowing hot air, but who knows? Maybe she has a new sugar daddy to support her and her wild schemes. She always did in the past. She could be sleeping with this fucking attorney of hers for all I know."

Harry smirked. "Sounds like a lovely woman. I just need you to sign here to verify that I will be the attorney on record in the case if this goes any further, and that the club will cover any expenses."

Fuck. I cleared my throat awkwardly. "Uh, and what if the club doesn't want to pay your fees with this?"

"I handle this kinda shit all the time for you guys. It's no hassle.

CHAPTER 15

Now getting Reb's not-so-ex-wife declared legally dead and him the beneficiary of her estate—that was a shit ton of hassle. This is a cakewalk in comparison."

I nodded like I knew what he was talking about, but the shit with Reb's ex-wife was before my time. I just knew that after she hooked up with the VP of our rival club, some shit went down with them, and no one had seen her since.

I rubbed the back of my neck where a stubborn knot had formed in addition to a wicked headache. "If this ends up coming out of my pocket, how much are we talking as far as your fee goes? My standing in the club might be kinda shaky right now."

A loud *merrrrooow* sounded from the other end of the room, toward the hallway, and Harry swiveled. His eyes widened as he sucked in a breath. "Right. I can see that."

I turned, too, and found Amber standing at the edge of the room with Pixie burrowed into her arms. But it wasn't the cat that held our attention. Amber was wearing one of my black T-shirts, and it fit her like a dress, hanging down almost to her knees, but still somehow left a lot of long, smooth leg exposed. Her hair was tousled like she'd been rolling around in a bed all night, and honestly I couldn't wait to get her back into it.

Harry cleared his throat. "I gotta tell you, kid, privilege gets a little murky when someone else is paying your legal fees. I mean, I can't—"

"They know Amber's here, Harry." I cut in. "It's fine. But I think you see why my standing in the club is shaky."

"Do you want me to put some coffee on, Bam?" Amber's voice was husky first thing in the morning, and brought to mind all sorts of wicked thoughts.

"Thanks, baby. Could you feed Pixie, too?" It took all my resolve, but I stayed on the couch and didn't devour her like I really fucking wanted to.

"None for me, thanks. We're almost through here." Harry threw a professional smile at Amber, his eyes staying on her face. After clearing his throat, he turned back to me, his poker face in place. "Okay, how about we hold off on the paperwork for now? I'll have a talk with Reb and make sure that he wants to cover my fees on this matter. I'll also call your mother's attorney, regardless of who's paying, and replay your stance to him. I'll contact you before the end of the week to let you know our progress. Any questions?"

"Nope. Sounds good. Thanks for coming over, Harry."

"Answer the fucking phone next time, you hear?"

"Yes, sir. Thank you."

"Bye, Harry," Amber called from the kitchenette as Harry walked to the door.

"Bye, darling. Give your mother my best." Harry smiled then closed the door behind him.

I stared at Amber for a beat, then smiled. "So, I'm gonna guess that you know Harry."

Amber bit her lip and shrugged. "He helped out with a few things after my dad died. Life insurance policy, bank accounts, all that kind of stuff. He was really sweet."

I blinked. I'd never known Harry to be anything except cantankerous and ornery, but I still jerked my chin in a slow nod.

Amber must've seen my disbelief, because she smiled slightly. "I think he had a little crush on my mom. And he felt bad about my dad dying, so he overcompensated with his guilt. He brought over scones every time he visited. I don't think my mom even noticed."

"Now I feel cheap. He didn't bring a single thing for me today, aside from a lecture and some paperwork."

Amber snorted as she turned to the burbling coffee pot. "Yup, you sold yourself cheap. All the legal work and none of the fringe benefits."

"Fuck me. I hope it's cheap. Knowing my mom, though, she'll make

CHAPTER 15

it difficult just because she can." I shook my head then braced my hands on the bar as I took in the sight of Amber barefoot in my kitchen. She stretched up to get a coffee mug off the shelf, and my shirt rose until I could see the curve of her ass cheek peeking out. I bit back a groan. How much coaxing would it take to get her back into my bed? Maybe next round we could go with her still wearing my shirt. That sounded hot as hell to me.

"Your mom's contesting your grandma's will? That sounds kind of awkward."

Nothing killed a boner quicker than talking about my mom. I sighed. "Yeah. She ignored her own mother for years—including her last one on earth when Grandma was dying and suffering through chemo treatments. Ma didn't lift a fucking finger to help, and now she's got the nerve to threaten to sue me because she doesn't believe Grandma would leave her outta the will. More like she's hoping the judge will take one look at me and side with her. Fucking cunt."

Amber paused with the coffeepot in her hand and sucked in a breath. "Sorry. It's just . . . I really don't like that word. Except you know, when you used it last night."

"Well, if it helps, I really don't like that woman, so it fits."

"Right." Amber nodded slowly. "I can see that. Family, huh?"

"Yeah. Family."

She poured two cups of coffee, then set the pot back on the burner and turned to me with a tremulous smile. "You look like you need a hug."

"Kitten, I am never gonna turn down an offer like that from you."

Amber closed the distance between us, and I went back on a foot at the force she landed with. Her arms closed around me as she hugged me with a grip that surprised me. She was so small; I hadn't expected it. I closed my arms around her and hugged her back just as hard. After a moment, her grip loosened slightly, and her hair tickled a bit as she burrowed her head into my chest.

"I'm sorry your family is sucking so much right now," she whispered.

"Ditto," I whispered back. "Although I don't really consider her family anymore. That ship sailed when she kicked me out in high school. Now she's just some chick that I share half of my DNA with."

Amber pulled back to frown up at me. "What about your dad? Is he on your side about your Grandma's things?"

"He died when I was six. Closest thing I've had to a father since is Maverick. He let me help him when he was tinkering with his motorcycle. The man taught me everything I know about bikes."

"What about brothers? Sisters?"

I shook my head. "Only child. Ma didn't have time for me after Dad died. She was too busy chasing after her boyfriends."

"Cousins? Aunts and uncles?"

"Maybe? I don't know. None on my mom's side, anyhow." I shrugged. "Grandma never mentioned any. Never really knew my dad's family. I think they live back east in Ohio or something."

Amber's brow wrinkled. "So, you don't have any family left?"

"I have my Brothers. Or I did. I guess we'll have to see how this next meeting goes." I lifted a shoulder like I didn't give a shit whether the men I'd come to see as family wanted me to be a part of them. For the first time, a niggle of regret burned in my stomach. I might've lost my friends—the guys I'd considered family—for this girl. Was she worth it? Was what we had together enough? Was any girl worth losing everything for?

Amber took a step back and crossed her arms over her chest. "I didn't know you had zero family outside of the club. It would've been nice if you'd told me the stakes last night before we . . . you know."

I snorted derisively. "I wasn't thinking of the stakes. I wasn't thinking about anything aside from you." Remembering how I felt last night, high off the confrontation with Ruslan and later with

CHAPTER 15

my Brothers, then seeing Amber all gorgeous and barefoot in my apartment—and worried about me—I couldn't regret what we did. She was the first woman in my life, aside from my grandma, who gave a damn about me. Nothing about having this woman in my life was regrettable. "It's too late to go back now, kitten. We're here. And I don't give a flying fuck what anyone thinks. You're mine for as long as you're willing to put up with my shit. So, what do you say? Are you in?"

"I just . . . I don't like the idea of me costing you everything. I'm not worth it, Bam. You have to see that."

I grabbed her hand and pulled her to me until I could feel the heat of her body through my thin T-shirt that covered her. "Never say that about yourself. You are the best thing to ever fucking happen to me. Believe it. Believe in us. Everything else will fall in line or it won't. But never doubt that I want you. I'm in this one hundred percent. No regrets."

Amber searched my eyes like she'd find something there to contradict my words, but after a beat she bit her lip and nodded slowly, then she said in the sweetest, softest voice. "Okay. I'm in."

"Fan-fucking-tastic. Let's go celebrate." I gave her a smacking kiss, then punctuated it with a smack on her ass that had her wincing. "Unless you're not feeling it. Are you sore?"

Amber ducked her head, her hair mostly obscuring her flushed, red cheeks. "Kinda, but we could probably still—"

I snorted. "Not happening. I want you a hundred percent with me, not suffering through the motions, kitten. Let's get you in a bath and soak those aching bits. I suddenly feel the urge to pamper my girl."

Bending down, I put a shoulder into Amber's stomach, then lifted her up and onto my shoulder. Amber's hair tickled my back as I grasped her bare ass cheek in one hand to help her balance.

She shrieked in surprise, then groaned when my hand flexed on her ass. "Bam, come on. I can walk all on my own. And I really think I'm okay. At the very least, we can take care of you instead."

I laughed as I started down the hall. "I always take care of you first, kitten. That's something you can count on. And I'm carrying you to the bathroom. If we're not gonna have sex, I'm at least gonna have a little bit of fun while we get there."

"What about our coffee?"

"I'll bring it to you. Do you want three teaspoons of sugar or four?"

"Oh my god, Bam, really?"

Chapter 16

Amber

We spent most of those first days lost in a sexual fog—learning everything about each other's bodies, cuddling—just enjoying the bliss of a new relationship. I discovered that Bam's feet were ticklish—but not his armpits—and he had this one spot on his neck near his left ear that made him groan when I ran my teeth over it. I spent hours tracing his tattoos with my fingers and tongue. He showed me how one orgasm could roll into another and another and another until I thought my heart would explode. The man was a master of lovemaking.

He'd called in sick to work that Monday, and I didn't have to work until Wednesday night, so we had plenty of time to get to know each other. We spent most of that first day in bed. After my bath, I'd practically had to beg Bam to make love to me. Fortunately he'd caved with a little coaxing and some not-so-subtle licks of my own. Then Bam had made me stay in bed while he cooked me breakfast. And after breakfast, some more rolling around between the sheets. But by then I was pretty sore, so most of our time was spent with soft touches and giggles and whispers.

Later that night Bam told me about his mom and moving in with his grandma, how he didn't even really remember his father. I told him about my losing my dad and trying to keep my family together. He knew most of the details, but wanted to hear them from me. He held me close and rubbed my arm like he was trying to soothe all my hurts away. I fell asleep that night wrapped in his arms. It'd been a long time since I felt so cared for and safe.

But eventually Bam had to get back to work, and meanwhile, I was avoiding my house, mostly because of my mom. I didn't know if she'd heard about me and Bam yet, and I wasn't ready to have that conversation with her. So like the responsible adult I was, I hid. I sent her a few texts that I was hanging out with Sydney since she was off, too, and added a few imaginary scenarios about how we were catching up on girl time.

To make up for the lying liar I was being, I went over to Sydney's house Wednesday while Bam was at work to catch her up on all that'd happened.

"A tongue? He sent you a freaking tongue like it was a box of chocolates or something?" Sydney gaped at me, her eyes wider than her mouth. "Oh my god. That's so . . . so deranged."

"I think it's safe to say that Ruslan has different ideas about seducing a girl. It's pretty sick that he even kept it, you know? And stupid. If he was ever tied to the guy's disappearance, they'd have him if they found that jar. It's ridiculously blatant to keep a freaking body part lying around."

"And now you have it? Oh my god. What if the cops search your house? Your fingerprints are all over it."

"I've got nothing to worry about. Bam returned it. Or I think he did. Last I saw he was leaving with the jar, and he sure as hell didn't bring it back."

"So, it's *Bam*, huh? Are you and him . . . you know?"

I flushed bright red. Only Sydney could go from eviscerated body parts to sex at the blink of an eye. "Yes."

CHAPTER 16

"I knew it! Didn't I tell you he was the one?!" Sydney lifted her hands like she'd made the game-winning goal and wiggled in her chair. Dropping her hands into her lap, she leaned toward me with avid interest. "Oh my god, you have to tell me everything. How was it? How was *he*? Did he take care of business?"

"Sydney." I groaned. "I'm not giving you details."

"I've told you everything about my partners. Girth, length, duration—"

"Number of freckles," I finished for her. "Yes, I'm pretty sure I could pick your last three exes' penises out of a lineup. Not that I ever asked for that kind of detail. Ever."

"Well, I am. So, spill! Please tell me it was worth waiting for. That man better have taken care of you."

I rolled my eyes as I caved in. Like we both knew I would. "He did. It was amazing. I think I had, like, three or four orgasms before we even . . . you know. He was just so sweet and tender, and then rough and dirty when I wanted it." I sighed as I remembered our first time together. "And he's been just as gentle and dirty every time since."

"Wait, so are you guys together? Like together-together?"

"Yeah, we're together."

Sydney squealed and tackle hugged me. "Oh my god. This is amazing. I thought you guys were just doing the nasty, but you got him to commit? I thought he was one of those can't-tie-me-down bad boys."

I laughed as Sydney settled onto to sofa next to me. "I guess he is, but he was the one who wanted it crystal clear that it wouldn't be a one-night stand before we even slept together. Like it was a deal breaker for him if I didn't agree."

Sydney squealed again. "That's amazing, Amber! You must teach me your ways. I can't get a guy to agree to breakfast the morning after, let alone have him be the one to demand a commitment. That's insane."

"I guess. I don't know. It just feels right, you know? Like he was the one I'd been waiting for."

"And little did you know he'd been under your nose all this time." She leaned toward me and raised her eyebrows. "And now he's got *you* under *him*."

"Subtle, Syd. Really subtle."

"Maybe that's what I've been doing wrong. Maybe I need a tough-as-nails, hot, bad-boy biker to tame me. Do you think you could get Bam to hook me up?"

I snorted. "Good luck. If things go how I think they're gonna go, Bam won't have any biker buddies to hook you up with."

"What are you talking about? I thought he was in your father's club."

"He is for now, but I guess the club isn't happy that he's defiling a daughter of one of their members. From what I gather, they told him that he has to choose: the club or me."

"And he chose you. That's so romantic." Sydney sighed with a faraway look in her eyes.

I snorted. "It's stupid is what it is. I couldn't get him to see that I'm not worth it. He won't have anyone once he tells the club about us. His dad died when he was little, his mom is a horror show that any talk-show host could make a week of shows with, he's an only child, and his grandma died last year. The club is all he has." I shook my head. "Had."

"He'll have you, though. And it sounds like that's all he wants right now."

"But it's ridiculous. How can I ever be enough? How can I live with that weight on my shoulders, knowing I'm the reason that he's lost his makeshift family?"

"That does suck, Amber. But who says it's permanent? If you guys really stick together, wouldn't the club come around? Maybe it was just an idle threat."

"The guys in the club don't make idle threats. They're going to jump

CHAPTER 16

Bam the first opportunity they get, and I'm going to be the one to pick up the pieces."

"But isn't that what you wanted?" Sydney winced and backpedaled a bit. "Not the beaten boyfriend part, obviously. But you've been saying for weeks now how you didn't want to date a biker. It was the entire reason you thought Bam was unsuitable."

"I never wanted this. The club is a huge part of who Bam is. How can I live with myself, knowing that I'm the reason he doesn't have that anymore? How can this ever last? He's going to look at me and remember that I'm the reason his friends kicked him out. I'm the reason he's not a True Brother anymore."

"You can't take the weight of their decisions on yourself. You're not doing this to him. They are. And at the end of the day, it's Bam's choice to make, right? And he chose you. Let that be enough. You deserve to be happy, Amber. Don't let those guys keep it from you."

I nodded slowly as Sydney's words sank in. It was scary as hell to know that everything might change when Bam went to his next meeting, but Sydney was right—I couldn't take the weight of the club's decision on my shoulders. I hadn't done anything wrong. I was a grown woman who wanted to be with a great guy. Everything else was just background noise.

"Good, now how about you give me all the details about Bam's sweet, sweet loving."

"Sydney!" I groaned.

"Okay, no gritty details. How about something vague? On a scale from one to ten, how was the first time?"

My face burned, but I couldn't lie. "Fifty?"

"Oh my god!" Sydney squealed. "Now you gotta give me the gritty details. Tell me everything and don't leave out a single moment."

Chapter 17

Bam

"I think I've created a monster," I groaned as Amber nuzzled against me. We'd spent most of our time together in bed or in the shower or on the sofa. Pretty much all the areas we could be naked. Apparently I'd unleashed a nymphomaniac. Not that I was complaining. I'd enjoyed every minute. But we'd just had an intense quickie, and both of us had to be somewhere soon.

When I'd come through the door after work, she'd practically attacked me with her sweet kisses just before she all but dragged me into the bedroom.

A woman after my own heart. Or, technically, dick. *Heh.*

"Are you saying you don't have another round in you?" Amber whispered huskily as she nibbled on that spot under my ear.

"Christ, woman, don't you have to go to work?" I rolled over so I could play with her tits. I palmed her left one in my hand while my thumb passed over her nipple, rolling the budded tip round and round.

Amber groaned. "Yes, but I don't wanna. I'd rather be in bed with you and play some more."

"Sucks being an adult sometimes," I murmured just before I ducked my head and drew her nipple into my mouth. With how fast the last

CHAPTER 17

round went, I really didn't have the time to give her lovely tits the attention they deserved.

"Is this you encouraging me to go to work?" Amber laughed. "Because I gotta tell you that your actions don't really match your words."

It was a toss-up which sound I loved more—her laugh or that little mewl she made when she was teetering on the edge of orgasm. Both sounds made me feel like I could do anything, that the whole damn world lay at my feet.

Amber moaned and arched her back. I tossed a quick glance at the alarm clock on my nightstand and winced. We really didn't have the time. Any minute tonight's Brother with guard duty would be knocking at the door, and I didn't want her naked when they showed up. That amazing sight was for my eyes only.

Even if a lot of it peeked out of her uniform at work. Christ, I hated that fucking thing. I really didn't like it when I had to shadow her, but now that she was my woman, it made me itchy to think of all those men leering at her. Itchy in that I-want-to beat-them-all down kinda way.

My lips pulled away from her tit with a pop. "Sorry, kitten. But we don't have time. Roscoe will be here in a minute, and you gotta get ready for work."

"Wait, you're not taking me?" Amber propped herself up on an elbow as she frowned at me. The sheet fell to her waist, perfectly framing her tits and distracting me. "Bam, eyes up here. We're having a conversation."

"What? Sorry." I focused on her face and the disgruntled look in her eyes. Now was not the time for fantasies from my spank bank. "No, I can't take you to work tonight. I have a club meeting."

Amber's eyes took on a shiny glow as she bit her lip. "That's tonight? I thought you guys were meeting Sunday."

"Nah, that's for something else. Tonight's our regular monthly meeting." I ran my hand up her arm to soothe the goosebumps. "It's gonna be okay, kitten. I don't want you worrying about me."

"How can I not?" Amber sat up and wrapped the sheet around her. "The guys don't want you with me. Tank is going to shit a brick and Axle—I don't even get why Axle's panties are in a twist. He was hardly ever around when I was growing up, not like Tank. But still. I don't want you to get hurt because of me."

I sat up and pulled her in my arms. "I know you feel like this is all on your shoulders, but it's not. It's okay. *I'll* be okay. And given the choice again, I'd choose you. I'll always choose you."

Amber shook in my arms as she took a deep breath. Then she whispered, "I'd choose you again, too."

My heart did a free fall in my chest. I was wrong. Apparently *that* was the sound that made me impenetrable and capable of leaping buildings. Unable to articulate the feelings coursing through me, I bent my head and passed my lips over Amber's blond head as I squeezed her tight. Christ, I'd do anything for this woman.

The sound of someone pounding on my door had us both jerking apart.

"That'll be Roscoe. You go get ready for work, and I'll tell him you'll be a few minutes." I drew my arm away from her and made to scoot across the bed when Amber's exclamation stopped me.

"Wait." She reached out and clutched the back of my neck and pulled me toward her, then covered my lips with the sweetest, softest kiss with her luscious lips. A beat later she took it deeper as her tongue teased mine.

Pound, pound, pound. Roscoe knocked at the door again while the melody of "Enter Sandman" blasted through the apartment from wherever I'd left my pants. I pulled back and, unable to resist, planted another quick kiss on her. I smiled. "What was that for?"

CHAPTER 17

"To thank you for being you."

Pound, pound, pound.

"Shit." Unable to process her words with all the endorphins surging through my veins, I leapt from the bed—and away from temptation—to search for my pants. Finding them in the hallway, I hopped as I struggled to pull them on. Behind me, the bathroom door softly clicked shut, and I winced in regret at missing out on Amber's naked departure. With my jeans finally on, I got to the door and ripped it open just as Roscoe lifted his hand to knock again. "Hey man, come on in."

Roscoe's wide eyes took in me with my disheveled state and wisely didn't say a word. Tucking his hands into the front pockets of his pants, he brushed past me to step inside my apartment. He stood next to the couch and awkwardly rocked back on his heels as he took in the room.

I shook my head as I watched the prospect say nothing with his mouth and everything with his body language. He was intimidated as hell and afraid to show it. Christ, that took me back to my prospecting days with the club. Everyone was larger than life and had me by the balls. I'd wanted to be a member so fucking bad.

And now, in a few hours, it'd probably all be over.

I sighed as I closed the door. "Amber will be out in a few minutes. Want something to drink?"

"No, sir. I'm good. Thanks." Roscoe crossed his arms over his chest then fidgeted and shoved his hands back into his pockets.

I smirked at the *sir* since I was pretty sure Roscoe was a year or two older than me. "Did Reb go over what to expect tonight?"

"Keep my eyes on Amber no matter where she goes. No drinking, and if I see anyone who even looks out of the ordinary, call Reb, then confront them."

I nodded slowly, even though it bugged the shit out of me that Roscoe would be calling Reb and not me. I was the fucking man in Amber's life, and after tonight's meeting the whole damn club would know it.

"I've been driving Amber out, but tonight you'll follow her. If everything goes like it should, I'll be at the Mother Lode before she gets off shift to relieve you." I'd be damned if Amber was on the back of another Brother's bike after I'd claimed her as my woman.

Roscoe frowned. "Reb didn't mention—"

"Reb doesn't know yet. I'll fill him in at the meeting tonight."

Roscoe jerked at my terse delivery, then nodded tightly. "Gotcha. Sir."

Awkward silence hummed between us while we stood there. Roscoe's eyes passed over my living room furniture, then briefly met mine before he stared, fascinated, at the tips of his boots. I chuckled quietly as I crossed to my kitchenette. Grabbing a glass from the cupboard, I filled it with tap water, then gulped it all down. All that playing with Amber really took it out of me. I was refilling my glass when she finally appeared.

"I just need another second. I've got to get all my gear in line," Amber muttered as she frantically searched through her overnight bag.

I set my glass down with a clink, then walked over to her. "Baby, it's gonna be okay. What's got you all twitchy?"

Amber bit her lip as she looked up at me. Her eyes glanced over at Roscoe, and she shook her head.

"Roscoe, give us a few seconds." I ordered without taking my eyes off Amber.

A moment later the door clicked closed.

"What's going on? You've got plenty of time to make it to work, so I know it's not that. Why are you all twitchy?"

"You. Okay? I'm worried about you."

"Me? I thought we sorted all that out in the bedroom when Roscoe got here. I'm gonna be fine."

"No, you're not. They're going to . . . I can't even say it. You're going

CHAPTER 17

to lose *everything* because of me. How can I not worry about that? I'm freaked out. What if they put you in the hospital? Or worse?" Her eye sheened with tears as she whispered, "I'm so fucking scared, Bam."

I closed my eyes and pulled her into my arms. I wanted to tell her that she was wrong, that everything would be okay, but I couldn't lie to her. To be honest, I worried about how tonight was gonna go down, too. I didn't want to lose my friends, my pseudo family, but the die had been cast. I'd made my decision, and I couldn't go back. Looking down into Amber's worried eyes and knowing all I knew now, I wouldn't go back. As long as this amazing woman was willing to put up with me, I wanted to be with her. In her life, her bed, wherever the hell she was willing to let me be close to her.

"Whatever happens tonight, I want you to know that I don't regret anything. You are the best thing in my life. And that's including the club."

A tear rolled down her cheek as she shook her head. "You're crazy. I'm just a girl. The club is everything to you. I can't be the reason you lose everything."

"As long as I have you in my arms, I do have everything." Before Amber could say something else ridiculous about her worthiness, I kissed her. Amber's lips were tense at first, but quickly softened as I deepened the kiss. In moments she was panting and arching toward me. But unfortunately for both of us, we didn't have the time to do anything more. Roscoe was waiting outside. With a sigh of regret, I broke the kiss and rested my forehead against hers. "So, we good now?"

Amber released a shaky sigh. "We're as good as I'm gonna be on the subject, I guess. Call me when the meeting's done?"

"I'll do you one better. As soon as the meeting's done, I'm gonna come to you."

Amber planted a peck on my lips, then pulled away to grab her bag.

"That could be difficult. What if I'm at home sleeping in my bed?"

"I'd scale the wall to get to you."

Amber rolled her eyes.

I laughed. "Okay, how about this? I'll give you a key, and if I'm not done by the time you get off shift, you come over here?"

Amber had been sneaking back to her mom's house to change clothes and whatever else while I was working, but she'd spent the majority of the past few days in my apartment and in my bed. Giving her a key was kinda crazy soon, but also made sense. I wanted her here where I knew she'd be safe. And I really didn't want her sleeping anywhere else but in my bed.

Amber's eyes widened as she fiddled with the strap on her bag. Then she squeaked, "A key?"

"Yeah." I walked over to the hall closet and rummaged through the shelves for a few seconds until I found it. Crossing back to Amber, I held it out to her. "If I don't get through with the meeting by the time your shift ends, have Roscoe follow you back here."

Amber took my key with a wary expression. "You sure this isn't too fast?"

"Probably." I laughed. "But since when have we done anything the normal way?"

"True." Amber placed the key in her bag, then stepped forward and hugged me tight. "Be careful. And take care of yourself, okay?"

"Will do. Have a good shift at work."

She laughed wryly like that wasn't possible. I gave her another quick peck, then opened the door to find Roscoe slouched against the opposite wall, waiting for her.

"Take care of my girl, prospect. Don't take your eyes off her for a second."

Roscoe straightened with a grimace. "Yes, sir."

Amber gave me a little wave, then the two of them disappeared down

CHAPTER 17

the hall.

I closed the door behind them with a sigh, then leaned against it. Comforting Amber took all of my bullshitting skills. I was between a rock and a hard place. And I was pretty sure the rock was gonna crush me in a few short hours. Pushing away from the door, I walked wearily down my hallway toward the bathroom. I might as well wash up. Wouldn't do to show up to my own funeral reeking of sex.

Three hours later, I walked into the meeting room at the clubhouse. Unlike every other meeting, where I'd show up early to hang out with the guys at the bar and shoot the breeze, this time I got there right before the doors closed. I couldn't stomach the idea of them confronting me before, during, and after the meeting. Why give them extra time to give me shit?

Instead, I avoided everyone and took my customary post at the back of the room, holding the wall up. A moment later, I flinched in surprise as a body slumped against the wall next to me. I looked over and smirked at Maverick. I shouldn't have been surprised to see that he had my back. Maverick was the best fucking guy I knew. I gave him a chin tilt in appreciation, which he returned. Then we both gave our attention to Reb at the podium.

"All right. All right," Reb barked. "If you all pipe down, we can get this shit started. I wanna get home to the soft woman in my bed, not be shooting the shit with you all."

The general rumble in the room subsided until only the sound of chairs squeaking broke the silence.

"Good." Reb grunted. "First order of business. Our meet is still on for Sunday night. Those of you with job assignments report to your designated areas. No chatter on phones or texts or anything that could be bugged. I wouldn't put it past those fucking Wild Riders—or hell, even the fucking pigs—to have a bug on someone. We're going radio silent on anything to do with this job. It's face-to-face communication only."

A few heads in the room nodded.

I had an assignment on the job, but given how shit was going this week, I wasn't sure if I'd actually be going. Not that I was gonna bring that up now.

"Second, I'm sure you all heard we had a rumble with the Bratva over the weekend. We had a little misunderstanding about club property, but I've been assured that it's all been handled on their end. Until I'm confident that they've backed off, we'll be continuing to have a few of the girls escorted everywhere they go. Stitch's family will be under guard for the time being."

A few heads swiveled my way, and I knew everyone in the room knew what was up, regardless of Rebel's glossing over the details. I crossed my arms over my chest and stared stoically back at Reb. In all honesty, I was surprised that Brittany had been added to the guard detail. I hadn't heard about that. Although, given the fact that I'd been hiding from everyone this week, it wasn't exactly shocking that I wasn't in the know.

"I'll turn it over to our treasurer to update us on the finances." Rebel stepped away from the podium, his eyes scanning the crowd until they lighted on me. He scowled as he stared me down. I didn't move a muscle, but also didn't break our impromptu staring contest. Gunnar droned on in the background about dues and something about a charity run, but I wasn't paying attention. I was too busy holding my ground with Reb.

After several minutes, Reb finally looked away as he retook the podium. "Thanks, Gunnar. That's all the official business we have for today's meeting, so unless anyone has anything else . . ."

And here we go. I pushed away from the wall and cleared my throat before saying, "I move to claim Amber Bennett as my old lady."

A few guys groaned in front of me and a couple of whispered

CHAPTER 17

conversations broke out, but I didn't look away from Reb.

Oddly, his narrow-eyed stare softened, and I could've sworn he almost smiled. Was the bastard really that eager to deliver a beat down on me? *Shit.*

Reb gripped the podium and turned his attention to crowd. "Any objections?"

I held my breath as I waited. Then my stomach sank as Tank and Axle both raised their hands. Tank stood up and crossed the room toward me with determined intent. He stopped in front of me and before I could open my mouth to say anything, he punched me in the stomach. A beat later I saw stars as another blow landed just below my right eye.

"Anyone else?" Reb asked.

I leaned against the wall and looked over Tank's shoulder. Most of the heads shook in the negative.

Then Axle piped up. "I think Tank said it for all of us. Don't fuck it up. Or we'll fuck you up."

"Motion passed." Reb thumped the podium. "Amber Bennett is now recognized as Bam's old lady, with all the respect and protection due to her."

"May the Lord have mercy on your soul," Maverick intoned.

Reb paused for a second then shook his head. "Anything else? Then meeting adjourned."

"That's it?" I blinked at Tank in confusion. "I thought you guys were gonna hand me my ass."

"We can always do that for you if you really wanna." Tank smirked. "We wanted to make sure that you understood that Amber wasn't a hookup kinda girl. If you wanted to be with her, you had to commit."

"And you couldn't have just told me that?" I groaned.

Axle came up and clapped Tank on the back. "More fun this way. Too bad Tank beat me to the punch. Literally."

"Come on, Bam. I'll buy you a drink to celebrate." Tank laughed as he helped me off the wall.

"Drinks are free," I grumbled as I held my sore ribs.

"You gonna bitch, or are ya gonna come have a drink with your boys?" Maverick snorted.

"Fine. Just one. I gotta go see about a girl. My girl," I added with a smile.

My girl. That sounded pretty damn good.

Chapter 18

Amber

I spent my entire shift freaking out about Bam's meeting—and avoiding the gropey hands of my customers. Despite what Bam had said, it was my fault. If it hadn't been for me, he wouldn't be faced with the decision to lose everything or lose me. It was insane. I wanted to march into that meeting and give everyone there a piece of my mind. They didn't even give a shit about what I thought. Bam was an awesome, amazing man who was totally worthy of my time and attention; I wouldn't be with him if he wasn't. Why couldn't they see that? But I knew my presence at the clubhouse wouldn't help. If anything, it'd make the situation worse.

So instead, I worried. I tried to hide my emotions from my customers, and at the same time keep their hands off my ass.

"Here you are." I set a beer bottle down on the craps table next to an old cowboy. "One Coors Light. Good luck."

"Wait, darlin'." The cowboy—who was easily old enough to be my grandfather—put his arm around my waist. "Give me some luck. Blow on the dice."

I stiffened when he touched me and tried to sidestep out of his reach, but despite his age, his grip was firm. Flashing a "help me" look at the dealer, I found no aid as he stared disinterested back at me. With a brittle smile, I blew on the man's dice, then stepped away when he threw them. "Good luck."

Fortunately, I was already forgotten as the game continued, and I barely resisted the urge to shudder. I hated this job. I hated everything about it except for the wage, but it still wasn't enough to make up for having to walk around in practically nothing while men pawed at me. And the son of a bitch didn't even tip me.

It was days like this that I really missed college.

And Bam. I wanted to feel his arms around me and know that everything was going to be okay. What were they doing to him? Would he be well enough to go to work tomorrow? I know he was worried about paying the attorney, so he needed every hour he could get at work.

"There you are, beautiful."

I stiffened at the words before it sank in who was delivering them. Ruslan.

Ruslan was here. At my work.

My eyes scanned the crowd frantically for security or Roscoe, but I found no one but gamblers and bored tourists around me. I bit my lip as I let my empty tray fall to my side. "What are you doing here? I wasn't expecting to see you. I'm working."

"And I wasn't expecting to see you dressed like this. What are you doing, *moya zvezda*? How can you let everyone see you dressed like a hooker? It is unacceptable."

I shook my head, stunned at his commanding tone. Why did he think he got a vote? Like his opinion mattered to me. My heart pounded in my ears, and I couldn't seem to get my mouth to work, so all I could do was glare back at him.

Ruslan's lip curled with his sneer. "You must give your notice immediately. I cannot have everyone looking at my woman dressed

CHAPTER 18

like this."

"I'm not your woman."

"What?" Ruslan's eyes narrowed. "I thought we had an understanding."

"We haven't even spoken in, like, three weeks. Why would you think we're together? I'm with Bam."

"Yes. She is." Bam's voice came from somewhere above my head just before his arm curled around my waist. "*And I thought* we had an understanding after we spoke Sunday."

Ruslan's eyes darted between me and Bam before he rose from the slot machine. "I wanted to hear it from Amber's lips."

"Now you have." Bam's arm tightened around me and I sank into his embrace as he continued. "She's club property—protected. So no more gifts, no more threats, no more love letters. She's done with you."

Ruslan brushed his hands down the lapels of his suit as he faced us. "When you change your mind, *moya zvezda,* I will be waiting."

Bam's fingers bit painfully into my waist, and I knew he was fighting the urge to plant his fist in Ruslan's face. I covered his hand with mine and rested my head on his chest as we both watched Ruslan leave. Then I turned to Bam and looked at his face. He was totally intact. Only a hint of red shaded his cheek, which I put down to his anger over Ruslan. "You're here. And in one piece. What happened?"

"Everything's fine. We can talk about it later. Are you okay?"

"Yeah. I'm fine. Dealing with overzealous customers is all part of the job," I joked with a slight smile.

If it were possible, Bam's expression went darker. I held my breath as I waited for him to say something biting about my job, but he only shook his head. "It was my fault. I was relieving Roscoe, and we both missed Ruslan's approach. I'm sorry, kitten. It won't happen again."

"It's okay. I'm okay. I'm just so happy to see you." I put both my arms around him and hugged him as tight as I could with my tray still in one hand. It was then that I noticed that Bam was still wearing his True Brothers vest. I pulled back as my heart gave an unsteady thud. "You're still wearing your colors. Does that mean you're still a Brother?"

"Yeah, kitten. I told you everything's fine. Finish your shift. I'll fill you in later."

"Okay," I whispered, even as happiness coursed through my body.

"I'll be sitting over there at the bar if you need anything."

I nodded as I squeezed him one more time before letting go. Bam tossed me a smug little smile, then turned and walked in the direction of the bar. The grin on my face was so big it practically enveloped my face. Ruslan's brief appearance fell to the back of my mind. All I could think about was Bam and the fact that he was here and safe. Nothing else mattered.

Suddenly I couldn't wait for my shift to end. But for a whole new reason.

I was gonna screw his brains out the second we got to his place.

I turned around and there was a new sway to my step as I looked for thirsty gamblers.

Bam was waiting for me when I cleared the locker room doors. I jumped into his arms and planted the biggest, wettest kiss on him. We were both panting when I finally pulled back and whispered. "Let's get out of here."

Bam's laugh was deep and dirty as we practically sprinted down the hall, across the street, and up the four flights of stairs, holding hands the entire time. Anticipation and lust coursed through me as I stayed pressed to Bam's side. We didn't even need to discuss who was driving. He led me to his bike and climbed on, passing me a helmet while he strapped his on. Helmet buckled onto my head, I jumped on behind him and wrapped my arms around his trim waist. In moments

CHAPTER 18

we were blasting down the parking garage ramp, then onto the Reno streets.

The stitching from Bam's vest bit into my breasts. I couldn't believe he was still wearing it. Things were finally going our way—he had the club at his back, we were together—life was finally starting to look up after this long, dark year. I grinned into Bam's back. Maybe this thing between us could work out after all.

I was split between my sudden optimism and my continued horniness. And Bam's motorcycle wasn't helping. The vibrations from the engine had me throbbing. The slightest movement from Bam had my nipples tingling. I was one huge erogenous zone, so much so that it wouldn't take much to send me over. But I didn't want to cheat Bam by letting him miss out on my first orgasm as an official couple. So I rested my cheek against his back as the wind whipped through the ends of my hair. And I just held on.

Minutes later we pulled into the parking lot of Bam's apartment. He let the engine idle as I swung off and unhooked my helmet. Bam pulled his off and his long Viking hair fell to his shoulders. The purr of his engine covered my groan. He could've been on a cover of a romance novel—all that hair, the muscles, and tattoos. And he was all mine.

Bam grabbed my hand, and our rush into the building was more frantic than ever. I laughed with delight as we ran through the parking lot and up the flight of stairs to his place. He didn't even pause next to the elevator anymore. He knew me so well. And it was probably quicker this way. When we reached his door, he pulled me to him and gave me a quick, hard kiss, then broke away and muttered a curse under his breath.

"I can't kiss you how I want *and* fit the key into the fucking lock."

I buried my face into his neck to muffle my laughter as he stabbed frantically at the doorknob.

"Finally," Bam muttered as he grabbed me and shoved us both through the open door. We staggered inside as his lips claimed mine in a torrid kiss, wilder than any other. His lips pressed against mine, and I opened them to him. Clutching at his back, I struggled to hold myself up as my head swam since my body was tingling all over. Even his hand on the small of my back felt good.

I groaned when his lips cruised down my neck, and he nibbled here and there. All the while, he was pushing my clothes off. His hands were eager and hungry as he pushed my jeans down my legs. We staggered backward toward his bedroom, and I tripped as the fabric wrapped around my shoes.

With another muttered curse, Bam caught me and hoisted me into his arms as he crossed to the kitchen. "I can't fucking wait. Stupid bed is too far away."

Standing a short distance away from the counter, Bam dropped me onto my jeans-covered feet, then pressed against my back until I slumped forward and braced my arms against the counter. He kicked against my feet so I widened my stance, then muttered, "Perfect."

I had about a second to wonder at our new position. Did he really mean to take me against the counter because he couldn't walk ten feet down the hallway? And then I heard a telltale crinkling behind me. I looked over my shoulder and found Bam, still entirely clothed with only his fly undone and his cock out. He rolled a condom down the long, hard length, then threw me a wink.

"You ready to rock and roll, baby?"

"Are you kidding me? Really, Bam? Here?"

"What's wrong with here? I've been picturing you all week bent over my counter looking back at me just like you are now." Still holding his dick in one hand, he bent over me and teasingly plucked at one of my still covered nipples.

I felt an answering throb between my legs and closed my eyes. "Oh

CHAPTER 18

God."

"Or even better, how about after, we put you up on this here counter, spread your legs, and let me eat you until neither one of us can stand it? Do you like that, baby? You want to be my meal tonight?" His hand plucked and twisted my nipple until I wasn't capable of a coherent thought, let alone forming some words to answer him.

I jumped slightly when I felt his condom-covered cock probing between my thighs. Looking. Searching. Teasing me. I couldn't help myself. I arched my back and helped him find his home.

We both groaned as he sank deep inside me. He didn't stop until I felt the press of his zipper against my ass. Bam's breath was hot against my cheek as he whispered, "I'm gonna need you to hold on, kitten. It's gonna be a bit of a rough ride."

His withdrawal was slow and steady, and he hesitated a moment before he pounded back in. And then I couldn't do anything but hold on like he'd said. He set a furious pace, pounding in and out, driving inside me as we both panted. The only sound in the quiet apartment was our slapping flesh and my low moan. I let go of the bar with one hand and searched for that bundle of nerves between my legs. My fingers brushed against Bam's balls as he swung up into me, and he bit off a curse. I flattened my hand so it brushed against me and him as he pounded inside me.

I was close. So close. I closed my eyes and bit my lip. Seconds later I saw a flash of white behind my eyelids as I went over. Shudders shook my body with my orgasm, and my knees went weak. Bam abandoned his hold on my breasts and clutched at my hips as he pounded into me. Once. Twice. Three more times. On the fourth he let out a noise that sounded suspiciously like a sob, then burrowed his head into my hair as his body shook behind me.

We stood there motionless as aftershocks quaked through our bodies. I was half afraid to move because movement seemed to feed them, and I wasn't sure how many more I could take. Finally, after a few moments, Bam stood and stepped away from me. His cock pulled out of my body with a soft slurp.

Still holding me by my waist, Bam turned me until our fronts collided. I wrapped my arms around his neck and smiled up at him. "Ready for round two?"

Bam laughed. "You have to be shitting me. No way can you be ready for more. You had at least three orgasms by my count."

"I don't know if you can count those aftershocks as separate orgasms. Not really the same thing. It's like one big one, then a littler one, then a littler one. So really you only get credit for the first one."

"I made you come like a banshee while standing in the kitchen. Do I seriously not get credit for *that*?"

"You're the one who said something about eating me out on the countertop. Kinda got my hopes up. It's sad to find out that you're all talk and no follow-through."

"I'll show you follow-through."

I squealed and turned to run, only to trip over my bound feet, still covered with my jeans. I pitched forward, my arms windmilling, but I couldn't find anything to grab onto. I landed with a grunt and skidded a few inches on my knee and right palm. Then I turned and glared at Bam. "Really? You couldn't catch me?"

Bam snorted, then tried to cover it with a cough as he rubbed his hand over his face. He bent down and picked me up, cradling me in his arms. "Sorry, kitten. You were too fast for me. Are you okay?"

"Nothing wounded except my pride. And maybe a little rug burn on my knee." I ran a finger over my reddened skin, and Bam's brow wrinkled.

"Shit, that's not good. You didn't even get your battle wound in the fun way. Let's go put some antiseptic cream on your knee."

"What about eating me out on the countertop?"

CHAPTER 18

"After the cream," Bam retorted as he carried me down the hall to the bathroom.

I was mostly joking. After his hot lovemaking against the bar, I wasn't really up for more.

But I did like to tease him.

After an hour, some cream, and another round of Bam between my legs, we were lying on our backs in his bed. This was the part of the night I loved the most. Don't get me wrong, Bam in action was hot as hell, but I loved knowing that I was the only one who got to see him like this—when he was all soft and vulnerable. It was the time of the day when we shared our thoughts and hopes, and I got to snuggle into his big, muscular arms.

"So, you never told me what happened at the meeting. I assume everything's okay with the guys, and we're still together?"

"Yeah, babe. It's all good." Bam gave me a barebones description of what'd happened when he claimed me as his old lady. He had to explain the darkening bruise on his cheekbone.

I sat up on my elbow and turned Bam's face so I could examine it in the moonlight. "He sucker punched you? Why?"

Bam shrugged and brushed away my prodding hand. "I'm fine. It's a guy thing. I shouldn't even be telling you this much about the meeting, but since it's about you I'm making a onetime only concession. You can't tell anyone about this shit. Clear?"

I rolled my eyes. "Crystal. So, Tank punched you. Did you at least punch him back?"

"Didn't really have the chance. And I was afraid it'd turn out into an all-out brawl since Maverick was at my back. I didn't want Mav to get hurt."

"So, the guys didn't want you to be with me unless you committed? That's—that's just so . . ."

"Sweet?"

I snorted. "Insulting is what it is. I'm a grown adult. I think I get to decide for myself who is in my bed." I paused and looked down at the bed I was in. "Or whose bed I sleep in. Whatever. It's my body, my decision."

"No one's arguing that. It wouldn't have been an issue but for the fact that I'm a Brother. That vest means something. Our brotherhood means something. You don't just screw around with a Brother's daughter. If your dad was alive, he would've been the one to kick my ass, then make sure I made a commitment to you. But since he wasn't there, Tank did it for him."

I sighed. "You're right. That's sweet . . . *and* insulting."

"You're thinking too hard." Bam wrapped an arm around my shoulders and urged me to lie back down next to him.

"I still can't believe you were willing to give it all up for me," I murmured as I lay in the cradle of his arms. "They're your entire life. Your family."

"They're yours, too. And now I don't have to give them up."

I snorted. "You make it sound incestuous when you put it like that."

"Shut up and go to sleep," Bam muttered, but gentled his command with a soft kiss to the top of my head.

I gave a quiet laugh and decided to obey him. This time.

He had fucked me into exhaustion, after all.

Chapter 19

Bam

I was twitchy as I waited in the clubhouse parking lot for my partner to show up. Tonight was a big night—over a year in the making. We were finally going to get our biggest revenge on the Wild Riders MC after all the shit they pulled last year. Sure, we'd gotten our eye-for-an-eye revenge when we turned Bear—the fucker behind the whole attack—over to the Bratva, but it wasn't enough. They'd killed Amber's dad—Stitch, one of our own—torched our motorcycle shop, and almost blown up our nightclub. Tonight was the beginning of the end. They'd fucked us, and we were going to fuck them back harder.

We all had our assignments. And Axle was fucking late. He and I were kinda the lynchpin of the whole fucking operation. Without us, the job couldn't go down. Where the fuck was he? I leaned against the chain-link fence and scowled. We had ten minutes to get into position before the whole fucking thing fell apart.

Almost as though I'd conjured him with my frustration, his beat-up old Ford pickup truck rolled into the lot. I pushed away from the fence and walked over to where he was idling. Pulling open the door, I swung inside and slammed it shut behind me. Axle didn't wait to exchange pleasantries; he tore out of the lot like we were late and everything hung in the balance. Mostly because it did.

"Nice of you to finally show up." I folded my arms over my chest and scowled.

"Nice of you to finally man up and claim Amber."

"What the fuck does that have to do with anything?"

Axle took a corner too fast, and I slammed into the door. It seemed like the kinda thing he'd do on purpose. Ass.

"You've been sniffing around her for weeks. Or do you think you're so smooth that no one noticed that you took the majority of guard duty shifts? You couldn't have been more fucking obvious if you tried."

"I liked Stitch—he was a great guy—and I didn't like the idea of that fucking Bratva asshole trying to move in on True Brothers' property. It didn't take a fucking genius to figure out that Stitch would've hated that. It had nothing to do with Amber at first."

Axle snorted. "If you think I'll believe that, you're more naïve than any fucking biker should be."

"It's the truth. I don't give a shit if you believe me or not. We couldn't stand each other at first. She didn't want anything to do with me."

"Now that I'll believe."

"Just get us there already. We've only got a few minutes until the checkpoint." I reached into my pocket and pulled out my black leather gloves. After pulling them on, I rubbed my hands up and down my jean clad thighs. I was already pretty twitchy, given what was about to go down. I really didn't need the mindfuck from Axle right now.

"All I'm saying is that a girl like Amber deserves to be publicly claimed. Not hidden like she's some kinda dirty secret."

"You think I don't know that? I risked everything for her. Once we decided to be together, I thought I'd have to give up the club. And I still picked her. I get it. I might look like a dumb fuck, but there are some functioning brain cells in here." I tapped my temple.

"You're smarter than I was at your age," Axle muttered as he pulled

CHAPTER 19

up to our checkpoint and parked in the center of the small two-lane road alongside three other pickups and eight or so motorcycles.

I turned to say something sarcastic and biting, but the miserable expression on his face had me hesitating, and I let it go. Clearly Axle was lost in his own thoughts or memories because he didn't even notice the approaching motorcycles or the box truck trailing behind.

"Get into position," I barked as I opened my door and crouched behind it, my pistol pointed at the vehicles driving toward us. Tossing a quick glance Axle's way, I saw he'd unglued his ass and was in a similar stance.

With the road and the shoulders blocked by us, the two approaching motorcycles slowed to a crawl. The rider on the left pulled out a gun and fired wildly at our blockade. Someone down the way returned fire and the biker fell off his bike with a groan. The other rider whipped his bike around and pulled out his gun. Axle shot him in his midsection. The biker tumbled off his bike, its wheels still spinning as it fell on top of him.

Meanwhile the box truck had slowed to a crawl, then stopped in the middle of the road. A beat later, a shrill series of beeps pierced the night as the backup alarm wailed when the driver threw the vehicle in reverse.

But he was too slow.

Tank jumped up on the side rail of the truck and ripped the door open. Grappling with the driver a short moment, Tank threw him to the pavement, then climbed inside to deal with the passenger. Axle jumped from behind the door and in seconds had the unconscious driver's arms tied up behind him with zip ties. I helped him drag the guy to the back of the truck. Tank met us there with the other unconscious and bleeding Wild Rider members and the keys to the truck. I unlocked the padlock and pushed the rolling door up.

We all stood there in stunned shock at the bounty in front of us.

Boxes and boxes towered over us. There almost wasn't enough room for our passengers. I hopped up into the back of the truck and ripped open the nearest box. Half a dozen gallon-size bags filled with a white powder stared back at me. We had them. I tipped the box down for the guys to see.

"Hot damn." Tank grinned as he held his unconscious Wild Rider with one hand.

"Makes me miss the days when we weren't so straight." Axle sighed as he propped up his unconscious Wild Rider. "That shit could set us up for life."

I shook my head. "I need to move a few boxes around to make room for our passengers."

"Hurry the hell up. This fucker's getting heavy." Axle staggered a bit before rightening.

A few guys hopped into the back with me and we moved some boxes around, stacking them to a huge height over our heads. I couldn't guarantee that they wouldn't fall on the fuckers, but it wasn't like we gave a shit. Once there was enough room, we hoisted the four Wild Riders into the back of the truck, then closed and locked the door.

"You got the route memorized?" Tank asked.

I took the keys from him and nodded. "All good to go."

"Okay. Axle will follow you as planned. We'll all meet up at the Pay Dirt Casino. Reb and a few of the other guys are already there. Drive safe." Tank clapped me on the shoulder then headed for his bike.

"You got your ski mask?" Axle asked.

"Yes, *Dad*."

Axle snorted as he walked with me around the truck. "Let's get one thing clear, kid. I'm not and never will be your father."

"Learn to take a joke, old man."

"I will, however, fuck you up if you break Amber's heart. I think of the girl like she's my own. I always thought . . . Never mind. Just don't

CHAPTER 19

fuck up. With this job or with Amber. We clear?"

"Crystal. It's really sweet how you all care so much about me." I faked wiping a tear away then clutched my chest. "It really gets me. Right here."

"Fuck off." Axle snorted a laugh as he shoved me toward the driver's door. "I'll follow behind and park across the street as planned. Think you can handle this without fucking it up?"

I gave him a one-finger salute as answer, then climbed into the cab. Shoving the keys into the ignition, I turned them and the engine purred to life. I took a second and pulled on my seat belt. Despite the fact that it was after midnight, I didn't want to give a cop a reason to pull me over when I had a truckload of drugs and four guys tied up in the back. The vehicles in front of me pulled off the road, clearing a path. Most would be heading toward the Pay Dirt Casino, where the rest of the club were waiting to provide alibis. Only Axle would be following me to my destination.

Adrenaline sang through my bloodstream as I slowly pulled out. I had easily a dozen or more felony counts in the back of the truck if I was caught. I cursed the fact that I'd drawn the short straw. Although, given how shit had been going up til the last meeting, it wasn't surprising. Axle in particular seemed pleased when I got my assignment for tonight, almost like the fucker hoped I'd get caught.

I obeyed every traffic law. And at my first turn, a few muffled thuds sounded from the back of the truck as the load settled. I didn't hear any shouts or calls for help, so I mentally shrugged and kept driving.

Ten long, agonizing minutes later, I pulled up to the Reno Police Department on East Second and parked on the blue curb out front. Given the late hour, the parking lot and the building out front were deserted. I pulled on my ski mask and left the keys in the ignition and the engine idling as I jumped down from the cab. Opening my pocket knife, I sank the blade into the front driver's tire and twisted, then dragged the blade through the wheel. The truck sank lopsidedly toward the hissing tire. After quickly repeating a slash through the back wheel, I darted across the street to Axle's waiting truck. I jumped inside, and we sped away.

As I ripped my ski mask off, I hooted with laughter. "Christ, that was fun. Really makes me miss my teen punk days."

Axle looked over at me while he dangled one wrist off the steering wheel. "Feel like knocking off a liquor store?"

"Nah, I think we've graduated from liquor stores. How about a casino? That was some *Ocean's Eleven* shit right there."

"All right, kid. Calm down. You've successfully pulled off *one* job. Let's not get ahead of yourself."

The combination of the adrenaline and Axle's grating tone had me barking, "Call me kid one more fucking time, and I won't be responsible for the ass whipping *I'm* gonna give *you*."

Axle smirked as he turned into the parking lot for the Pay Dirt Casino. "We might make a real biker outta you yet."

I rolled my eyes as I rubbed my hands on my thighs and didn't give Axle another thought. At that moment, I felt like I could do anything. And right now, more than anything, I wanted to do Amber. I wanted to hold her in my arms and tease her sweet little body until we were both crying for mercy.

But unfortunately for me, we had an alibi to make, so my little fantasy with Amber would have to wait.

Chapter 20

Eight hours earlier

Amber

There were lots of things about my job that I hated. The hours, how much my feet hurt from the shoes, the leering looks from scumbags, the ass grabs. And they all merged into a huge fuck-you on the Sunday afternoon shift. Something about weekend day drinking made my job as a cocktail waitress suck the big one on Sunday afternoons. A lot of assholes made their last hurrahs before their workweek started. Although I doubted a few of these asses had paying jobs.

I couldn't wait until I got off work today.

Smiling brightly at a craps player while I unobtrusively set his drink down, I thought about the night ahead. For the first time in over a week, I was on my own. Bam had some vague "club business" to take care of, so we wouldn't be burning up the sheets in his bed. I accepted a tip from the craps player and gritted my teeth as he slyly patted my ass as I walked by. Fucker. I know I could say something and get his ass booted out of here, but Shannon had been suspiciously "let go" yesterday, and everyone was humming that it was because she complained too much about gropey customers and not the bullshit reason management came up with. Given all my drama with Bam and that customer a few weeks back and Ruslan continuing to pop up at work, I really couldn't afford to draw more attention to myself with management. At the end of the day, I still needed a paycheck.

I left the gropey craps player behind and searched for new customers as I thought through my evening plans. I'd been avoiding my mom since I hooked up with Bam, so it'd be kinda awkward if I went home early enough tonight when she'd still be awake. Maybe I should swing by Sidney's house and see if I could bunk with her tonight.

"Cocktails?"

"I'll have something, honey."

I froze at the sound of my mother's voice coming from my right.

Closing my eyes, I mentally ran through every curse word I knew. But it wasn't enough. Because when I turned and opened my eyes, I found not only my mom, sitting at a slot machine, but all her biker chick friends. And they were all grinning like fools, happy to see me when I was feeling anything but.

I held my tray like a shield in front of my body, trying and failing to hide behind the tiny circle of plastic. "Mom, what are you doing here?"

"What does it look like, honey? We're gambling!" My mom grinned hugely, and I took a step closer and subtly sniffed the air.

Or so I thought.

My mom's smile fell off her face as she bit her lip. "I haven't been drinking, Amber."

I winced. "Sorry, Mom. It's just . . ." I trailed off and shrugged helplessly. There was really nothing I could say to make it better.

"Right."

I cleared my throat and tried to reclaim my professional outer shell. "So, what can I get you ladies?"

"A diet coke for me," my mom ordered quietly.

CHAPTER 20

"Sprite," Mom's friend Emily requested.

Nicole smiled. "Full sugar coke for me."

"Diet," Jessica said.

My mom turned and blinked at her friends. "You guys don't have to order sodas because of me. It's okay if you drink; I swear I can handle it."

"It's not even five o'clock yet." Nicole scowled. "Has nothing to do with you."

"Right," my mom drawled. "When was the last time we went out on a weekend, and you didn't drink?"

"You're gonna drive me to drink today," Nicole muttered before turning to me. "Regular coke. Please."

I turned and beat a hasty retreat as the ladies quietly bickered behind me. Hunching over the bar, I repeated their drink order to the bartender. While I waited for their sodas, I peeked at my watch and mentally cursed the fact that I still had several minutes on my shift, and that it hadn't ended ten minutes ago. Why? Why me? At least they hadn't commented on the ridiculous outfit that I had to wear.

Accepting the sodas from Sean, I carefully arranged them on my tray, then slowly walked back to my mom and her friends like I was approaching a death squad.

"Two diets, a Sprite, and a regular Coke. I'm off in ten minutes, but I think Tracy is on shift after me. She'll take care of you ladies." I smiled brightly and was halfway through my pivot when my mom shouted.

"Wait, you forgot your tip, Amber."

I turned back; all the ladies were holding out dollar bills. My cheeks burning brightly, I tipped my tray down and let them place their tips on the tray. I don't think I'd ever felt more like a stripper than I did at that moment.

My mom looked at me with wide, knowing eyes and asked, "Can you hang out with us after your shift ends? We wanted to celebrate your new status in the club."

"My status?" I repeated as I stacked the singles and discreetly folded them so they wouldn't be visible to customers.

"The guys told us that Bam claimed you as his old lady." Emily smiled. "That's something to celebrate!"

I shot wide eyes over at my mom and caught her wince before she smiled bravely at me. "She's right, honey. We should celebrate."

I didn't know if my mom's wince was from my new biker bitch status or the fact that the information hadn't come from me. I bit my lip and nodded slowly. "Sure. I don't have any plans."

"Fan-fucking-tastic," Nicole hooted. "Get changed out of that crazy getup, and we're gonna tear this place up!"

"Or we could go to the Pay Dirt Casino." I held my tray in front of me again. "I don't really like to hang out where I work. Some customers might recognize me, and it can get a little . . . uncomfortable."

My mom's eyes narrowed. "I see."

"Sounds good, Amber." Jessica nodded. "I worked here a few years back, so I totally understand. We'll play the machines in this area while we wait for you, and then we'll make our plans."

"I like the sound of Pay Dirt." Emily tossed in. "They have that risqué cabaret show that we never got around to seeing for Jessica's bachelorette party."

Because I totally wanted to go see a male strip show with *my mother*.

"Wow, being with Reb really has changed you." My mom smiled. "I remember how . . . tense you were that night. And now you're the one all excited about going to a strip show."

"Well, it'll be kinda my last hurrah. I know Reb won't want me to be seeing any other naked guys once we get married in the fall," Emily announced as she held out her left hand where a huge solitaire diamond ring sat on her ring finger.

All the ladies squealed with excitement as they crowded around her.

CHAPTER 20

My mom hugged her. "When did he propose?"

"How did we miss seeing this huge rock today?" Nicole scowled down at Emily's ring.

"When are you getting married?" Jessica asked.

I slowly backed away. It was a toss-up which I was more excited by: Emily's engagement or the fact that the attention was off of me. And then my mom's eyes met mine.

"Here. Fifteen minutes," my mom commanded.

I nodded and disappeared into the rows of slot machines. Making my way toward the locker room, I was lost in my thoughts of old lady titles, vests, and engagement rings—not to mention that look in my mom's eyes—when I became aware of someone walking behind me, following me in a not-so-subtle way. I turned, ready to give Jackson a piece of my mind, and locked eyes with Ruslan.

I froze as my mind whirled. What was he doing here? After our last confrontation, he knew I was Bam's. Where was everyone? I looked frantically over his shoulder, but we'd entered a deserted back hallway of the casino where only employees and deliveries were allowed.

"So, he has claimed you, and yet you still walk around this casino dressed like a common prostitute? Begging for tips dressed like that when I can offer you so much more?"

"I, uh, Ruslan. Hi. I'm not, uh, dressed like a common prostitute. It's supposed to be an 1800s saloon girl. You know, the gold rush, cancan dancers, that kinda thing." I smiled weakly as my heart raced.

"I could have given you so much, *moya zvezda*. How could you choose that lunkhead instead of me?"

The depth of pain in Ruslan's voice stole my breath. I didn't know how anyone could feel that much about me after such a short amount of time. Clearly this was more wounded pride than anything to do with me. And he was crazy. I had no idea how to handle this.

I bit my lip. "I'm sorry, Ruslan. Believe me, the last thing I wanted was to fall for a guy like Bam, but it just happened."

"I could give you so much more. The entire city would lie at your feet if you were by my side."

I shrugged helplessly. "I'm with Bam."

Ruslan's eyes narrowed. "I see."

A shiver shook my body, and I gripped my tray tighter. Something about the way he'd said that made me more worried than anything he could've said. "Bam's really a great guy. I don't—"

Ruslan waved a hand, cutting me off. "I understand. I hope you are happy with your . . . *biker*."

He'd bit the last word off like it was an insult. I was trembling from the combination of his unspoken threat and his raw anger when someone jostled me from behind.

"Sorry, Amber," Sean muttered as he walked by me to the men's locker room.

And when I turned back, Ruslan was gone.

I sprinted to the ladies' locker room, where I collapsed on the bench in front of my locker and panted. I didn't know what to think. That was the weirdest confrontation with Ruslan to date, and I'd had a few to choose from. Was he threatening Bam's life? Should I tell Bam? Why was Ruslan so fixated on me? Was it because I was the one that got away? More bruised ego than obsession? Or was he just plain crazy?

The only thing I did know was that I was definitely not telling my mom.

Chapter 21

Still Amber

I had to wait until my hands stopped shaking, so I could change into my street clothes. Hopefully nothing had happened to Jackson, who was my guard for the afternoon shift. I didn't want anyone hurt because of me.

When I finally returned to the casino floor, I found the ladies still haunting the same group of slots, only this time in the company of my brother.

My eyes found him in the crowd and I slumped in relief that he was unscathed. Although now that I knew he was safe, I was more than a little pissed that Jackson hadn't done his job. Maybe if he'd stepped in, I wouldn't have had my little run-in with Ruslan.

But it was too late to bitch now, and I was pretty sure Bam would have more than a little to say about this. That is, if I told him about it.

"You okay, sis? You look a little shaken." Jackson's eyes narrowed on me. "Did something happen to you between here and the locker room?"

I bit my lip and did what any good sister would do. I lied. "No, no. I'm fine. I'm just . . . I kinda need to talk to Mom. You know? Girl talk?"

Jackson's eyes didn't leave my face as he nodded slowly. "Sure."

"What's up, honey?" my mom asked as she bounced up from her slot machine's seat.

I tore my gaze away from my brother's probing eyes and smiled weakly at my mom. "Can we talk? You know, alone? Maybe over there?"

My mom nodded, and we took off for the weird divider between the bar and the slots. Reaching the wall, my mom turned and gave me a look. "Okay, what's really going on?"

"What do you mean?"

"I know that look. That's your I'm-hiding-something-that-I-don't-wanna-talk-about look, so spill."

"I don't have a look."

"I've raised you. I know all your looks. What's going on?"

This. This right here was why I'd been avoiding her for so long. "It's not important." I sighed. "I just wanted—"

"It's important enough that you don't want Jackson to know. Jackson who was supposed to be watching you but instead came over to talk to us. Something happened. What. Was. It?"

"It's not a big deal. I was going to tell Bam about it later. Maybe."

"Amber."

"Ruslan was here. Okay? That's the big secret. Ruslan came up to me when I was outside the locker room alone, and we had a few words."

"Ruslan? Is that the Bratva guy who's been stalking you?"

"Yes. I know I should've told you about the whole thing, but—"

"Yeah, you should've. You had a crazy mafioso stalking you—sending you gifts, probably watching the house—you damn well should've told me about it. What if something happened, Amber? Did you ever think about that?"

"Of course I did! But I thought you had enough on your plate. I don't want to worry you."

CHAPTER 21

"I'm a parent. That's the job. Of course I worry about you. I worry about Jackson. I worry about him following in his father's footsteps. I worry about you dropping out of college, working here. I worry all the time."

"I know you do. It's what drove you to drink. I didn't want to be the one adding to your worries, and cause you to fall off the wagon."

"No, grief drove me to drink. And my insecurities. That has nothing to do with you. My drinking is on me. I don't want you to ever hold things back from me because you're worried I'm going to go over the deep end."

"You're kidding, right? Do you not remember who's been cleaning you up for the last year? Who's been paying the bills because Dad didn't have much life insurance, and you couldn't scrape yourself off the floor in the morning to make it to work on time? It's all been on my shoulders and has been ever since Dad died."

My mom looked at me like I'd sucker punched her, and I pulled in a breath as regret burned through my stomach lining. This was why we kept everything inside and never talked. I always said something the wrong way, or was too honest and biting. A little bit of honesty was good; too much tended to burn. Happy fake family was so much better than truth-telling wounded family. I never wanted to be the reason that my mom was so hurt.

I bit my lip. "I'm sorry, Mom. I shouldn't have—"

"No. It's fine. We needed to get this out." My mom's eyes glistened as tears welled, and I felt so low. "I know I haven't been there for you this last year. I know it's been hard. And I'm so sorry that you had to pick up the slack and become an adult so much sooner than you should've. You should be at college parties and worrying about boys and grades, not working a full-time job, shaking your ass to pay *my* bills."

My face burned at her ass-shaking remark. I'd never enjoyed this job, but it paid so much more than any other I was qualified for. I could've worked the reception desk or cleaned rooms, but the tips alone paid our mortgage. And we needed the money. "Mom . . ."

"No. I'm so thankful that you worked your tail off for me, but it ends today. You're quitting. Give them your notice. Turn in your tiny skirt and bustier, because you're going back to college next semester."

I sucked in a breath. It was everything I'd wished for.

And yet . . .

"We can't." I sighed. "It's not that easy. There's the mortgage and tuition and all the paperwork for admission and financial aid. I wish we could, but I can't."

"We can and you will." My mom waved a hand when I tried to interrupt her. "No—I got a job, so the mortgage is covered. And as far as the paperwork goes, we'll talk to the admissions office tomorrow. If it's too late to apply for this year, you can do a semester or two at the community college, take some classes that will transfer over. We're done with you living your life for me."

"I'd do it again in a heartbeat." I smiled at my mom as tears streamed down my face.

"I know you would, honey." She grabbed me in her arms and pulled me into the tightest, warmest hug. It'd been so long. I wrapped my arms around her and hugged her right back. I'd missed this. I finally had my mom back after a long, hard, painful year. My breath shuddered.

We stood there for a minute, tangled in each other's arms. Finally, my mom squeezed me one more time, then took a step away. "You go give your notice, then we'll go find the boys, and you can introduce me to your man."

I groaned even as a giddy sensation swept over me—I had no idea that we were meeting up with the guys tonight. "I was totally going to tell you about Bam, I just—"

CHAPTER 21

"Had to figure out how you'd explain it first?" My mom interjected.

"Kinda. I'd been so anti-biker since Dad died, and I knew you knew how I felt, but you didn't know about Ruslan and the Bratva thing, so it was kinda hard to explain."

My mom laughed as she put her arm around me and led us back to the group. "Well, now you know for the future. If you tell your mom everything, it doesn't make it awkward later."

I rolled my eyes. "Yeah, I love you, Mom, but I'm not telling you everything."

"You can and you should. Speaking of, does Bam have his you-know-what pierced? Quite a few guys in the club do, you know."

"Mom," I groaned.

Six hours, I don't know how many drinks, and one job quit later, I was feeling no pain. The ladies and I had left the Mother Lode for the Pay Dirt Casino across the street, and had taken up almost half of their Gold Bullion Bar with our mix of biker chicks and True Brothers patched members. Bam hadn't shown up yet, but after the first hour or so, Tank and Reb and a few of the other guys slowly trickled in. My mom and I were dancing at our table to an old eighties song while my brother rolled his eyes and sipped a beer. He might be too cool for school, but I was having the time of my life. I'd quit my job. I'd be going to school next semester. I was laughing and drinking with my friends and family. Life was pretty damn perfect.

The only thing that could've made my night any better was the man who'd just walked in the door.

"Bam!" I squealed as I pushed away from the table and practically ran for the door.

Bam spread his stance and caught my flying leap with a grunt.

"You're here! You're here!" I peppered his face with a thousand kisses. "I was beginning to think the guys were lying. They were here, but you weren't. But they kept saying he's coming, he'll be here, don't worry about it. And you're here! You're here!"

He laughed as he held me in his arms. "Holy shit, kitten. How many have you had?"

"How can you say that?" I pushed away from him with a glare. "You know you're the only man I've ever slept with!"

Axle snorted a laugh as he slapped Bam on the shoulder and walked by us. I didn't know what the hell that was about, but Bam hadn't acknowledged him. His eyes were trained on me and only me.

Finally he rumbled, "I meant, how many drinks have you had?"

"Oh." My face burned from a combination of my drinks and my blush as I thought over his question. Giving up, I shrugged. "I dunno. I lost track. Come on! Let's get you something to drink so you can catch up."

Bam laughed when I squirmed down his body to break away. I grabbed his hand and led him toward the bar.

"One huge-ass beer for my man, Raymond!" I shouted—by this time I was on a first-name basis with the waitstaff at the bar. Which reminded me. I turned to Bam and let out another squeal. "Guess what?!"

Bam's eyes danced as he smiled down at me. "What?"

"I quit my job! As of the end of the month, I will no longer have to shake my ass to pay our bills."

"Ah, babe, that's great. It'll make my life a hell of a lot easier if I don't have to watch other men ogle your ass on a nightly basis."

"Yup. I'm going back to school. I talked it over with my mom, and I'll enroll next semester. Or the one after. Or the year after. I don't really know how the whole thing works since I've never gone back. But since I was in there before, it shouldn't be too hard to figure out." I leaned hard against his side and blinked up at Bam. "What were we talking about?"

He laughed as he accepted the large beer mug from the bartender.

CHAPTER 21

"I think you've had way too much to drink tonight, kitten."

"No, it's just that I'm so excited that you're here." I nuzzled my face against his arm, and that amazing aroma of Bam filled my head. Leather, bergamot, and Bam. God, he smelled so good. My nipples tightened as a faint buzzing sound drowned out the background noise. If we were alone, there was so much I would do to this man. But we weren't. We'd have to wait till later to play drunk and horny night.

Bam choked on his beer. "What the hell did you just say?"

"I didn't say anything. I was just thinking about how hot you are and how good you smell. How long do you think we need to stay to celebrate Reb and Emily's engagement?"

"Considering you just offered me a drunk and horny night, I'm thinking we're leaving right now. Where's your car?" Bam put his barely touched beer down and wrapped his arms around me, then kissed me like he hadn't seen me in a year.

After a long and heady kiss, I pulled away, panting. "Across the street. In the employee lot. Like usual."

"Fantastic. Let's go."

There were cheers and good-natured jeers as Bam swung me into his arms and headed for the door. I know I should've been more embarrassed by the fact that everyone in the bar knew what we were going to do, but I was too happy—and horny—to think much about it. We were ten feet from the door when Tank stopped Bam with a hand on his shoulder.

"I know you kids have somewhere you'd rather be, but we have a little business to settle first."

A steely look settled over Bam's face as he set me down on my feet then stepped in front of me, putting his body between me and Tank and leaving his hands loose at his sides. Bam's voice was a low drawl when he finally spoke. "I thought we settled everything we needed to at the last club meeting."

Tank stared back at him with a similar hard expression. The entire bar was silent, only the soft strains of Def Leppard's "Pour Some Sugar On Me" could be heard. I had no idea what their standoff was about. I thought everyone in the club was okay with me and Bam being together.

Bam tensed as Tank reached for something on the table behind him.

"Not quite," Tank said as he held out a leather vest with a flourish. He twisted it so the back was visible. Curving around the vest in the True Brother script were the words "Property of Bam Bam."

I sucked in a breath while I stared at the vest. My mom had a similar one, and had worn it so much the stitching had to be repaired. I never thought I'd wear one, too.

Bam laughed as he took the vest from Tank, then pulled him in for a one-armed man hug.

Tank slapped him on the back before he pulled away. "Sorry for all the shit we gave you. Well, not really." He laughed. "But this is our way of welcoming Amber officially to the club. You guys stay safe and enjoy the rest of your night."

The crowd around us hooted and cheered their approval. Bam was practically beaming as he helped me into the vest. It didn't exactly go with my outfit, but now wasn't the time to bitch about that. The leather smelled new and fresh as it enveloped me. I brushed a hand down the lapel and noticed the blank spot where my name patch should've been on the front.

"We didn't know if you wanted your name or if Bam had picked a road name out for you. We can fill that part in later." Tank saluted us with his beer before he melted back into the crowd.

"So, what do you say, kitten? Or should we have 'em put Amber on your patch?" Bam's grin was so wide. I don't think I'd ever seen him smile that big.

"Whatever you'd like, honey." I replied. "I'm your property, after all."

CHAPTER 21

"Fuck yeah. And don't you forget it." Bam pressed a quick peck on my lips, then slapped my ass with a loud spank. "Let's get going before you're no longer drunk for drunk and horny night."

"Yes, sir." I mockingly saluted him. I was able to take three whole steps away before I felt Bam grab me and heave me over his shoulder in a fireman's hold.

The crowd hooted and hollered as Bam carried me away, like the marauding Viking he was.

And I grinned the entire time.

Chapter 22

Two weeks later

Bam

"If all continues to go as scheduled, probate will close on Friday." Harry Hastings rumbled on the other end of the phone. "So far we haven't heard a single peep out of your mother or her lawyer. It looks like it was an empty threat."

I laughed bitterly. "I doubt it. My mom has a way of swooping in and ruining everything at the last second."

"Regardless, you have the upper hand—your grandmother's will was written years before you joined the club. She can't claim coercion due to the club, and you had cleaned up your act and were enrolled in a local trade school at the time. I'm confident that if it goes to trial, the judge will rule in your favor."

"Thanks, Harry. I appreciate all the work you've done for me on this."

"Wasn't much work, but I'm glad to have it. I'll let you know when it's official. Later."

I ended the call and tossed my cell phone onto the couch next to me. It was hard to relax when so many things were going my way. Amber

CHAPTER 22

had worked her final shift as a cocktail waitress and had enrolled at the local community college. And the Wild Riders MC had yet to strike back or even threaten anything after we'd hijacked their drug shipment and left it on the Reno PD's front doorstep. The drug delivery had made the news. The police had found the place where we'd hijacked the truck, but no one had come knocking at our door. They'd just arrested more Wild Riders. Dumb fucks. Everything in my life was finally running smoothly. I had an amazing woman, a great job, and my Brothers at my back. Life was fan-fucking-tastic.

Hence my tension. Nothing in my life had ever gone as good as these last few weeks. It was only a matter of time before it all came crashing down, one way or another.

"What did Harry say?" Amber asked as she came out of the bathroom wearing stretchy yoga pants and a T-shirt, rubbing her wet hair with a towel.

My dick hardened at the sight of her. I watched, mesmerized, as her tits bounced in rhythm with her vigorous rubbing. She was clearly braless, and given the little bit she was wearing, it wouldn't take much to get her naked again. I'd had to skip out on showering together when I saw the call come in from Harry. My only regret so far. But maybe we could rectify that.

"Bam? Hello?" Amber leaned toward me and waved her fingers in my face. "Is everything okay? What happened with Harry?"

"What? Sorry. You get me so fucking hard just being you." I reached out and grabbed her hand and pulled her until she fell into my lap. "You look so squeaky clean and wholesome; it makes me wanna dirty you up."

I burrowed my face in her neck as she squealed and wiggled in my lap.

"Oh my god. Stop, Bam! You're gonna give me a huge beard rash on my entire face, and I'm supposed to meet my mom in an hour."

I stopped tormenting Amber and sat up with a frown. "What? An hour? When did that happen? I thought we were gonna have the whole afternoon together. I had plans. Wonderful, dirty plans involving you and my beard and your thighs."

Amber bit her lip and groaned. "Don't tell me that. Now I don't want to go."

"Exactly," I murmured as I molded my hands over her perfect but still covered breasts. "Now let's get to getting naked."

"Bam, no. I can't." Amber wiggled until she fell off my lap and onto the couch next to me. "I haven't seen my mom in weeks, and she really wants to spend time together. Now that she's working, and I'm over here so much, we haven't had any time to just hang out. She wanted to do a fun family get-together. Jackson is even coming."

I nodded stiffly. "Fine. That's okay. I'll watch some TV or whatever. Maybe swing by the club and see if anyone wants to get a drink."

Amber's eyes darkened as she frowned. "I'm sorry I didn't tell you. It was kind of a spur-of-the-moment thing. She asked me about it last night when she called. Maybe—"

She was cut off as my cell phone rang. I checked the screen, and seeing the name of my grandma's seventy-year-old neighbor, Neil, I answered.

"Hey Neil. What's up?"

"Hunter, hi. I, uh, I'm sorry to be interrupting your Sunday afternoon, but, uh, I thought you'd want to know . . ." Neil fell silent.

"Neil? You still there?" I pulled my phone away from my face and looked at the screen. I had a full signal. "Neil?"

"Hey, sorry, Hunter. I, erm, dropped my phone." Neil paused and coughed weakly.

"Everything all right? You don't sound too good, man."

"I'm fine. I'm fine. Got one of those annoying summer head colds, but I'll be okay. Anyway, I wanted to call and let you know that a tree

CHAPTER 22

came down on your grandma's garage last night. Doesn't seem to, uh, be a lot of damage, but you should head over and check it out—today, if you can. You know how your grandma was about those trees of hers."

My head fell back onto the sofa cushion with a groan. A downed tree on top of her garage? That sounded like a fucking expensive headache. And given how little I had in the bank, it might be the thing that would make me have to sell her place. Fuck, I really loved that little house.

"I hear you. I'll drive up today and take a look. Thanks for calling, Neil."

"No problem. Hunter, listen, I um . . ." Neil trailed off and grunted softly then coughed.

"Neil?"

He groaned, then sighed. "Yeah—hey, I gotta go, kid. Take care of you."

"Bye, Neil." I shook my head as I put down my cell phone. Poor guy. Summer head colds sucked. I should swing by his place and see if he needed anything.

"Everything okay?" Amber asked, her forehead wrinkled in concern.

"Not really. I guess a tree came down on my grandma's garage last night. I gotta go check it out and see what the damages are."

"Oh no. I'm sorry."

"Fuck, I hope it's not bad. I don't have the money to fix something like that right now." I pushed off the couch with a groan. "But hey, you have fun with your bro and mom. Tell 'em I said hi."

"Bam, wait. I think I should come with you." Amber jumped up from the couch and grabbed my hand. "I don't want you to go by yourself."

"I'll be fine, kitten. I'm used to it."

"But you shouldn't have to be. What is it that my mom always says? A trouble shared is a trouble halved? Or something schmaltzy like that. But it's true. I'm here. You shouldn't have to stress about it all on your own. Let me help you."

"It's a tree on top of the garage. Not much you could help with there. Besides, you got that thing with your family. It's fine. *I'll* be fine."

"Give me a second, and let me call my mom. I know that once she hears about this, she'll want to come along, too. You're part of our family now, and we take care of our own."

Before I could reply, Amber walked away and grabbed her cell phone off the kitchen counter. Five seconds later her mom's voice was resonating through the apartment as Amber put her on speakerphone.

"Hey honey, are you on your way?"

"No, Mom, listen, you're on speakerphone, and . . ." Amber filled her mom in on the tree situation as I rolled my eyes and crossed my arms over my chest.

"Of course, sweetie. I'll call Jackson, and we'll meet you guys there. Text me the address. How about we swing by a deli on the way and grab some sandwiches? Make a day of it."

"Sounds great, Mom." Amber threw me a smug look then stuck her tongue out at me.

"And Bam Bam?"

"Yes, ma'am?"

"Don't worry about anything. If we can't figure things out between the four of us, we'll call in the guys and get your grandma's place straightened out. I'm sorry this has happened, but we'll get it fixed."

I had to clear my throat as I suddenly found it difficult to talk. "Thanks, Mrs. Bennett."

"It's Brittany, honey. And Amber? Don't forget to text me the address. We'll see you guys there."

"Bye, Mom. Love you."

"Love you, too, honey."

Amber ended the call, then crossed over to envelop me in a hug. Her arms tightened spasmodically around me. "See? I told you—part of

CHAPTER 22

the family."

I laughed huskily as I closed my arms around her, too. "Apparently."

"I'm sorry I didn't invite you to our family thing." Amber burrowed her head into my shoulder. "I wasn't thinking. I swear it won't happen again."

"It's okay, kitten. We don't have to be attached at the hip every moment of every day. You've got your family, and in a few weeks you'll have your school stuff. You can do some shit on your own. I'm a big boy; I can take care of myself."

"But you don't have to. That's what I'm trying to tell you. We're together, right? You claimed me in front of the club; they gave me a vest. It's kinda official now. So that means you're stuck with me. Your worries are my worries, and vice versa."

I had to laugh at Amber's commanding tone. She was explaining relationships to me like I didn't have a clue. Which to be honest, I didn't really, since this was my first. But she didn't, either. "Okay, okay. I guess you guys can come along."

"Mighty kind of you to offer, since we've already decided we're coming," Amber teased as she smiled up at me. "Let's get dressed and get on the road. If you're lucky, we'll have enough time for you to show me the local sights before my mom shows up."

"You've been to Tahoe before, haven't you?"

"Not the sights I was talking about." Amber pulled out of my arms and danced down the hallway with a seductive roll to her hips.

I growled. If we had it my way, I'd show her the sights before we even left the apartment.

Amber tossed a seductive look over her shoulder, and I took off. She squealed and ran for the safety of my bedroom.

Directly, unknowingly, into the trap I'd laid. I had her right where I wanted her. And I'd have her a few more times before we left for Tahoe.

Chapter 23

Amber

I loved the feeling of the wind on my face and Bam's large, hard body between my thighs. Riding on the back of his bike was second only to riding him in the bedroom. Although, given the way my body ached, it would've been better if we'd left a little more time between the two activities.

Not that I was complaining.

I wallowed in my pleasure-satiated body and the knowledge that I got to wear my "Property of" vest. My body knew it was the property of Bam, and I loved knowing that everyone who saw us knew as well.

My grin about swallowed up my face as Bam took a corner a little fast, and I had to tighten my grip around his body. Life was pretty damn near perfect. I wanted to shout it to the heavens and maybe have him make love to me again—this time in his childhood bedroom.

Okay, we'd do that last one *after* my mother and brother left. *Ick.*

Still, I had a wide grin on my face as we roared down the residential streets in Bam's old neighborhood. Then the houses got further and further apart. The fences got bigger and more elaborate. Bam hadn't said anything about his grandma living in the ritzy part of Tahoe. My confusion cleared up the further we rode. His bike weaved for a second

CHAPTER 23

as we left the pavement behind and the road got rougher. About half a mile further, he pulled up to what I could only describe as a cabin. It looked small from the road and only got smaller as we coasted down the driveway toward it. From here it looked like there were maybe five rooms inside at most; a small lean-to sat not far from it, with a ginormous pine tree speared through the roof.

Bam coasted to a stop twenty feet from the tree and killed the engine. His face was drawn as he surveyed the destruction. Closing his eyes, he whispered, "Fuck me."

My heart ached for him. I know he loved this house as it—and Pixie—were the only links he had to his grandmother. I gave his waist a squeeze before I swung off the bike, but I didn't say anything. What could I say in the face of this?

Unclipping my helmet, I watched with solemn eyes as he swung off his bike and paced toward the uprooted tree. He angrily eyed the torn earth and mess of roots jutting out, then gave it a swift kick. "Son of a bitch!"

I winced, but still didn't say anything. I'd been around enough alpha men to know that sometimes it was better to let them vent that anger—unless you wanted them to turn it on you. Instead, I turned my eyes toward the destroyed garage. Because it was destroyed. I knew almost nothing about construction, but even I could recognize a lost cause when it was this bad.

"I told her. You know?" Bam raged as his eyes flickered between the tree roots and the garage and back. "This tree was so fucking old, I was afraid this'd happen. I got her to agree to cut back the younger trees that were close to the house, but this one . . . She wouldn't let me touch this one. Son of a bitch."

I winced again at the vicious kick he gave the tree. I felt that one in my toes; I could only imagine how his foot felt. "I'm sorry, Bam." I bit my lip as we surveyed the damage. "But at least it looks like the house wasn't hit. Just think how bad it could've been if it fell the other way."

Bam looked at the house for a second, then tipped his jaw at me. I could tell he was holding back whatever smart-ass comment he wanted to say. He was just spoiling for a fight—something to get his aggression out since the tree wasn't fighting back. He just didn't want to take it out on me.

It was sweet in that badass-biker-who-had-feelings-for-me-and-didn't-want-to-piss-me-off kinda way. Something I'd seen my dad do for my mom a million times before. A warmth spread through my body that had nothing to do with the summer sun. I wiped at the smile that threatened to tug at my lips. The last thing I wanted to do was smile in the middle of Bam's heartbreak. He certainly wouldn't understand.

But I was beginning to.

I was falling for this big, behemoth, bossy-as-all-hell biker. Falling, hell—I'd already fallen. I loved him.

I loved Hunter "Bam Bam" Kincaid.

I loved the way he made me feel. In clothes and without. I loved the way he tried and failed to get Pixie to cuddle with him when he thought no one was looking. I loved the way he'd risked everything to be with me, and how he'd had no doubts. I loved the way he protected me when it felt like everything was falling apart.

And I loved the way he loved his grandma's house.

There had to be a way to fix this so he got to keep the house and land. We could figure it out together.

I walked across the barren yard as a bird chirped overhead. Bam continued to berate the fallen tree, and I couldn't help but smile—mostly because his back was turned to me. God, I loved this man. Sneaking up behind him, I wrapped my arms around his waist and held him tight. "I'm so sorry this happened, Bam, but we'll figure it out. You'll still have her house."

CHAPTER 23

Bam turned in my arms and wrapped his own around me. "I'm a fucking fool. Not only do I have the house, but I have you, too. Thanks for putting up with my shit, kitten."

"Anytime."

We stood there in each other's arms as a gentle breeze ruffled my hair and the scent of pine enveloped us. I loved him. Now I just had to figure out the perfect time to tell him. And I knew this definitely wasn't it.

"You know, in one short week this'll all belong to me." Bam rumbled under my ear. "That's what Harry called to say. My mom hasn't filed a petition, and near as he can tell, she won't. He thinks it'll cost too much on her end, and our case is too good. Which means probate will close Friday, and this heap of branches and needles will me mine."

"That's great, Bam."

He grunted. "I thought so at the time. I'm thinking less and less so now that I'm staring at this clusterfuck." His voice trailed off as he sighed. "Christ, she loved that tree. I guess my grandpa planted it when they first built the place. She just couldn't stomach getting rid of it when she didn't have him."

"Sounds like something you'd know a lot about." He'd held onto his grandma's cat and her house with everything he had. Apparently sentimentality ran in his family.

Bam laughed softly then kissed the tip of my nose. "Ya got me there."

We both turned at the sound of crunching gravel and watched as my mom's car pulled into the drive behind Bam's bike. A second later, she and Jackson stepped out of the car.

"Holy shit," Jackson whistled.

"Jackson, language," my mom barked. Then her eyes ran over what was left of the garage. "Okay, I take that back. Holy shit is right."

Bam laughed as he kept one arm around me and walked me toward my family. "Yeah, it's not pretty."

"You got that right." My mom's forehead wrinkled with her frown. "But you have insurance, don't you?"

"I don't even know how that works. I've been paying the mortgage out of my own pocket, and I think the taxes and insurance are all rolled up into one package, but I don't know how to go about making a claim or who to even call. Plus, it's all in her name, so who knows if they'll actually pay out. Those fuckers are always looking for a loophole to avoid paying."

My mom nodded. "First things first—let's unload the food, and I'll make lunch while you kids take pictures with your smart-ass phones. Then we'll dig through your grandma's paperwork and see if we can't figure out who and where we need to call."

She circled around to the trunk with Jackson lazily following behind to help.

Bam pulled me even closer to his chest and murmured into my ear, "Smart-ass phone?"

I bit back a giggle. "She's a little crazy. But this kinda crazy is so much better than the past year's crazy. I got my old mom back. Thank you."

"You're sweet, kitten, but I had nothing to do with that."

"We both know that's not right." I smiled up at him and for a second got lost in his gorgeous blue eyes. The words *I love you* hovered on my tongue, and I almost said them, but . . .

"Are you two going to stare at each other all day or is someone gonna help me with this heavy-ass cooler?" Jackson yelled from all of five feet away.

"I got you, bro," Bam yelled back before ducking his head again to murmur to me, "What is it with your family and asses?"

I snorted. "What can I say? We like butts." I slapped his jeans-clad ass. "It's half the reason I'm with you, bucko."

"You're gonna pay for that one, kitten."

CHAPTER 23

"I sure hope so."

Jackson rolled his eyes as he heaved the cooler out of the trunk. "If I knew I was gonna spend the day watching my sister making goo-goo eyes and talking dirty—" He shuddered. "I would've happily gone back to the clubhouse and cleaned the shop bathroom with a toothbrush. Hell, I'd've used *my* toothbrush."

"Enough, children," my mom commanded. "Amber, let go of your man for one minute. Bam, help Jackson with the cooler. And Jackson, try not to be such a child."

"She started it," Jackson muttered, and I snickered as he and Bam took off for the house lugging the huge cooler my mom had packed.

"I heard that," my mom hollered.

"Thanks again for coming out, Mrs. Bennett," Bam said, walking backward as he held up his half of the cooler. "It's been a while since I had family that I could count on."

"Honey, I told you, it's Brittany. And I gotta call horseshit on the rest of what you've said," my mom replied.

The light in Bam's eyes died as a grim expression came across his face. I opened my mouth to rebut her when my mom continued.

"Don't get me wrong, that ma of yours sounds like a train wreck. I just meant you've got the club. You need to start thinking of them as your family now. Sure, we are, too, now, but you've got the guys at your back. They're ready and willing to help you with anything you need."

Bam's eyes twinkled again as he smiled. "Sure. It's just hard to get out of the prospect frame of mind, ya know? I've been so busy busting my ass, sometimes I forget I'm a member and not a—"

Bam gasped and dropped to his knees. The ice chest landed with a thud next to him. A second later he fell to his side, clutching his left arm.

"Bam?" I shrieked. My heart in my throat, I ran the few feet separating us and kneeled next to his side. A bright red stain blossomed across his upper arm. "Oh God. Oh God."

My mom and Jackson dropped to their knees next to us just as the dirt exploded a few feet away. A faint pop echoed through the trees.

"Shit, shit, shit," Jackson said. "Everyone, stay down. Some fucker is shooting at us."

"We gotta get inside." My mom kneeled next to Bam, shielding him with her body. "We're sitting ducks out here. Where are the keys?"

Bam groaned as he rolled to his side and dug in his pocket. "Here."

I grabbed the keys from him as tears burned my eyes. "Oh my god. Are you okay, Bam?"

"We can take a goddamn inventory once we get inside the fucking house. Lucky for us whoever is out there is a bad fucking shot. Now get moving, kitten!"

"Right, right," I muttered to myself as I duckwalked/ran to the front door, trusting the others to follow along behind me. Bam didn't say, but I'd guessed that the generic-looking house key was the one I wanted. My hands shook as I tried to fit the key into the lock, and I missed my first try. Before I could stab at it again, Bam's hand covered mine as he helped guide the key home.

Shoving the door open, I jumped inside and held the door as my mom, Jackson, and finally Bam crossed the threshold. Just as I slammed the door shut, I heard the unmistakable sound of a bullet ricocheting off the metal door.

Chapter 24

Bam

My arm burned like a son of a bitch. Really, all I wanted to do was curl up into a ball and drink the fucking pain away, but we needed to get a handle on the situation. My girl and what was left of her family depended on me.

Apparently Brittany was of the same frame of mind as she crossed the room to my grandma's phone on the side table. Picking up the receiver, she put it to her ear before I could say anything. "It's dead. They must've cut the phone line."

I had to laugh at that. "I turned off the phone before I moved out. Who's got their cell on them? Mine's back on my bike."

"I think mine's in my purse, wherever that landed out front." Amber frowned as she patted down her pockets.

"Mine's in my car," Brittany replied.

Jackson held his up with a triumphant smile. "Good thing one of us always has his on him."

I gave him a chin jerk. "Fantastic. Call Reb tell him what's up. Amber, go grab the first-aid kit in the hall closet. Everyone meet me and Brittany in the basement. I have a few handguns stored there that'll come in handy if shit hits the fan before the guys show up."

"Uh, one little problem here," Jackson interjected, holding his phone up. "I don't seem to have any bars."

"Fuck, it's been so long since I was here, I forgot how shitty the signal is up in these hills. Shit, shit, shit." I scowled. "Move around the house and keep trying. But stay away from the goddamn windows."

Jackson nodded as he held his phone up, swinging it to the left then the right.

"Try sending a text!" Amber yelled from somewhere down the hall. "Don't need as much signal for a text."

"Good fucking idea!" Jackson yelled back as he bent over his phone.

The women shrieked as a window exploded on the other side of the room.

Fuck, fuck, fuck. I had no idea who was out there, but it didn't sound like they were going away anytime soon. It was only a matter of time before they breached the house.

"Jackson, try sending a text or make a call, then get your ass downstairs. Ladies, let's go." I ushered the pair of them down the rickety wooden staircase that my grandfather built in the late seventies into the unfinished basement below. Their eyes were wide with terror, and I ached to hold Amber in my arms. But then again, my arm also ached like a son of a bitch. Ignoring the emotion and pain in the room, I crossed to the corner where I'd stored some of my stuff. Swiftly loading my two Ruger handguns, I grabbed as much ammo as I had on hand, then led the ladies to the end of the room furthest from the two tiny windows.

Looking around, I took stock of the space. Like most basements, it'd been a dumping area for years, decades even. Stacks of boxes littered the room. An ancient sofa from the eighties sagged against the wall near the stairs. A single bulb swayed precariously overhead. An old dining table slumped beneath a heap of boxes. The whole place was a fucking mess. But I saw shit we could actually use. All of it could

CHAPTER 24

be used to barricade us in and keep whoever was out there out. The stairs weren't ideal, but we had a shitload of furniture and boxes to hide behind.

"Okay, sit down, champ," Brittany commanded. "Let's take a look at that arm."

"We don't have time for that shit. We gotta be prepared for when whoever's out there tries to come in here." I darted a look Amber's way and shut my mouth as her face crumpled, and a single tear rolled down her cheek.

"We've got time to take care of you first. Sit your ass down on the fucking sofa," Brittany barked.

It wasn't Brittany's command that had me sitting down. I wanted to do something—anything—to alleviate the fear swimming in Amber's eyes. "I'm fine, kitten. Pretty sure it's just a flesh wound."

"Okay," she whispered, crowding closer with her first-aid kit in hand.

I didn't take my eyes off her as she and her mom bent over my arm, passing cotton and bandages and whatever else back and forth.

"It's just a graze," Brittany proclaimed as she examined my arm.

It didn't feel like "just a" anything. If it burned like a son of a bitch before, all this probing at it didn't make it or me feel any better. I mentally cursed myself for not bringing any liquor downstairs. Tequila paired nicely with a bullet wound, right? Maybe whiskey.

"Fuck," I hissed as Brittany none too gently wiped at my arm.

"Here, let me," Amber said softly as she brushed her mom's hands away. "I was studying nursing before I left school."

"Yeah, but it's different when it's someone you care about, honey. Let me."

Amber frowned. "Mom, I've got this."

"Someone do something and finish it already! We don't have all goddamn day!" I shouted.

"What the hell is going on down here?" Jackson asked as he tromped down the stairs.

"Finally," I muttered as Amber won the staring contest with her mom and started dabbing at my wound. "Did you get a signal?"

"I think so. Enough to send a text, anyhow. Didn't get a reply. The way that bastard is shooting out windows, I thought it best to get the fuck downstairs." Jackson surveyed the scene with a scowl. "If you Florence Nightingales are finished, maybe we could plan what the fuck we're gonna do next. It'll be at least an hour before the troops arrive, and that's only once Reb sees the fucking text, assuming it actually went through. So, what do we do in the meantime?"

Amber's hands were shaking as she tried and failed to affix the bandage around my arm. Tears still swam in her eyes, but she was fighting bravely against letting them fall.

I lifted a hand and swept the hair out of her eyes. "I'm gonna be okay, kitten. *We* are going to be okay. I'm not gonna let anything happen to you. I swear it."

Amber bit her lip, then she shook her head. "You can't promise me that."

"I can and did. I'd die before I'd let anything happen to you." I looked deep into her eyes and said the words that'd been on the tip of my tongue for the last week. "I love you, Amber."

"Don't say that. You can't say that. Not now. Not here, like this." Her tears spilled over and ran down her cheeks. She swiped at them with the back of her hand. "I don't want you to die. You can't die on me."

"We're gonna be fine. I'll take care of you."

"That's what my dad always said," she whispered as she avoided my eyes.

My heart fell into my stomach. *Shit. Stitch.* This had to be bringing up the worst of shit for everyone here. How did I not put that together? I raised my eyes and took in Brittany, who was carefully avoiding them

CHAPTER 24

as she balled up all the bloodstained cotton balls and bandages while tears swam in her own eyes. She was hurting for her daughter, and most likely for herself, since she'd been there the night her husband died. I was probably the last fucking guy she'd wanted to see her daughter hooked up with. I shot a glance at Jackson and found him studiously avoiding the emotion on the couch while he hefted one of the handguns we'd laid out. But even he had a glimmer of moisture in his eyes.

Before I could get a handle on the situation, a loud crash of glass sounded from upstairs. The women squealed and ducked against the couch. My eyes went to the silent staircase. After a few seconds when no other sound came, I relaxed slightly.

"Okay. He's still shooting at the windows. Probably doesn't realize there's a basement under the house. Let's get set up." I stood and grabbed the remaining handgun, shoving it into the small of my back. "Let's get some boxes and shit stacked against the bottom of the stairs. Don't wanna make it easy for those fuckers to find us. I want that table against the wall so we can access the windows. Everybody move."

"Is that smart?" Amber asked. "What if they build a fire to smoke us out?"

"Shit. I didn't think of that." I rubbed my palms against my thighs as I thought out a few different scenarios. My gut said they wouldn't use fire, since it would attract attention. Single gunshots could be mistaken for so many things, especially out here in the hills. No one would think twice. But I didn't want to put us in a position where Amber and her family died because I was wrong. "Okay. Change of plans. You and Brittany build a barricade in that corner, furthest from the staircase. Jackson and I will go up and make sure we're secure and hopefully get a few shots in of our own."

Amber bit her lip. "Bam, no. I don't want you to go."

"I'll be okay, kitten. Stay here and help your mom out."

"You're already not okay. Going up there will only lessen your odds of being okay."

My lips twitched at her eloquence, and she glared at me.

"Whatever. You know what I mean."

"I do." I grabbed her hands and pulled her up next to me so I could wrap my arms around her again. "But if we want to widen our odds of getting out of this okay, we gotta do something. So, you do something down here, and I'll do something upstairs."

"Okay," she whispered. "Just take care of you. And Jackson."

I gave her a quick peck on the lips. "Will do."

I pulled back and tossed a look at Jackson. "You ready?"

He nodded tightly.

"Let's roll. Stay clear of windows and follow me." I made for the stairs and felt Amber's hands slide over my shoulders and back as I walked away. I know she wanted to cling to me, and I was proud as hell that she didn't.

"Stay safe," Brittany added as we started up the stairs.

My heartbeat was louder than my breathing at that moment, but I kept up my stoic mask for the people depending on me. Really, I was scared as shit. What if I was wrong? What if they did try to smoke us out? How was I gonna get Amber and her family out of this? *Fuck, fuck, fuck.*

I sucked in a breath then let it out in a slow exhale as I stared at the door at the top of the stairs. Okay, I could do this. I had to keep Amber safe.

"Do you know who's out there?" Jackson asked in an overly loud voice.

"No. Why, did you see something? You know who it is?"

"No, just thought it might be nice to know who's trying to kill us," Jackson replied in a sardonic tone.

I had to laugh at that. "Could be the Wild Riders MC or their support

CHAPTER 24

club, since this is their territory, and we've been fucking with them lately. I've also pissed off the number two in the Bratva by claiming your sister, so it could be them."

Jackson grunted at that.

"Slight possibility that it's my mom."

Jackson sucked in a breath, then shot me a look. "Your own mom? Really?"

I hitched a shoulder. "We don't exactly have the best relationship, and she's pissed off my grandma left all this to me instead of her."

"So, she shoots it up? And you, too? That doesn't make a lick of sense."

"Killing me would be cheaper than fighting me in court. She's also not the brightest bulb, so who knows?"

"Are you guys gonna do something?" Brittany shouted up the stairs. "'Cause I don't want to sit down here for the rest of my goddamn life!"

"Yes, ma'am." I replied before turning back to Jackson. "You ready?"

"Let's do this."

I turned the doorknob and slowly pushed the door open.

Silence greeted us on the main floor. But it appeared that whoever was out there had been busy while we were downstairs. Most of the windows had been shot out, and glass littered almost every surface in the house. I signaled to Jackson to go for the front door, and I made my way toward the kitchen and the back door.

I think I only took two steps when I felt a searing pain in my right arm that took my breath away. I grunted and fell to my knees, clutching my arm. There must've been glass under me, but I didn't feel it. I couldn't think of anything aside from how much my arm hurt. "Fuck, fuck, fuck."

"Shit, Bam. You okay?"

"Do I fucking look okay?" I roared as blood flowed over my arm. "Fuck, it must've hit a vein or something. Grab some towels in the kitchen. Third drawer left of the stove. No, your other left."

Shit. I was gonna bleed out on my grandma's linoleum while Jackson hunted for a fucking towel. The basement door burst open behind us as Brittany and Amber crowded into the room.

"Fuck, get down!" I shouted.

Amber and Brittany dropped to a crouch behind me, but that didn't stop my anger.

"I told you two to stay downstairs," I grumbled as Amber wrapped a towel around my arm.

"Well, it sounded like you guys need us upstairs," Brittany drolly retorted.

I thought maybe Amber's face was pale, but it was hard to tell with the room swimming around like it was.

"Lay him down more." Amber barked out commands like a drill sergeant. "Elevate his feet. Jackson, get over here and apply pressure to his arm. Not that one. His other arm."

Everyone moved to follow her instructions. And the hills around us were surprisingly silent. No more gunshots came. Maybe they thought they'd got their guy.

Maybe they had.

The towel around my arm had already turned bright red with my blood. I was bleeding to death on my grandma's kitchen floor.

"He's losing too much blood. We gotta get him out of here," Amber whispered to her mom.

"Did you get a reply from Reb?" Brittany asked.

"Nope," Jackson answered from my other side.

"Shit," Brittany whispered.

"What do we do? Text someone else for help? The police?" Amber's voice shook. "We can't just sit here and watch him die."

I opened my eyes and looked at Amber's pale, drawn face. "I'm gonna be fine, kitten. Help me up, and I'll shoot that motherfucker."

CHAPTER 24

"You're not going anywhere." Amber's lips quivered. "And you better not break your promise."

"Let's make a run for it," Jackson said. "I'll lay some cover fire while you guys go for the car, and I'll follow once it's safe."

"Did you hear the part where I said he's not going anywhere?" Amber angrily whispered. "Besides, Mom and I can't carry him to the car."

"It's just a little flesh wound. I'll be fine. Here, help me up," I muttered.

"Not. Going. Anywhere," Amber bit out.

"We can't just stay here, Amber. I watched your father bleed out in a goddamn parking lot. There's no way in hell I'm letting that happen a second time." Brittany's breath hitched with her suppressed sob. "We're going with Jackson's plan. Get him up; we're heading for the car."

The Bennetts fussed around me for a minute, sweeping away glass and securing a makeshift wrap on my arm. My head swam, but I ignored it as Amber and Jackson helped me to my feet. I took a staggering step toward the door, but Amber stopped me with a touch.

"Whoa. Hold up there a minute, champ." Amber patted my chest. "We need you to get your bearings for a second. Make sure you're not gonna pass out on us. Take a few deep breaths for me. How you feeling?"

"I'm fine. Let's do this." I felt anything but, not that I was gonna tell my girl that. Bile tickled the back of my throat, and my vision swam. But I was doing this. I'd be damned if I'd be the reason they were left here as sitting ducks. We were getting the hell out of here.

As a group, we took a few steps toward the door, then froze in shock as it burst open.

Ruslan stood in the doorway, a handgun in his right hand pointed at the sky. "Thank God, *moya zvezda*. You are all right."

Amber jumped in front of me, blocking my view of the Russian. "Are you fucking crazy? You shot my boyfriend? Did you think that would make me want you?"

"Fuck," Jackson muttered as he pointed his gun at Ruslan. "Stay the hell away from my sister." He took a shot, but judging from the lack of a pained grunt from Ruslan, Jackson must've missed.

"Whoa, whoa, whoa," Ruslan shouted. "I will do you a favor and forget that you took a fucking shot at me, *malchik*. But only because you're *moya zvezda*'s brother. You only get one favor. Clear? Now let's put the guns down and have a little talk."

"We can talk when you're dead." Jackson lifted and pointed his gun again, but froze when I put my hand over his and took his gun away.

If we weren't careful, he'd probably shoot one of us, even at this close range. I had to get the kid some time at the gun range.

Passing the gun to my left—and nondominant—hand, I pushed Amber out of the way and pointed the gun at Ruslan. "Time to talk is over. You fucking come here and shoot up my grandmother's place, scare the shit outta my girl and her family, *and then* you wanna have a conversation? How about you say hey to fucking Satan on your way down."

"I didn't shoot you!" Ruslan yelled. "Why the fuck do you think I'm here?"

"Seriously?" Amber shouted. "You've been stalking me for months. Sending me creepy gifts and showing up at my work—"

"What? Did I know about that last part?" I cut in as I swayed behind her.

"I might've forgotten to tell you about that. Sorry." Amber stayed close to my side and took some of my weight after she wrapped her arm around my back. "But really? Do you think this is the way to get me? Do you really think I'll want to be with you after you kill my boyfriend and scare the hell out of me?"

Ruslan raised an eyebrow. "The only person I've killed was the Wild

CHAPTER 24

Rider who was out there shooting at you, but I'm beginning to think that might've been a mistake. Should I call the rest of the club and let them come out and finish the job?"

"Wild Rider?" Amber repeated weakly.

"Yes." Ruslan opened his suit jacket and holstered his gun before continuing. "The guy I had tailing you reported you'd picked up another tail as you drove through Incline Village. Fortunately, I was close by, as I was inspecting our property in Kings Beach. I met up with Viktor, and we got rid of your little problem."

"You sure took your goddamn sweet-ass time," Jackson muttered, then reddened as Ruslan sent him a glare. "But, uh, sorry about shooting at you."

"Wait," Amber said. "You're still having me followed? Almost a month after we last talked? After I told you that I was happy that I was with Bam? That's . . . That's insane."

"That's how much I want you, *moya zvezda*." His voice grew husky as he continued, "That's how much I want to protect you. I would kill—and have killed—for you."

"I can't—do you really think that's going to be the thing that makes me leave Bam for you?" Amber asked incredulously. "He's been doing that for months for me, *because of you*. He's been protecting me since before we were an item. Because that's the kind of guy he is. He wasn't doing it for payback or to get some. He did because it was right, and I was scared. And you were the one who scared me. You were the one who drove me into Bam's arms. So thank you for that. Because if it weren't for you—"

"Kitten?" I interrupted as the room swam alarmingly around me. Bile tickled the back of my throat.

"Just a second, honey." Amber patted my chest. "I wanna tell this maniac off for once and for all."

Brittany cut in, sotto voce. "Maybe it's a bad idea to piss off the

Russian with a gun who just saved our lives."

"Mom, I got this."

I grunted. "Okay . . . it's just—"

And that was the last thing I could remember right before everything went dark.

Chapter 25

Amber

"Bam!" I shouted as he keeled over right in front of me. I tried to catch him, but his behemoth body was too big and heavy. Instead, he landed on me, pinning me to the floor. "Mom! Jackson! Help!"

There was a flurry of action in the room, but I couldn't see what anyone was doing. Bam's face was frozen and slack above me. My heart in my throat, it took a few moments for me to realize that he was still breathing. He'd just passed out. He was breathing. He was alive.

For now.

The thought haunted me as they shoved his prone body off me and onto his back. I pushed myself to my feet and stared down at Bam. The bandage wrapped around his right arm was bright red and dripping with blood. He was losing too much too fast. Oh God. Oh God. All I could do was stare at the proof that he was slipping away from me. It felt like I was at the bottom of the ocean. Sounds were muffled and far away. Everything except the drip of Bam's blood on the linoleum floor.

"Amber!" My mom shouted two inches from my face. "Get your shit together! We gotta get Bam loaded in the car and down the fucking mountain before he bleeds to death!"

"Right. Okay," I muttered.

"No, keep him here," Ruslan's accented voice butted in.

My mom turned, scooped up Bam's gun from the floor where he'd dropped it when he fell, and faced down the Russian. "We're not going to let him die to clear your way into my daughter's pants. Either help us or get the fuck out of the way."

"What happened to not pissing off our savior with the gun?" Jackson asked in his typical smart-ass way.

"Are you fucking kidding me?" I shouted. "My boyfriend is bleeding out on the floor, and you all are bickering? What the fuck is wrong with you?"

"Our family doctor is on the way. He'll be here shortly to assess the situation." Ruslan paused and raised an eyebrow. "In the future, if your . . . pants are free, I'd appreciate a phone call."

I stared at him, stupefied that he still—after everything I'd shouted at him and everything that'd happened—he still wanted to be with me. I couldn't wrap my brain around it. It was too much. I wasn't worth this amount of fuss. Bam had taken two bullets protecting me. This crazy SOB had shot someone for me. Why? This was insane. This couldn't be my life.

Two men I'd never seen in my life wearing formal suits crowded into the room, pushing me away from Bam's side and muttering in guttural Russian. A moment later, they hoisted Bam up and carried him down the hallway to where I guess the bedrooms were.

"If you ever need anything in the future, please call me, *moya zvezda*." Ruslan held out a business card. "I wish—" Ruslan grunted and clutched his chest as he fell to his knees. His eyes took on a vacant expression as he collapsed in the doorway.

Jackson yelled something, but all I heard was my heartbeat in my ears. And then, suddenly, a huge biker I'd never seen before stood in

CHAPTER 25

the open doorway with a handgun pointed at my head.

I opened my mouth to scream as guns exploded all around me. My mom fired from the floor a few feet from me. There had to be more, but I couldn't look away from the strange biker as his body jerked as bullet after bullet pierced him. He collapsed on the floor next to Ruslan, displaying the logo of the Wild Riders MC on the back of his vest. There was another flurry of action as more suited men swarmed the room and carried Ruslan's lifeless body out the front door.

My mom bent in front of me and said something, but I couldn't hear anything aside from the ringing in my ears. That underwater sensation came back to me as I watched a few suits cart off the biker's body. All I could do was look down at the red stains on my hands. Bam's blood. And I remembered the night, almost a year ago, when my mom came home, staring at her hands. I would hear later that Dad had died in her arms, bleeding out in the parking lot. When I saw her later, she'd been clean of blood, unlike me now, but I'd known something was wrong. She'd looked shattered. And that was when I knew.

That was the night when everything in our lives had changed.

And if this kept going—the way it was going—it was only a matter of time before that was me. If it wasn't me already.

"Amber? You want to clean up, honey?" My mom sounded like she was under water as she rubbed my back. "Then I'll take you back and see how Bam is doing."

I guess we were going to do that thing where we ignored what was really going on—like when she'd been drinking, or like now when she, along with a few others, shot a rival biker. My family. I bit back the hysterical laughter burning the back of my throat. This was insane.

"I just need to get my purse," I mumbled.

"Why don't you start washing up? I think we should stay inside until we get the all clear from the guys. There could be more Wild Riders out there."

I shook my head, still staring at my hands. "I doubt they stuck around after all that went down. They're stupid, but they're not that stupid."

"That might be, Amber, but I really think—"

"I want my purse."

"Okay, honey," she said in that placating tone of hers. "How about I send Jackson out to get it for you while you clean up?"

"I SAID I'LL GET IT!"

My mom flinched at my shout.

I closed my eyes with a wince. "I'm sorry, Mom, but I'll get it. Do you have the car keys? I think I have my gym bag in your trunk."

My mom watched me with wide eyes. "I don't. I think I dropped them somewhere outside, or maybe in the basement. I wasn't really keeping track, but I didn't lock it. You shouldn't need the keys to get into the trunk."

"Right." I rubbed my palms on my jeans-clad thighs, but the blood had dried and still stained my hands. "I'll just go grab my stuff. Would you go check on Bam for me? Please?"

"Sure, honey. It's all going to be okay. You know that, right?"

"Funny. Bam said the same thing to me right before he got shot for the second time today. Didn't seem to work out all that great for him."

"Amber . . ."

"Just go, okay? Please make sure that they're taking care of him, and not . . ." I couldn't even say it.

"Okay, honey. You go clean up, and I'll stand over your guy until you come back." My mom squeezed my shoulder once, then took a step away before coming back and enveloping me in a hard, tight hug. "I'm so glad that you're okay. Both of you. I don't know what I would've done if I lost you guys, too."

My composure slipped as my body shuddered with a suppressed sob. "Me, too, Mama. Me, too. Thank you for saving us."

CHAPTER 25

I flinched as another set of arms wrapped around the two of us, but relaxed when I realized it was my brother. I'd forgotten he was here.

His voice was husky when he finally spoke. "Bam and I would've died before we let that happen."

My mom laughed. "Which two do you think I was talking about, dingus? By the way, I know what I'm getting you for your birthday this year—a membership to the shooting range. Didn't your dad ever take you out to practice?"

"Very funny." Jackson pushed away from us and buried his hands in his pocket. I knew from his red cheeks that he was afraid this would become a thing.

And he was right.

My mom laughed. "Well, at least one person in this family can hit a stationary target at five feet."

"Right." Jackson nodded as he rocked back on his heels. "Because nothing bad would've happened if I'd been the one to shoot the number two in the Bratva when he was the guy who'd actually saved our asses today."

They were still bickering as I slipped out the lopsided front door. Two steps later, I turned over the car keys lying in the dirt with my foot. A minute later dust was flying in the rearview mirror as I whipped the car in reverse down the driveway. Three blocks later I dodged a fleet of motorcycles riding in the opposite direction. I caught a glimpse of Reb's face on the lead bike, Zag riding next to him, and Maverick in the middle of the pack. I tightened my hands on the steering wheel and just kept driving.

My mind was blank at first. I concentrated on the road and its tight turns as I wound down the mountainside. I hadn't driven to Tahoe myself more than a couple of times, so I wasn't confident about the route. I followed the signs pointing toward Reno and drove.

Soon the pine trees thinned out while buildings and other cars and people pressed against the road. I had to slow for traffic, and I sat there in the middle of the road as I watched a family of four—a mom, a dad, and a boy and girl in their teens—cross in the crosswalk in front of me. It hadn't been that long ago when it was my family dressed for the beach in Tahoe. Frolicking in the water. Lying out on a towel in the sun. Watching my brother crash and burn with the cute tourist girls. My life had been that carefree before.

Before.

The word haunted me. My life had become a dichotomy. Before. And after. Before, when we were happy. Then after, everything had changed. It didn't escape me that I was following in my mom's footsteps. In a few short years, or maybe even sooner, it could be me in the parking lot holding onto my dead husband. After all, I'd just watched two men die in a hail of bullets. It was only a matter of time until it was Bam dying in front of me.

A horn blared behind me, and I jumped. Looking around, I finally noticed that the road was clear and probably had been for too long. I stepped on the gas and drove.

The next thing I knew I blinked, and I was sitting in the parking lot of Sydney's apartment. I must've been on autopilot because I literally had no memory of what'd happened after I watched that family cross the road in Tahoe.

"Shit," I muttered to myself as I stared down at my bloodstained clothing. It looked like I'd killed someone or something. I wasn't too keen about walking into Syd's apartment building looking like this, but where else could I go? I didn't want to talk to my mom or anyone from the club right now, so home and her friends were out. And I couldn't go to any of my other friends—my life had narrowed since my dad had died, and they were all busy with their budding careers and stuff. I didn't have anyone else to turn to. That was really fucking sad.

CHAPTER 25

Looking around the empty parking lot, I debated for a second about turning my shirt inside out, but somehow I didn't think that'd help my problem. Instead, I shoved open the car door and ran for it. Two flights of stairs later, I was out of breath as I pounded on Sydney's door. I hoped like hell she was home. Since I had no clue where my phone was, I couldn't text her first to make sure, and silly me hadn't taken the time to look in the parking lot for her car. I lifted my hand and knocked again. The longer I waited out here, the more nervous and fidgety I got.

Shit, shit, shit.

I was debating whether I should leave when the door finally ripped open.

"What the hell is so . . . important," Sydney finished weakly as she looked at me. "Holy shit, what happened, Amber? Get in here. Are you okay?"

The tears I'd been holding at bay for so long broke free and coursed down my cheeks. "Syd, oh my god. I can't—I can't . . ."

Sydney gathered me in her arms and kicked the door shut behind me. "Sssshhh, you gotta pull it together for one second and just let me know that you're okay. I'm kinda freaking out here. Where'd all this blood come from?"

"B-B-Bam Bam. Bam was shot at his grandmother's house."

"Holy shit. Is he okay?"

"I-I-I think so. I mean, he was when I left. I don't really know. I don't know where my phone is. I should probably find my phone."

"Okay. Shit. Okay, I think you're in shock. We should probably call for an ambulance."

"No!" I shouted, and Sydney jumped. I shook my head frantically. "We can't. I can't talk to the police or whatever. It'll get Bam in so much trouble."

"But honey, if you're in shock, you need help. I can't, I'm not qualified to—"

"I'm fine." I took a deep breath and gave her a tight smile. "See? I'm fine. Nothing to worry about. Totally fine."

"Right. That's why you're grinning at me like a Batman villain. Totally fine. Nothing to worry about here."

Her typical smart-ass reply did something that all the miles between Tahoe and here didn't—I finally relaxed a little. I felt some tension draining out of my shoulders as I laughed hoarsely.

"Okay." Sydney sighed. "We should at least clean you up. Let me run you a nice warm bath." Syd put her arm around me and guided me down the hall to her bathroom as she muttered under her breath. "While I Google shock on my phone."

I rubbed my arms and silently walked with her into the bathroom.

An hour later, I was wrapped in Sydney's warmest blanket and lying on the sofa with a few pillows under my legs to elevate my feet. I felt ridiculous, but Sydney had insisted.

"So, what do you want to do?" Sydney asked from her chair across from me.

"I don't know. Should we order some food or something?"

"I'm talking about with Bam, Amber! What do you want to do about Bam?"

I'd filled in Sydney about the whole big mess as she sat on the toilet seat while I'd washed the blood off of me. She'd been adamant about not leaving me alone while I was "in shock." It was sweet, but it'd been a long time since someone had supervised my bath. I mean, there had been those few showers with Bam, but that was different.

Bam.

Shit.

I wanted to know if he was okay. It was killing me not to be by his side, but I couldn't do it. I was afraid. So fucking afraid of following in my mom's footsteps. I'd watched her fall apart this last year, and I

CHAPTER 25

just knew that I didn't have it in me. If that was how a strong, capable woman handled losing her biker, what hope did I have?

Tears sheened my vision and my shoulders shook as I fought against the tears.

"Oh shit." Sydney jumped out of her chair and kneeled by my side. "Are you okay? Does anything hurt?"

"Nope, just my heart." I buried my face in my hands as I cried. The tears were endless. I cried until my chest burned. I cried until my eyes hurt. I cried until I had no more tears left inside me. All I had was an aching hole where my heart used to be.

I scrubbed my face with the robe Syd had lent me. I didn't know what to do. I loved Bam. I knew I did. Otherwise this wouldn't hurt so much. I just didn't know if I wanted to live this life. I'd just watched two men die. What if next time it was Bam? Was I the kind of girl who could happily cook dinner while her guy was out "taking care of club business"? Always wondering if the next time the phone rang it would be with the news that he'd never be coming home again? Or, like last year with my parents and what'd almost happened a few hours ago with Bam, having a front-row seat to the end of us? I didn't know if I had it in me.

"So, bad news."

I jumped at Sydney's declaration. In all my moping I'd forgotten where I was.

She continued. "Or not, depending on how you're feeling. That was your mom. She's on her way over."

I hadn't even heard her phone ring. *Shit.* I wasn't ready for my mom. I didn't have to be psychic to know that she wasn't happy with how I'd run away. Hell, I wasn't happy with how I ran away. I just . . . it was so much, and I was scared.

I looked at Sydney and bit my lip. "Maybe now it's time for tequila?"

Sydney shook her head. "Web Doc says you can't have any food or drink."

"Oh my god, Sydney. I'm not in shock. I'm fine. I just saw my boyfriend get shot twice and two men die in front of me."

Syd's face blanched, and I panicked.

"Is it Bam?" I pushed off the sofa and all but ran to Sydney's side. "Did my mom say something about Bam? Is he okay? Is he alive?"

"What? No. I mean, Bam's fine. I think. Your mom didn't say anything about him. She was worried about you."

"Do you think that's why she's coming here? She wants to tell me in person that he didn't make it?"

"I think she's worried about her only daughter and wants to see if you're okay. Truth be told, she sounded kind of pissed."

"Yeah." I relaxed and let go of Sydney's shirt. I didn't even know I'd grabbed it. "That sounds like my mom."

"So, tequila?" Sydney asked.

"Tequila."

Chapter 26

Still Amber

My mom showed up somewhere after shot number four. Honestly, I'd kinda lost count by that point. Sydney had joined me on the couch, and after we called for a pizza, she'd grabbed the shot glasses and a bottle of tequila, and we went to town.

Fifteen minutes and many shots later, someone knocked on her door.

"Pizza!" Sydney shouted as she jumped up from the couch. And promptly tripped over the coffee table.

I giggled uncontrollably as I grabbed at the toppling bottle of liquor. I caught it and held it aloft in triumph just when Sydney opened the door.

"Hey, you're not pizza."

"No," my mom replied as she walked inside. "And I don't have to guess what the two of you have been doing. I can smell the booze from here."

"That's because your daughter is awful at body shots," Sydney snorted while she closed the door.

"Oh my god, Syd. Shut up. My mom is going to think you're serious." I covered my mouth as a giggle slipped out. "But we totally should try that. You've got the perfect rack for body shots."

"You don't have to tell me that." Sydney laughed as she bounced down on the couch next to me. "How do you think I made it through my one year of college? Body shots make the campus go 'round."

"I think that might've been the hangover that spun your campus around." My mom stood in front of us with her arms crossed over her chest. "You mind giving us a few minutes alone, Sydney? I'd like to talk to my daughter alone."

I took in the grim expression on my mom's face, and my heart fell to my feet. *Oh God. Bam.* I couldn't . . . I don't know if I could handle what she had to say to me. I grabbed Sydney's hands before she had a chance to get up. "No, I want her to stay. Just say whatever it is you have to tell me."

"Oh, honey. It's okay." My mom kneeled in front of me and took my hand in hers. "Bam is fine, I promise. They had to stitch him up, and I think he got a transfusion from that Mafia doctor, but he was alive and sleeping when I left his grandma's house. I just think that there's a few things we need to talk about."

"I think I need another shot first." Relief coursed through my veins at the news that Bam was fine. It only took a second for me to take in the tension in my mom's body. And I knew I needed a little medicinal pain relief before whatever blow came next from my mom.

"And I think the two of you have had enough." My mom pushed to her feet and loomed above us, every inch the disapproving mom that I'd remembered from my teenage years. "Syd, would you please take the bottle with you into the other room."

It was phrased like a request but sounded more like a command.

"Sure thing, Miz Bennett. More for me." Sydney grabbed the tequila off the coffee table and was out of the room before I could come up with an excuse for her to stay.

"Are you okay, honey?" my mom asked as she took Sydney's seat on

CHAPTER 26

the sofa.

"Yeah. I just . . . it was all a little too much, and I needed some time to think."

"Tequila will help with that. I know I do my best thinking when I'm blitzed out on booze." My mom's sarcasm was biting, and I had to look away due to all the shame oozing out of my pores.

My mom's voice grew softer. "If I've learned one thing, it's that there is no answer at the bottom of a bottle. There's no answer in any part of a liquor bottle."

"Well, apparently bikers aren't the only thing I'm following your footsteps in. Now, according to you, I'm an alcoholic as well. Awesome."

"No, smart-ass, I'm not saying that. You're nothing like me." My mom bit out the words, and something about the way she said them made me feel very small.

Or maybe that was my own self-loathing talking because what she said next almost sent me to the floor.

"You're so much better than me." Her voice shook with her words, and I knew she was fighting back tears.

"Mom." I sat up and tentatively touched her leg. "Don't say that. You're the strongest, bravest woman I know. If it wasn't for you, that biker could've—" I couldn't even say it. Every time I closed my eyes I saw that gun pointed at me.

"No, you are. That was . . . that was time at the range with your dad, and pure dumb luck. But you, you took the blow of your dad dying and kept going. While I was falling apart, you gave up your college career and took a menial job and kept me from choking on my vomit because I was getting drunk off my ass every night. And day. I just . . . I'm so sorry, honey. I'm so sorry I put you through that. I wish I was strong like you and was able to hold it together for my family."

"You're joking, right? I just ran away while my boyfriend was bleeding out from a freaking gunshot wound. Two gunshot wounds. I'm not strong. I'm weak." I scrubbed a hand over my face. All the wonderful mellowness from the liquor was gone. Now I just felt like an empty shell. My voice was husky when I whispered, "So fucking weak."

"Oh, honey, no. It's a lot to take in. You just watched two men die, and your guy was down the hall bleeding like a faucet." My mom reached over and squeezed my leg. "It's easy for a bitch to say that she's in—that she's okay with the life—but it's another thing entirely to see it and live it. And unfortunately, today you got the live in-person view of how bad it can get."

"But he was bleeding when I left, Mom. Who does that?"

"You only left once you knew he was getting help. If he was in a hospital, you wouldn't have been able to stay by his side. It's okay if you need to take a minute or a day to breathe and figure out where your head is. He's being taken care of. You need to take care of you."

I shook my head. "I don't know if I'm cut out for this life, Mom. I don't know if I can handle everything that happened today. Ruslan and that biker were killed. Bam was shot. Twice. After Dad, I don't know if I can be with someone like that."

"It's not the life I would ever wish for you, honey. It's not easy."

"No, it's not." And despite everything my mom just said, I still didn't feel right with how I'd left Bam. Guilt weighed heavily on my shoulders. I loved him, but I still left before I knew he was all right. I left before someone made me. Shouldn't I have been torn from his bedside wailing about how I couldn't leave him? What kinda biker bitch was I?

The kind who ran away at the first sign of trouble.

"No, you didn't."

I flinched as I realized I was so drunk I couldn't keep my thoughts inside my head.

CHAPTER 26

"You're gonna piss me off if you keep talking about yourself that way. I am so proud of you, Amber. The way you kept your cool and helped out? You bandaged Bam's arm and didn't fall apart. You stood up to that bastard Russian and let him have it. You didn't lose your shit after watching two men die. I couldn't be prouder of you. So please, give yourself a little slack. If you need some space to breathe and think, then take it. Talk things over with your girl. Figure out where your head is. Bam will still be there tomorrow."

"I don't know if I can wait that long to see him, Mom."

My mom's lips twitched with her soft smile. "Then I guess you have your answer right there."

I let out a sad laugh. "If only it were that easy."

"Do you love him?"

"Of course."

"Then you need to decide if how he lives his life is a deal breaker for you. After everything you told me about how the two of you got together, I think he might leave the club for you, but do you want him to? Do you want to start your life together with an ultimatum?"

I shook my head. "The club is his family. I can't take that away from him."

"Then you need to decide if you can handle him being who he is—warts and all. I'm a firm believer that you should never want to change the man you're with. Remind me to tell you about a few of the guys I dated before your dad. There were some doozies."

Doozies compared to my dad? The mind boggled. "Like what?"

Mom laughed. "That's a conversation for another time."

"I'll hold you to that." We smiled at each other. I remembered how she'd wanted to share some of her wild dating stories with me once I'd started dating, and the look of panic in my dad's eyes before he'd shut that down. Like he was petrified that even hearing about what my mom had done would make me want to do the same. And how my mom had smiled, then mouthed behind his back that she would tell me later. Not that she did. Dad had won that round.

Which was rare. Usually he gave Mom anything and everything she'd ever wanted.

"Do you regret it, Mom?"

"What? The guys I dated before your dad?"

"No." I bit my lip. "Choosing Dad. If you knew then what you know now, would you still choose Dad?"

Tears sheened her eyes, and her lips quirked before she answered huskily. "Yes. I'd go through that pain every day if it meant that I'd have your father. Had your father. He was worth it. You and your brother were worth it. You guys mean everything to me. Your dad most of all. I will love that man until the day I die. So yes, I'd choose him again and again and again."

My eyes teared up at her passionate answer. I knew the love my parents had, felt it every day I'd lived at home, could feel it over the phone when I was away at school. That was what I wanted with the man I chose.

"You just need to decide if Bam is worth the pain."

I blinked at my mom. She smiled and patted my leg. "And no one can tell you that but you. Can't help you there, honey. Sorry."

"Nothing to be sorry about, Mom. Thank you."

"You're welcome. I hope this helped."

"It did. Thanks. I love you, Mom."

"Love you, too, sweetie." She leaned over and gave me an awkward—given our positions on the couch—but amazing hug.

A second later we both flinched and jumped apart as someone pounded on the door.

"Finally!" Sydney shouted as she swayed down the hall. "Pizza!"

She opened the door and smiled drunkenly at the pizza guy. "I love you. That smells so good."

CHAPTER 26

Mom laughed as she got to her feet. "How about I pay for the pizza, girls?"

Sydney held onto the door as she swung around to smile at my mom. "Miz Bennett, you are the best! I love you!"

Mom handed some money over to the delivery guy and took the pizza. "And you two need some food in your bellies." She shut the door with a hip bump. "We can't make important life and love decisions on empty stomachs."

I bit my lip. "I think I've already decided."

My mom's smile spread across her face. "Pizza first. Then, if you still want to go after your man, I'm driving."

"Deal."

Chapter 27

Bam

I blinked blearily at the ceiling. It took a second for the room to come into focus. And then confusion set in. I saw my Metallica poster, the trophies from my high school football team lining the top of my old dresser, and piles of old *Easyriders* magazines I'd liberated from Maverick's garage forever ago. Wait, I was at my grandma's house?

I went to push myself up and fell back against the bed as my arms wouldn't work. What the hell?

"Hey champ." Maverick jumped up from his chair in the corner. I hadn't noticed him in my first sweep of the room. "How you feeling?"

"Confused. What the fuck is going on? What am I doing at my grandma's house?" I looked down at the bandages covering my arms, and I remembered. The call from Neil about the downed tree. The gunshots. Ruslan. Amber.

Amber!

"Where's Amber? Is she okay?" I looked around the room but didn't see her anywhere. "Where is she?"

Maverick rubbed at the back of his neck and winced. "She's, uh, she went back to town to get a handle on shit."

"A handle on shit? What does that even mean?"

CHAPTER 27

"She, uh, left." He sighed heavily. "She left you, Bam. There's no other way to put it. Shit got hard. You were bleeding like a stuck pig, and she took off. I'm sorry."

I blinked as my eyelids got heavy; Maverick sounded like he was talking at the end of a tunnel, his words echoing. *She took off. I'm sorry. Bleeding like a stuck pig. Took off. Took off.*

It took a minute for his words to sink in. And when they finally did, I was pissed. "Fuck that."

I rolled over and tried to sit up, but found myself tangled in a web of IV tubes and sheets.

"Whoa, hold on, son. You need to lay back and get some sleep. You keep fighting like that, you're gonna open up your stitches and shit. And after all that nice doctor did to fix you up."

"Fuck that. I'm going down the goddamn hill and getting my girl back."

Maverick pushed a wrinkled hand against my chest, keeping me down with a pitiful amount of effort. "Bullshit, son. A girl like that isn't worth the spit you took to make that sentence. You were bleeding like a son of bitch, needed a fucking transfusion, and that girl drove away like the hounds from hell were on her heels. She didn't stand by you. She doesn't deserve you."

I shook my head and the room swum around me. I had to lie back against the pillow before I could make my brain work enough to form a goddamn sentence. "I think you've got that backward, Mav. I'm the one who doesn't deserve her, and I'm gonna do everything I fucking can to make sure she doesn't realize that."

"She isn't worth it, kid. You'll find one someday that is worth all the bullshit. But it's not her."

"But I love her, Mav."

"And sadly, sometimes love isn't enough."

Then a new voice spoke from the doorway. One I knew so well it made me close my eyes in relief.

"And sometimes love is everything," Amber said, her voice strong and sure.

I opened my eyes and drank in the sight of my girl in skintight jeans and a T-shirt.

And over that, my Property Of vest.

"Where the hell you been, girl?" Maverick huffed. "This kid has been through the fucking wringer, and you hightail it off for town? What the hell kinda love is that?"

"Mav, I appreciate you, man, but can we have some privacy?" I asked.

"No," Amber cut in. "I'd like to answer him."

Maverick grunted and crossed his arms over his chest. I knew that expression well. Last time was when I fucked up as a prospect and fell asleep on watch. What I'd done reflected on him since he'd been my sponsor. Mav wasn't impressed with me, and it'd taken a hell of a lot of groveling to make it right with him.

Amber bit her lip as she took in Maverick's expression. She turned her eyes to me and spoke. "I did run. I'm sorry, Bam. Maverick. I just freaked out. So much of it was so similar to what happened last year with my dad. And I was scared. I didn't want to lose you, Bam. I didn't want what happened to my mom to happen to me. Dad died in her arms, and you almost died in mine. I couldn't deal."

"So, you ran away with your tail between your legs," Maverick muttered, every inch the disapproving papa. I kinda loved him for it, while at the same time I wanted to wring his neck.

Amber nodded. "I did. And I cried the whole way because I'd already lost him. I left him and lost him, but by my own hand this time. It was a chickenshit thing to do, and I'm so sorry, Maverick. I'm so, so sorry, Bam. I'll do anything and everything to make it up to you. I love you so much."

"Nothing to make up. Come here, kitten." I tried to hold my arms

CHAPTER 27

out to her, but they still wouldn't move. Amber still got my weak gesture, though, and I hardly felt it when she collapsed against my body. I needed to get off these fucking drugs so I could feel my baby in my arms again.

Over Amber's shoulder, I saw Maverick shake his head, but he didn't say anything.

Amber buried her face in my chest and spoke in a husky whisper. "I'm so, so sorry, Bam. I love you so much. I just was afraid to face my life without you in it. I watched two men die today, and I knew it could so easily be you. But I talked it over with my friend and my mom, and I realized that I'll take whatever amount of time I have on this earth with you. I'm just so sorry that I freaked out—that I wasn't here when you woke up. It's just . . . damn. I'm so, so sorry, Bam."

"I love you, kitten." I tried to hug her back and cursed the medicine and bandages that kept me from squeezing her. "I'm so fucking glad you found your way back to me before I had to go find you and drag you home. Because you know I would. I'd do anything—whatever it took—to keep you in my life."

Maverick cleared his throat. "I'll just give you kids some privacy. I'll be down the hall if you need anything, Bam."

I rested my chin on Amber's shoulder. "Thanks. And Mav? Give her a break. Please. You're the closest thing I've got to family, and I'd appreciate it if you and my girl would get along. Love you, man."

"Right back at you, son."

I could swear I saw a sheen of liquid in his eyes, but I blamed the drugs I was on. Maverick wasn't the kinda guy to cry. His voice was warm when he addressed Amber.

"Bye, Amber. Thanks for coming back for my boy."

"Always, Mav," Amber replied, but Maverick had already left, closing the door quietly behind him.

"I'm so glad you're okay," Amber whispered.

"I am, baby. Do you really think I'd let something like a few bullets from a damn Wild Rider keep you from me?"

"That's what kept my dad from my mom."

My stomach felt hollow. It could've been the cocktail of whatever drugs I was on, but one look at the fear in Amber's eyes and I knew. She'd been to hell today. No amount of kissing or joking around would fix this. Last year she'd lost her dad because a fucking Wild Rider shot up the parking lot Brittany, Stitch, and a few others were standing in. She knew more than most the cost of living our life.

"I know, kitten. I shouldn't have joked about it. I'm sorry. But I'm fine. The first bullet wound was only a graze—"

"And the second hit an artery or something. No one bleeds like that from a little flesh wound. Don't diminish it, Bam."

"Okay. You're right."

"Damn straight."

"I'm sorry I put you through that. I guess one of the guys saw us riding through town and decided to get some retribution. And your family got caught in the scrap. Again. I'm so fucking sorry that this touched your family again."

"I'm not."

"What?" I blinked at Amber in confusion.

"At least now we've got this whole conversation out of the way. I won't have to wonder if I'm cut out for the lifestyle. I've seen the worst that can happen, almost had it happen with you, and I'm still coming back for more. If that doesn't say I love you, I don't know what does."

"Baby," I whispered before I kissed her hard. Tears stung my eyes, but I was man enough to call them what they were. I loved this woman. She was so fucking strong and smart and gorgeous. I don't know how the hell I got so lucky to call her mine, but I was hanging onto her with everything I had.

Or I would be, once I got feeling back in my arms.

CHAPTER 27

I fell back onto my pillows with a frustrated groan.

"Oh God. Are you okay?" Amber sprang off the bed and hovered over me with a worried expression. "Does it hurt somewhere? Of course it hurts; you were shot twice. I should go get someone."

"Kitten, come here. I'm fine." I tried to reach out to her but still couldn't function. "I swear to God, I'm fine. I'm just frustrated that I can't hold you."

"Oh." Amber's lips trembled, then she smiled. "Okay."

"So how about, in the meantime, you climb into bed with me and hold me? You look fucking exhausted, kitten."

"I am kinda tired." Amber rolled her eyes, then crawled into bed next to me, taking a ridiculous amount of care not to jostle me. She curled up to my side and cautiously wrapped her arm around my abdomen, settling her hand near my heart.

The combination of the adrenaline, the drugs, and the comfort of Amber's presence had my eyelids drooping. I wanted to say something deep and meaningful to let her know that I was so fucking happy to have her in my life, but I couldn't make my brain or mouth work. Instead, I mumbled, "Love you, kitten. So glad I didn't have to drag you back to my place like a caveman."

I was on the edge of sleep when I heard Amber whisper back with a smile in her voice. "I always thought you looked more like a Viking. Love you, Bam."

Epilogue

Three months later

Bam

I couldn't think of a better way to spend my Wednesday night. I was sitting on my bike outside the English building of the community college, waiting for Amber. It'd been too late for her to get back into her college this year, but my girl wasn't letting any grass grow under her feet. She was busy knocking out a few required classes that would transfer when she finally enrolled next semester. I was so fucking proud of her.

She'd also moved out of her mom's house and into my place. Her mom hadn't put up a fuss. Brittany—as she demanded I call her—had actually helped, schlepped more than her share of boxes and suitcases, and even helped Amber unpack. If that wasn't a ringing endorsement of our relationship, I don't know what was.

Speaking of rings, I had a square ring box burning a hole in my pocket.

I was gonna propose to Amber tonight. Maverick had helped me plan the whole thing out. After dinner at the fancy steak joint in the Mother Lode Casino—with me wearing a button-up shirt; Mav had been adamant about that part—I'd get down on one knee and pop the question. Then champagne, and then drunk and engaged sex. That last bit was my part of the engagement night planning.

Amber would be wearing my ring by the end of the night.

Life was finally turning around for the both of us. My arms had healed up fine. Got all the function back and everything. My mom had apparently been full of shit. She'd never filed anything about my grandmother's will. All Grandma's wishes had been carried out, and the Tahoe house was officially mine—downed tree, bullet holes, and all. A few of my Brothers had helped me sort out the tree, and one of our members was a carpenter who took his pay from me in beer, so we were slowly fixing the damage the Wild Riders had done. Our war was nowhere near over, but now we had a firm alliance with the Bratva since the Wild Riders had killed Ruslan in cold blood. Both our organizations had lost family members to those bastards, and neither one of us would rest until the Wild Riders were six feet under. Every last fucking one.

And the Bratva were proving to be an excellent alliance since they'd dealt with all the Wild Rider bodies. We hadn't heard one fucking peep from the local LEOs about any of the shit that went down that day in Tahoe. It was almost like it'd never happened. Well, aside from the bullet holes in the house and me. And Ruslan.

The doors of the building burst open, and an odd mix of twenty- and thirty-somethings, and a few older students, left the building. My eyes skimmed over them, then snagged when I saw the one I was here for. Amber walked next to a girl about her age; both had backpacks slung over their shoulders. My girl was laughing at something her friend had said. Then her eyes locked with mine, and her smile grew even bigger. She said something to her friend and didn't wait for a reply as she took off toward me.

I barely had time to swing off my bike before she was in my arms.

She laughed as I caught her.

"Funny meeting you here like this. I didn't take you for the kind of guy who hung around college campuses."

Something about what she said reminded me of our first conversation outside of Howl. The night that everything changed for me. Deciding to screw with her, I repeated what I could remember of it. "Did you drive yourself out here, or am I taking you home?"

Amber's brow wrinkled, and it took her a second to catch on. Then she bit her lip to hide her smile. "I left my car at home and took an Uber."

"Fine. I'll take you home." I couldn't stop the smile that spread across my face. "Get on the back of my bike, kitten."

"Always, Bam. That's where I belong."

Damn right. And after tonight, she'd belong to me forever.

A few minutes later Amber wrapped her arms around my waist, and we rode home.

Together.

The End

Dedication

To all my fabulous readers who begged me for Bam's story. This one's for you!

Acknowledgments

First, I have to thank you, the readers! You have all been so passionate about my True Brothers MC series. I love hearing from you, how excited you are to read my books and your eagerness for certain characters' stories. You guys make my day with every email, FB message, and tweet! You're the reason why I do this! Thank you!

To my awesome husband, Dave—Thank you for putting up with all the dirty dishes, cold meals, and our fussy toddler while I'm busy chasing deadlines. I love you and all the wonderful things you do for me!

To my awesome crit partners, Amy Isaman and Paisley Hendrix—Thank you for all early morning Starbucks meetings and thoughtful feedback! You two always keep me on track and true to my characters.

Also By Gillian Archer

Star Studded
Falling for Rome
Coming soon:
Fighting for King
Burning for Phoenix
Burns Brothers Series
Build
Fast
Spark
Torque
True Brothers MC Series
Ruthless
Rebellious
Resilient
Rough Ride
HRH Series
Reluctantly Royal
Standalone Short
King of Hearts

BIO

GILLIAN ARCHER has a bachelor's degree in mining engineering but prefers to spend her time on happily ever after. She writes the kind of stories she loves to read—the hotter the better! When she's not pounding away on the keyboard, she can be found chasing her grade-schooler, or surfing the couch while indulging in her latest reality TV fixation, or reading awesome romance ebooks by her favorite authors. Gillian lives in the wilds of Nevada with her amazing husband, gorgeous little girl, and goofy dog. Please visit her at gillianarcher.com/

Gillian@GillianArcher.com

Facebook.com/GillianArcherWrites

Twitter: @gillianarcher

Sign up to receive important news and new-release info from Gillian Archer straight to your inbox: eepurl.com/n3UWf

Read on for an excerpt from Build

Burns Brothers #1 out now and free at all retailers!

Build Chapter One

Austin Burns

Badass Builds

Sacramento, CA

Days like today, I really wish I'd been an only child.

"You're full of it if you think the West Coast Kings are going to be happy with a fucking paint job like that." My younger brother by eighteen months, Nathan, growled as we stood in our workshop with all my brothers gathered around the cans for the Kings build. "It's streaky on that side, and you totally jacked up their logo. We'll be lucky if those sons of bitches don't fuck us all up."

"I know it's not my best work," our youngest brother, Dylan, groaned as he stared morosely at the cans in question. "I had some shit on my mind. I guess I wasn't concentrating. I fucked up."

"*I fucked up*," Nathan mocked. "I'm sure the Kings will find that hilarious when they show up Saturday to pick up the goddamn bike. You know, after they give us a beat down."

And I wished I hadn't gone into business with my entire family, like a moron. My temples began to throb in that special way that only my brothers could make me feel.

My middle brother Ryan laughed and muttered something under his breath that sounded suspiciously like, "I'd like to see them try."

"Really?" Nathan scoffed. "You think you could hold your own with the one-percent motorcycle club that runs this city? They would eat you for breakfast."

"They could try," Ryan retorted as he straightened from his slouch. He closed the distance between him and Nathan in a slow, measured saunter. "We all remember who ended up with a broken nose the last time me and you danced. Wanna go again?"

There was a reason the Urban Channel was in talks with our lawyer to make our previous hour long special into a weekly reality show. The four of us together defined drama.

And dysfunction.

"*ENOUGH!*" I roared, finally at the end of my patience. "We don't have time for another run to the E.R. because you two can't figure out how to get along. We gotta fix this mess and build the bike before we piss off the Kings. They're our biggest client right now. We don't have time for finger pointing. So calm the hell down, or get the fuck out. Either way, this bike will be done by Saturday. We clear?"

"Clear," Nathan muttered with a glare Ryan's way.

Ryan smirked. "I could use the weekend off."

"If you're not careful, you're gonna have a whole lot of weekends off." I shook my head.

"Wait, what?" Ryan turned and blinked at me.

"I'm tired of your bullshit." I crossed my arms over my chest. "This is a fucking business. Do you think you'd get away with any of your screwing off if you worked for someone else? It's time to grow up. You're twenty-seven years old for Christ's sake."

"Are you serious?"

"As a heart attack. I'm done bailing you out—both literally and figuratively. You need to start treating this like an actual job. What time did you even come in this morning?"

"Ten," Ryan muttered.

"I was here at seven. Nathan showed up at eight. Dylan too. How is that fair?"

Ryan hitched a shoulder and studied the tips of his boots, all his earlier bravado gone.

I shook my head. "Maybe try being an adult for a change. God knows I've had to be one since I was eight years old."

Ryan narrowed his eyes at me. "That's a low blow."

Dylan and Nathan shot me sidelong glances, but neither said a word. Dylan's face took a reddish hue. He hated confrontation of any kind, but I was too tired to give a shit at the moment. Especially since he was the reason we were in this mess in the first place.

"So, if we're all done measuring our dicks, can we come up with a plan to finish this bike? Preferably before the Kings make us regret ever taking this job?" I looked from one brother to another.

After a beat, each gave me a grudging nod. Except Ryan.

"What's it gonna be, bro?" I asked. "You staying or going?"

"I'm still here, aren't I?" Ryan retorted. Like that was an answer.

Or a fucking apology.

I suppressed the urge to give him the beatdown he clearly wanted. Despite how much he'd pissed me off. We didn't have the time, and I really didn't want to spend the whole day in the E.R.

Again.

"Fantastic," I muttered sarcastically. "Dylan will repaint the cans tonight, and the three of us will be here first thing tomorrow to finish the build. If it all goes smoothly, we shouldn't have any problem finishing the bike by Saturday. But no more screwups. Clear?"

"Crystal," Nathan snarled. More than likely he was still pissed that he hadn't been able to swing on Ryan.

Join the club.

Dylan picked up the cans and left the room without a word. He'd been oddly silent through most of the exchange. Usually he'd have something to say in Ryan's defense—those two were thick as thieves—but today he was practically a zombie stumbling around the shop. I made a mental note to check in with him later today and find out what had crawled up his ass.

"I'll call T-Bone and move the reveal a few hours back. Maybe we should bring the bike to them, instead of having the reveal at the shop."

Nathan hitched a shoulder. "Could be a good idea. If they have one of their infamous parties, they'll be more mellow."

"Anything to avoid a fight, huh, Nate?" Ryan taunted.

Nathan took a threatening step in Ryan's direction.

"Whoa, okay. You—" I said pointing in Nathan's direction. "Go home. Get some sleep. Maybe have some booze first, so you mellow the fuck out."

Nathan lifted his upper lip in a snarl before turning on his heel and stomping away. Before he reached the door, he picked up an empty gas can and hurled it into the wall with a thunderous crash. It fell to the floor with one side completely caved in.

A beat later, the office door slammed shut with a wallop that shook the walls.

Fan-fucking-tastic.

"And you," I turned to my only remaining brother, and the biggest literal pain in my neck today. "You'd better be here bright and early tomorrow."

"Sure," Ryan replied sullenly.

"I'm not screwing around. We're cutting it close as is. We don't have time for you to keep needling Nathan and pulling this bullshit."

"Whatever, bro." Ryan pushed away from the cabinet he'd been leaning against.

"You gotta grow the fuck up and be an adult. I'm not kidding, Ry. If you're not here at seven tomorrow, you're gone."

He lifted a middle finger in salute as he walked away from me.

It probably sounded like an empty threat, since it wasn't the first time I'd made it.

But it would be the last because I was done.

Done with their bullshit. Done with E.R. visits (and bills) because my brothers were at each other's throats. Done with all the family drama. I needed a tropical island getaway—somewhere far, far away from my crazy family.

Running away was a regular fantasy of mine. I craved somewhere quiet, secluded, and just peaceful. Maybe I'd hit up my friend, former client, and rock star great, Cole Jackson, and see if I could borrow his Tahoe retreat. The place was crazy—super luxe with a freaking media room and every amenity you could think of. Apparently it was vacant most of the season since Cole was on the road right now.

I sighed. One day.

Instead, I retreated to my silent office, passing my cousin and Badass Builds' CPA, Sabrina, on the way.

"Is it all clear?" Sabrina asked, as she tugged on the cuffs of her oversized sweater then crossed her arms over her chest.

"Yeah, sorry about the fireworks. Nate and Ry took off for the night. Dylan is in the paint shed fixing the cans. It'll probably be a late night for him."

Sabrina nodded then gave me a sad smile. "Did you mean it?"

I tilted my head in confusion.

"Ryan. Are you really going to fire him if he doesn't show up on time tomorrow?"

I closed my eyes with a muttered curse. "You heard that part, huh?"

"Pretty sure the nail salon down the block heard your threat. And Nathan. You all get kinda loud when you're uh, discussing stuff."

That was Sabrina's nice way of saying we get loud when shit hits the fan.

"I don't know. He's my brother and I love him. But shit's gotta change. I've worked almost every weekend since I started building motorcycles. Ryan's had it too easy. I'm tired of holding his hand. He's a freaking adult. He needs to start acting like it." I rubbed a weary hand over my face. "And with Dylan's fuck up, we're cutting it crazy close to get the Kings' build done in time. I'm just so fucking tired, Sabby."

"Well, when's the last time you took a vacation? Oh wait, I can answer that. When you finished the bike for Cole Jackson, and he took you all up to his cabin. That was what? Over six months ago? That's not healthy, Austin. You need a break."

I chuckled wearily. "I can always sleep when I'm dead."

"The way you're going, that'll be sooner than later. I'm worried about you."

"You're sweet, Sabby, but I'm fine. I'm gonna go do some paperwork, but I'll knock off early tonight. I promise."

Sabrina shook her head. "Still not good enough. Maybe you should hit Mom's diner on the way home. She'll get you straightened out."

I snorted. "I definitely don't have the energy for Wendy tonight." My aunt was a ballbreaker and lifelong meddler. The last thing I needed tonight was a dose of Aunt Wendy.

"Think about it. Goodnight, Austin."

"Night Sabrina." I shook my head as I walked past her and down the hall toward my office. I'd have to have a death wish if I went to Bette's Diner when Wendy was working. The food was amazing, but the lecture that came with it wasn't worth the price of admission.

I spent the next twenty minutes on the phone with T-Bone, promising him everything but my firstborn to push the reveal a few hours back and bring the bike to him at the Kings' clubhouse. I finally hung up the phone with a groan. If this reveal didn't go well, we could kiss our business goodbye.

Along with our loved ones, more than likely.

I hung my head between my knees and let out a muted roar. When was this gonna get easier? We'd been doing this for years. *Years*. When would the shitstorm finally end?

My phone pinged with an incoming email.

I was almost afraid to look. But the Kings were too smart to put any threats in writing.

The words in the subject line made the blood freeze in my veins.

Parole granted.

No. No. It couldn't… They wouldn't…

I clicked on the email and every word made me feel sicker. The usual bureaucratic jargon followed by George Burns. Parole granted. The words swam on my screen. I couldn't believe it. I never thought that bastard would see freedom for the rest of his life. After the first parole hearing, my brothers and I had stopped attending. We had our lawyer send victim impact statements and our declaration forms because we weren't spending another second breathing the same air as that bastard. And because we knew there was no way an evil son of a bitch like him would ever be paroled.

Apparently the California Department of Corrections and Rehabilitation disagreed.

What the fuck was wrong with them? How could they not see past his bullshit? Oh God, I was gonna have to tells my brothers. Sabrina. Aunt Wendy.

I couldn't.

I couldn't breathe.

I needed to get the fuck out of here.

*Get **Build** (Burns Brothers #1) today. Ebook is free at all retailers!*

www.ingramcontent.com/pod-product-compliance
Lightning Source LLC
LaVergne TN
LVHW091547160125
801479LV00006B/54